ALSO BY DARRYL BOLLINGER

The Pill Game

A Case of Revenge

The Medicine Game

THE
CARE
CARD

A Novel

DARRYL BOLLINGER

JNB
PRESS

Copyright © 2014 by Darryl Bollinger

JNB Press
Tallahassee, FL

www.jnbpress.com

Printed in the United States of America

First Trade Edition: December 2014

ISBN 978-0-9848432-6-8

In memory of my mother.

Chapter 1

Warren Thompson hung up the phone and glanced at his new watch, a birthday present to himself. Though the Patek Philippe Nautilus was not the most expensive watch made, at more than fifty thousand dollars it made a Rolex pale by comparison.

A warm smile crossed his face as he thought back to his first watch, a hand-me down Timex, the only thing of his dad's that he still had. The smile faded when he remembered that his dad had given it to him the night before he left.

He shook his head and turned his attention back to his next appointment. Warren was late, as usual. He grabbed the file on the corner of his desk as he headed out his office door. Becky, his assistant, started talking as soon as he emerged, but he waved her off and kept walking, almost running, down the hall to the conference room.

As head of the largest hedge fund based in southwest Florida, with over twenty billion dollars in assets under management, he had a full schedule. This was an important meeting, with one of his largest clients who was vacationing at his winter home on Sanibel Island.

Warren burst through the conference room door and strode over to the elderly, silver-haired man standing at the window. As usual, the man was dressed casually in khakis and a short-sleeved plaid shirt.

"Clay. Hi, sorry I'm late. I was on the phone with New York."

Clay Fortson smiled and extended his hand. "Warren, you'll be late for your own funeral. Have you ever been on time for anything?" He chuckled as he took a sip of coffee out of the Everglades Investment Fund mug in his hand. Fortson was one of the wealthiest real estate tycoons in the Midwest and owned more of Chicago than many people realized.

Warren shook his head and laughed. "Not recently," he said, shaking Fortson's hand with genuine warmth and affection. The old man liked making money, and that's what kept him tolerating Warren's tardiness—a courtesy he didn't extend to many people. Fortson was in the one percent of the one percent—what Warren called "screw you rich." While Warren's fortune could be measured in hundreds of millions, Fortson was in the billionaire ranks, which earned him a perennial listing near the top of the Forbes 400.

"How have you been, Clay? You look great."

"Not bad for an old man. Glad to be down here. It was twelve degrees and snowing when I left Chicago."

Warren shivered. "Makes me cold just thinking about it. Glad you don't want me to come up there this time of year."

The old man laughed and sat down. "Hell, you don't have to worry about that. Why do you think I bought that place out on Sanibel? Gives me a good excuse to get out of Chicago in winter."

Warren felt his phone vibrate in his pocket, but ignored it and turned his attention back to his guest.

"How's Martha?" Warren asked. Clay and Martha had been married for fifty years, a record in Warren's opinion. She was a gracious and classy lady.

Clay beamed at the mention of his wife. "I dropped her off in Atlanta to see her sister. They're both coming down here next week."

Warren gestured toward the table, where they sat.

"We did a swap on the Claiborne derivatives and that worked out well," Warren said. He started with the highlight. Unfortunately, there wasn't much good news after that. It had been a tough quarter, and he dreaded the rest of the conversation, but he spent the next hour reviewing the fund's performance over the past three months. By the time he'd gotten to the end of the review, he could tell that Clay was getting antsy.

"I don't know shit about derivatives and that fancy stuff," Clay replied, cutting straight to the bottom line. "What I do know is that my whole portfolio only improved by two percent overall. That's probably the worst quarter we've had since we started."

They had met when Warren was a young manager with Jenkins-Gilmore, a large Wall Street firm. Having made a mere four million dollars that year, he'd walked into his boss's office and demanded an increase—to eight million. His boss laughed and told him to take a hike.

Warren called Clay that afternoon, told him he'd been fired and was starting his own firm back in Fort Myers. Clay told him his business was going with Warren.

He wanted Clay's account, but he cited his non-compete agreement with the Wall Street behemoth. Fortson assured him they wouldn't pursue it, but Warren said his hands were tied. Two days later, a fax arrived at Warren's makeshift office. It was a legal document specifically authorizing Warren to take Fortson's account. The document was signed by the CEO of Warren's old firm.

Since then, through a combination of complex derivatives and shrewd timing, Warren Thompson had established a track record that was the envy of Wall Street. Yet, he stayed in Fort Myers—his home—and refused to move back to the financial center of the world. In today's environment that was no longer necessary and business could be transacted remotely just as well. What was important was maintaining that personal relationship with his clients, something that Warren excelled at.

The squeak of Clay's chair brought Warren's attention back to the present. Clay leaned back, shifting his gaze out the window for a moment before returning his focus to Warren.

"Warren, we've known each other for a long time. And we've always been straight with each other." He took another sip of his coffee before continuing. "I'm considering moving my account with Everglades."

Warren started to interrupt, but Clay held up his hand.

"I haven't decided anything—yet, but I'm not happy with the past year's performance." He paused to let the words sink in. "Why don't you come out to the house this weekend for dinner, and we'll discuss it further. Say Friday around seven." The elderly man rose, signifying the meeting was over.

Warren stood to escort Clay out. It had been a tough year, he knew, but he had no idea that Clay Fortson was thinking about moving his account. He wanted to discuss it, but held his tongue, sensing this wasn't the time. Losing Fortson would be disastrous.

"That sounds good, Clay. I look forward to it."

As soon as Clay got on the elevator and the doors shut, Warren pulled out his iPhone and headed toward his office, swearing to himself. Clay was one of his biggest accounts and one that he could ill afford to lose.

He skimmed through the dozens of text messages and stopped when he got to one from Alex, his fiancée.

Don't forget-dinner @ 8

Damn, he thought. He'd forgotten. Warren had spent more time with Clay than usual, since the fund had performed below par and required more explanation. When there was mostly good news to report, the review went faster.

Alex had set up dinner with Ken Taylor, the CEO of Rivers Community Hospital, to discuss their annual foundation fundraiser. Taylor had asked Warren to be the Chair this year. The job was mostly name-only, with a cadre of foundation employees doing all of the heavy lifting, but it was an excellent way to mingle with moneyed clients in the community.

Alexis Sutton worked in the foundation office, and he'd been intrigued with her from the first time he met her. She was thin, with long black hair, and a charming smile that could thaw the coldest heart. He smiled as he thought of her. Her coal black eyes twinkled with mischief, and she was an incredible lover, though it had taken him some time to get to that point.

Unlike most of the women he had slept with, she did things on her schedule and was not swept away by his charm. She was equally at ease with him as she was with a panhandler on the street. She was assertive and independent—characteristics he admired. He liked the way she carried herself.

As Warren walked back to his office, Becky followed behind with messages and reminders all the way to his desk. When they got there, she handed him a new inhaler, and said, "I picked this up for you this morning."

Warren had had asthma since childhood, and he never went anywhere without an inhaler that contained the life-saving medicine. Becky usually got his prescriptions refilled for him.

"Thanks," he said, taking the device and putting it in his pocket.

He returned the calls that were important and ignored the others. Monitoring the steady stream of information flowing across one of the four large computer screens on his desk, which looked like a NASA command center, he executed several trades.

He could multi-task like few people, which was part of the reason for his success. The ability to quickly sort through the chaff and focus on the critical issues ahead of the pack was another of his strengths.

He finished a few things he was working on, and left the office at the last possible minute, still fretting over Clay's comment about moving his investment. Too impatient to wait for the elevator, he decided to take the stairs down to the parking garage. There, he climbed into his metallic grey Porsche 911 Turbo, a two-hundred thousand dollar land rocket with almost six hundred horsepower.

He fired up the engine, letting it warm up briefly before he threw the shifter in reverse. He turned his head to look behind him, mashed the accelerator, and heard the tires squeal as the car jerked backwards. Before he could get his head around, he heard and felt a crash as the car stopped as quickly as it had started.

He stared at the rear end of a silver SUV behind him, parked not in a parking space, but in the aisle next to the concrete wall. In the ten years he'd been in this building, there had never been a vehicle parked there.

Shit, he thought, looking at his watch. He opened his door, got out, and walked toward the rear of the car. The bumper of the Porsche had done its job and protected the sports car, but left a small dent in the rear fender of the SUV, a Tahoe. He looked around the garage. No one was there but him. He knelt and took another look.

The dent was hardly noticeable on the fender near the back bumper. The vehicle shouldn't have been parked there, and the owner probably wouldn't notice it. He shook his head, went back to the cockpit of his car, and dug around in the console for a pen. He scribbled a short note on the back of his business card and placed it under the windshield wiper on the driver's side of the Tahoe where it wouldn't be missed.

He jumped back in his car, maneuvered around the Tahoe and sped out of the garage, tires squealing as he turned left on Cleveland Avenue and made his way over to McGregor Boulevard and Alex's condo. Two miles later, downshifting the Porsche's gears as he turned the corner, he roared into the Rivergate condominium complex, screeching to a stop at the entrance to Alex's building. He drove like he did everything else—hard and fast, with no wasted effort.

He'd been trying to get her to move in with him, or at least to a more desirable condo. Although she spent most nights at his house, she was adamant about keeping her own place. Rivergate wasn't a dump, but it was an older complex, close to downtown, and had fallen behind some of the other more modern places. But it was hers and she was determined to hold onto it.

Just as he got to her door and raised his hand to knock, it opened. Alex stood there in a simple, elegant black dress and looked like a million dollars. The dress was short enough to display her long, well-shaped legs, but not so short as to be scandalous. The front was scooped and displayed the beginning of her cleavage, but again, with the stone pendent hanging down, it was tasteful and set the perfect balance.

He recognized the pendant—a Petoskey stone that he'd bought her on a trip they took to Mackinac Island this past summer. They spent a week at the historic Grand Hotel, in a suite with a beautiful view of Lake Huron.

She arched her eyebrows and held her hands down by her side, palms open, seeking his approval.

"You look stunning," he said, meaning every bit of it.

Her frown turned into a smile, and she said, "Thank you, but you're still late. I look okay? You're not embarrassed to be seen with me?"

He laughed. It was one of her constant worries. Alex was insecure that she wasn't from the same class as he and worried that one day he'd trade her in for a trust baby from his side of the tracks. Although he did his best to persuade her that wasn't in the cards, she still let it show at times.

He shook his head and said, "How many times do I have to tell you? People question what you're doing with me, not vice versa." Her grin broadened, and she shut the condo door.

Downstairs, he opened the car door for her, admiring the view as she sat in the seat of the sports car, swinging her legs inside. She caught him looking and smiled, not saying a word.

They left her condo, heading south on McGregor. At Colonial, he turned left and went to Summerlin Road, turning south toward the University Club.

As he threaded his way through the traffic on the six-lane highway, Alex reached over and put her hand on his shoulder.

"We're only a few minutes late. Let's just get there in one piece."

He smiled, shifted into a lower gear, and floored the accelerator. After a split-second hesitation, the turbo came to life. The engine roared and six hundred horsepower pinned them back in their seats. He moved over to the left lane, intending to shoot back into a tiny gap between the car in front of him and a car in the right lane next to them.

He glanced in the outside rearview mirror on his right to confirm he had just enough room to squeeze in. Before he could move over, he caught movement in his peripheral vision on his left. *What the hell?* Reflexively, he hesitated on changing lanes, and swiveled his head slightly to the left, only to see a large Cadillac coming directly at him. He jerked his head to the right, confirming the right lane was clear. Bracing himself, he cranked the steering wheel to the right, yelling at Alex to hold on.

The Cadillac slammed into the left side of the Porsche. He felt the car tip to the right. Airbags exploded around him and the car continued to tilt, rolling completely over. The last thing he remembered was wanting the motion to stop.

Chapter 2

Warren? Warren?"

Warren opened his eyes. The white light was bright and his eyes seemed as though they'd been glued shut. His mouth was dry and he was thirsty. He squinted, and tried to determine who was calling his name.

The familiar face of his friend, Dr. Gordon Pollock, came into focus above him. Warren realized he was lying on his back. When he tried to sit up, a dagger of pain shot through his left arm. That was when he noticed it was elevated and suspended from some sort of contraption hanging over him.

"Gordo?" he croaked, his voice sounding raspy.

"Hey, buddy. How're you feeling?"

"A little foggy. Where am I?"

Gordo explained that he was in a room at Rivers Hospital.

"What happened?" Warren asked.

"You were in a car accident yesterday, remember?"

He closed his eyes, then opened them. "Alex?" he asked, in a panic, as he remembered she was with him in the car. He was relieved to see Gordo smile.

"She's fine. She's up on six, but doing well. Bruises and scratches, but nothing permanent. She's running a little fever, so they're probably going to keep her overnight."

"You taking care of her?" Warren asked.

Gordo shook his head. "No. I'm not sure who's assigned to her, but she'll be fine. Don't worry."

Warren's arm throbbed, and he looked at it, wincing.

"You've had surgery on your left arm." Gordo explained that it had been damaged in the wreck, and emergency surgery was necessary to repair it. "You've been pretty doped up since you've been in here. The CT was negative, but we just wanted to make sure everything inside was fine."

"You do my surgery?" Warren asked.

Gordo laughed. "No way, my friend. You wouldn't want me doing it. Larry Kenner did it, and trust me, he's the one you want. Remember Javarious Croup?"

Warren winced as he thought about the name. Javarious Croup was a stellar wide receiver who played college ball for Florida State. In the Florida game two years ago, Croup had been streaking down the sideline, on his way to what looked to be a game winning reception. At the last moment, when he went airborne to catch the ball, he was smashed by the Florida cornerback who jarred the ball loose. Anyone watching remembered the camera zooming in on the writhing athlete. When someone in the control booth realized the white on Croup's leg was not a sock but the athlete's tibia sticking out, the network cut away. It was too late. The video went viral in the sports community.

Croup had suffered a compound fracture that the talking heads insisted was the end of his career. Two years later, he led the Tampa Bay Buccaneers to an NFC Conference championship.

"Larry's the one who did the work on him. He's the best in the country. You were lucky. He was down here on Sanibel to do some fishing. We pulled some strings at the hospital to get him temporary privileges. Larry came over and did the surgery on your arm."

"So when do I get out?"

"Probably not for a few days, but that's up to him. He'll want to keep it immobilized and watch for infection. Then you can go." He pointed to the IV bag hanging next to the bed.

Warren looked up and saw an IV bag with a clear liquid, labeled Zena, hooked up to a clear plastic line that he assumed was connected to his body somewhere.

"That's why he's got you on this—it's the latest broad spectrum antibiotic. Good stuff—the best—but not cheap." Gordo glanced at the clock on the wall. "Look, I've got to run. I'll stop by this evening to check on you." He patted Warren's good arm, turned and walked out.

Warren looked around the small room. He could see sunlight streaming in the window, and a flat-panel television hanging from the ceiling. The walls were covered with rich, patterned wallpaper in a pleasing neutral shade. The bedside table appeared to be cherry or some sort of real wood as opposed to the typical industrial furniture normally expected in this setting. The room was clean and well-appointed.

He wanted to see Alex, but he knew he wasn't in any shape to find her. Some of the details were coming back to him.

He needed to call Becky. He wondered where his cell phone was. He turned his head to the table next to the bed, but didn't see anything on it resembling a phone. He pressed the call button on the intercom speaker clipped to his bed rail. A male voice answered, "Yes?"

"Could you send a nurse in, please?"

"Certainly. It'll be a few minutes." The intercom clicked off.

He waited, and soon a petite woman with short blonde hair and wearing blue scrubs walked into his field of vision.

"I'm Micah, Mr. Thompson. Can I help you?"

"Can you take me up to see my fiancée?"

She frowned. "I'll have to check with your doctor."

"I need my cell phone. Do you know where it is?"

She smiled and shook her head. "They just brought you down from recovery a little while ago. The only thing with you is what you see."

"I need to call my assistant. Could you get her for me please?"

The nurse stared at him for a moment, her penetrating blue eyes matching the blue scrubs. "There's a phone built in your call device. Just press nine for an outside line." She turned to leave.

"I don't know the number. Can you get it for me?"

Micah turned back around and put her hands on her hips. "Mr. Thompson," she said, pausing for effect. "I'm a nurse, and I'm here to take care of you medically so that you can get out of here as soon as possible. I'm good at what I do, and I'll give you my best. But, I've got six patients to take care of. I'm not your secretary, and I don't have time to fetch for you."

Warren started to let her know what he thought about her attitude, then realized that probably wasn't a smart thing to do. He tried to stare her down, but without success. He caved, nodded, and she walked out.

Lost without his cell phone, he had to call 411 through the hospital switchboard for information and be connected to his office number. Thank God, Becky answered the phone.

"Becky. I'm glad to hear your voice. Have you talked to Alex? Can you come down and take me up to see her? Oh, and I need my cell phone."

She chuckled. "Well, I see you're feeling better, barking out orders as usual. That's a good sign."

"Sorry, I'm just worried about her. When can you—"

"I was just leaving the office. Be there in thirty minutes. And, I have you a phone."

Twenty minutes later, Becky walked in. "How are you feeling?" she asked, a worried look on her face.

"I'm sore, and my arm hurts like hell."

"You both were very lucky. After seeing the car, I'm amazed you look as good as you do."

"What happened to the person who hit us?" he asked.

Becky shook her head and lowered her eyes. "She didn't make it. She'd had a heart attack, which is why she ran the stop sign."

If he hadn't been in such a rush, maybe he could've avoided the accident, he thought.

"They said she was probably gone before the crash. Not your fault." She handed him a phone. "Your phone was destroyed in the wreck. I've already loaded your contacts and other information," she said.

"Have you seen Alex?" he asked.

"I'm on my way up to see her as soon as I leave you. And I brought her a phone as well."

"Good, you can take me with you."

Becky looked at him, frowned, and shook her head. "You're hooked up to an IV and your arm is immobilized. You're not going anywhere tonight. I'll check and see if maybe in the morning."

He started to protest, but recognizing Becky's stern look, knew it was pointless.

She brought him up to speed on what was going on at work, then left to check on Alex. He gave her a few minutes to get to Alex's room, then called Alex's number.

"Hey, how are you?" Alex said, answering the phone. She came across as weary.

"Miserable. I tried to get Becky to take me up there with her, but she wouldn't. I should fire her."

Alex tried to laugh, but ended up coughing.

"You okay?" he asked.

"Tired. Just need to get some rest."

He could hear people talking in her room. "Who's that?" he asked.

"Just the other people in the pod," she said.

He wasn't sure what a pod was. He frowned, puzzled. He figured pod was hospital-speak for something less than a private room.

"As soon as I can get moving, I'll come up to see you," he said. "Sweet dreams."

As he set his phone down, the nurse came in to check on him. It was the same nurse who'd previously lectured him.

She checked his IV line and made some adjustments to the equipment.

"You don't much care for me, do you?" he said, watching her work.

Her face was inscrutable and the blue eyes intense. "My job is to take care of patients. I like taking care of people, and I think I do it well. Whether I like them or not isn't important. I'm a professional, just like you."

He was surprised at her response. It was without malice, but all business.

He looked at her hospital badge. "Look—Micah, is it? I'm sorry if I offended you. I'm just a little disoriented. The last thing I remember was a Cadillac headed straight toward the car my fiancée and I were in. Next thing I know, I wake up in the hospital."

Smiling, he continued. "I understand she's on the sixth floor. Do you work on that floor as well?"

Her face softened, and she shook her head. She checked the bandages on his arm, then studied the bedside computer screen.

"Do you know who her doctor is?" Warren asked. "I'd like to speak to him, if possible."

"Sorry, I really couldn't speak about other patients," she said, turning to walk out of the room.

Damn, what a customer-friendly place. If he didn't get out of here soon, he was going to explode. This was the first time he'd been a patient in a hospital since he was a kid, and he hoped it was the last.

Someone knocked on the door. "Hey, buddy."

He looked up to see who the voice belonged to and recognized Tim McLaughlin. They had gone to high school together, and in college, Tim had tried to talk Warren into going to law school. It was a running argument between them, with Warren going to business school, and Tim opting for law.

"Hey, Tim. Come on in. Nice to see a friendly face."

"Tabby's on his way up. He got waylaid by his boss in the lobby. How you feeling?"

"Not bad. Ready to get the hell out of here before nurse Ratched kills me."

Tim laughed. "Surely you're not talking about the one who just left your room. She looked nice enough."

"Yeah, well looks can be deceiving."

About that time, a mountain of a man filled the doorway.

"Sounds like a party in here," he said, lumbering over next to them after shutting the door. He dwarfed Tim, and Tim wasn't a small man.

Tabby Wilkins, a lieutenant with the Lee County Sheriff's office, wore a permanent grin accompanied by a squint, hence the nickname. He looked like the proverbial Cheshire cat.

The three of them grew up in the same neighborhood in east Fort Myers. In high school, they all had motorcycles. They were cheap transportation, and none of them could afford a car.

After graduation, they came close to joining the Split Aces, a notorious Florida-based motorcycle club. Fate intervened, when an older classmate who'd joined them the year before was shot and killed in an armed robbery attempt, part of his initiation.

That event was a wakeup call for the three friends, much to the relief of their parents. Tabby joined the Marines. Warren and Tim decided to go to college.

Tabby had a brown paper sack with him and set it on the bed. Warren thought he smelled food.

Tabby opened the bag and pulled out three Styrofoam containers.

"We thought you might want something decent to eat," Tim said, smiling.

Warren opened the container, hoping it was what he thought. It was—whole fried mullet, his favorite.

"Stopped by the City Fish Market on my way here," Tabby said.

The three friends enjoyed their meal, laughing and licking their fingers after devouring every morsel of the succulent fish. Most people turned up their nose at mullet, but to Warren and his friends, nothing was better than fresh fried mullet.

By the time they left, he was tired and almost asleep when his phone buzzed. It was Becky.

"I just thought I'd check on you before you went to sleep."

He told her about the guys stopping by and bringing him dinner from City Fish Market.

She laughed. "I'm sure you enjoyed that. Tabby didn't bring beer, did he?"

Becky and Tabby were close friends, which is where Warren suspected Becky got a lot of her information, though he'd never pursued it with either of them.

"No, he was supposedly on duty." Changing the subject, he asked her what a pod was.

Becky hesitated, then said, "Alex isn't in a private room."

He frowned. He had figured that much. Something to check on tomorrow. Unable to stop, he yawned out loud, not bothering to stifle it.

"I heard that," she said. "Put your phone up and get some sleep. I'll come by in the morning."

He was too tired to argue. "Thanks, Becky."

He nodded, rested the phone on his chest, and fell asleep within minutes.

Chapter 3

The next morning, Dr. Kenner stopped in to see him. Warren was surprised at how old the doctor was. For some reason, he'd been expecting someone much younger. He didn't know whether he was comforted or troubled by the physician's apparent age, then remembered Gordo's ringing endorsement of Kenner's skills.

"How's my Sanibel project doing?" Dr. Kenner asked.

"I'll be better once you let me out of this place," Warren answered. "How's the fishing?"

"Good, good. I landed two nice tarpon yesterday after taking care of you. I'm going back out again today as soon as I leave the hospital."

Dr. Kenner glanced down at Warren's chart. "Everything's looking good here. I'm sure Gordon explained that you had an open fracture, which is why we had to do immediate surgery. You fractured both the radius and the ulna—the two main bones in your forearm—so I put a plate in. The surgery went well, but there's always a risk of infection, which is why you're still here and on a prophylactic antibiotic."

Kenner put the chart down and looked at Warren's arm. "If everything continues to look good, we'll put a cast on and you'll be on your way. I'll need to see you again in four weeks. We'll evaluate it then, and go from there."

"That's the best news I've had since I've been here. What about the arm?"

Dr. Kenner explained that it should be as good as new, after time and a lot of physical therapy. He'd had great success with this procedure when the patient had followed instructions, and mixed results when they didn't.

"I can take the hint, and promise to be a good boy," Warren said. "When can I get disconnected from all of this crap? I'd really like to get up and stretch my legs a bit." He pointed to the IV.

Kenner nodded. "We can probably discontinue the IV and switch you over to oral. I still want to keep you on the antibiotic for a few more days, just to be safe. I'll put the order in when I leave," he said and walked out.

"Thanks, doc," Warren said, smiling.

As soon as the nurse came in and disconnected the IV, he told her he wanted to walk down the hall.

She frowned, and Warren continued. "Dr. Kenner said it was okay. He put that in the orders, didn't he? My legs are fine, and I feel good."

She helped him get out of the bed, and watched as he walked across the room to prove his point. He turned to face her and held out his right hand, his left arm in a sling.

"See?" he said.

She nodded. "Just stay close to the handrails," she responded.

He gave her a few minutes before he went to the door of his room. On the way to radiology, he'd noticed the elevators were directly across from the nursing station, so that would be out. However, he'd noticed an Exit sign the opposite direction, and hoped that indicated a stairwell.

He walked out in the hall and stopped, getting his bearings. It was a busy floor, with people coming and going both directions. The nursing station was to the right, as he remembered. He turned and looked left. The Exit sign was four doors down on the same side of the hall as his room.

Turning to the left, he walked toward the sign, staying as close to the left side of the hallway as possible. Halfway there, he heard a female voice call his name.

"Mr. Thompson?"

Damn, he thought. *Who the hell?*

He stopped and turned to see Micah headed toward him.

"Mr. Thompson. What are you doing?"

"I . . . I was just stretching my legs."

She wrinkled her brow and stared at him, "Are you—"

"Dr. Kenner cleared me to walk. You can ask . . . what's the red-headed nurse's name? She was just in my room."

"Nancy?"

"Yeah, that's it. Nancy."

Micah appeared to give it some thought, then nodded. "Are you doing okay? No light-headedness?"

"No, no. I'm fine, really."

"Well, don't overdo it, okay. And if you feel dizzy, just hold on to the handrail and call someone. We don't want you falling."

"Sure. Thanks," he said, taking a deep breath as she turned and walked toward the nursing station.

He went through the door beneath the Exit sign, stopping first to make sure no one was watching. As he'd guessed, it was the stairwell. He took his time, holding on to the railing and walked up the two flights to the sixth floor, passing someone in scrubs headed down, who only gave him a passing glance.

When he got to six, he opened the door, and stepped out onto Alex's floor. He looked around, amazed, realizing it was a completely different layout. The elevators were in a familiar spot, along with a nursing station opposite, but the entire floor was more open.

Beds were lined up against the exterior walls, with flimsy curtains hanging from the ceiling on tracks, pulled around some beds to give the illusion of privacy. It reminded him of the hospital wards he'd see in an old movie, the name of which he couldn't recall. As he cautiously made his way toward the nursing station, he realized the beds were in groups of four, separated by walls that didn't even extend all of the way to the middle of the room. *So these are pods,* he thought.

He passed the first two pods, looking for Alex, but not recognizing anyone. He knew he had to find her quick, and he prayed she was in the next set of pods on this side of the central nursing station. *There, on the right.* Alex was lying in the bed, her head propped up on two pillows. At first, he thought she was asleep, but then she opened her eyes and smiled when she saw him.

He walked over, grasped her hand with his good one, and kissed her forehead.

"Hey, there, stranger. Glad to see you," he said. Her color wasn't good, and her skin seemed warm to his lips. Yet, other than a few visible scrapes and bruises, she seemed to be fine. He noticed she wasn't hooked up to any IVs or monitors.

"I'm glad to see you," she said, her voice weak. "What are—how did you—"

"I escaped, but probably not for long. How are you feeling?"

"Alright, just tired. What happened to your arm?" she asked, a concerned look on her face.

"Just a break, nothing serious," he answered, not going into any detail. "My keeper told me I'm going home soon. Said it will be good as new." He looked around at the meager surroundings. "Why didn't you tell me you were stuck in a ward? 'Pod' my ass."

She shrugged. "They didn't exactly give me a choice. I guess this is all my insurance covers. Why? Where are you?"

He was embarrassed to answer. "I'm down on four," he said, again skipping the details. "I'm going to get this straightened out when I get back downstairs."

"Who are you? What are you doing here?" a voice behind him barked. "Obviously a patient."

The voice was that of a female, but one that indicated no nonsense.

Warren turned his head to see a heavy-set woman dressed in scrubs standing there, arms on her hips and a stethoscope draped around her neck.

"This is my fiancée. I'm just visiting—"

"This is my unit and my patient and you need to leave—now. You still haven't answered my questions."

His face flushed, but he said, "Warren Thompson, and I'm a patient on four."

She continued her assault. "And, do you have your doctor's permission to be off your floor?"

He hesitated. Kenner hadn't really given him permission to leave fourth floor, but he hadn't forbid it, either. As he started to reply, she shook her head.

"I didn't think so. You are leaving—immediately."

"Not before I—"

A security guard appeared next to her, pushing a wheelchair. He was a large man with a smoothly-shaven head, and appeared to be in excellent shape. Definitely not your typical rent-a-cop, and not someone Warren wanted to provoke.

"Gary, please escort Mr. Thompson back down to four," she said to the uniformed man. "They're looking for him."

Warren kissed Alex and whispered, "I'll get this sorted out, don't worry. Talk to you later."

As soon as he got back downstairs to his room, he called Gordo's cell phone. No answer. He disconnected, not bothering to leave a message, and called Becky.

"Can you get a hold of Gordo?" he said when she answered. "Have him call me as soon as he can."

Thirty minutes later, Gordo walked in, still wearing scrubs. "I was busy with another patient when you called. What's up?"

"Gordo, will you check on Alex? I'm worried about her, and no one will tell me anything. I went up there earlier—"

Gordo frowned. "You went up there? You shouldn't be on that floor."

"She doesn't look good, at all. Plus, I want to get her moved to a private room. She's in a fucking ward, Gordo."

Gordo held up his hands. "Just settle down. Let me see what I can find out. I'll let you know."

Later that evening, Gordo stopped by on his way out of the hospital. "I went up and checked on Alex. I talked to Kevin Vann, her physician. She seems to have gotten an infection. That's why they didn't want you up there. Anyway, these things happen. Nothing to worry about."

"You sure?"

"Positive," Gordo answered. He didn't seem alarmed, which reassured Warren.

"What about getting her moved to a private room?" Warren asked.

"Her insurance won't—"

"I don't give a damn about her insurance. I'll pay the difference."

"Let me finish," Gordo said. "There aren't any private rooms available. I'll ask Kevin to put her on the list for one. Quit worrying."

He walked over to Warren's bed. "I hear you're getting out tomorrow."

"That's what Kenner said. It won't be soon enough, I can tell you that."

His friend laughed. "Not a fun place to be, is it?"

"Another day of this, and you'll have to take me to a psychiatric hospital."

After Gordo left, he read for a little bit, then called Alex. She didn't answer, and he left her a voice mail telling her good night.

After a restless night, a young doctor in a white lab coat and stethoscope draped around his neck walked in the next morning, accompanied by the female nurse from the day before.

"Mr. Thompson? I'm Doctor Bankston. I'm the hospitalist making rounds for Doctor Kenner this morning. How are you feeling?" The doctor held on to his clipboard as if holding a security blanket.

Warren shrugged and rotated his head around. "Sore. A little stiff, but ready to get the hell out of here."

Bankston set the clipboard on the bed and plugged the stethoscope in his ears. He leaned over and placed the disc on Warren's chest. After a few seconds, he nodded, and stood, taking the earpieces out and draping it back over his neck.

He flipped through the pages of the clipboard and said, "I'm going to discharge you, but you need to make a follow-up appointment with your regular doctor within the next couple of days—strictly as a precaution. Your labs and MRI look good. You were lucky."

"Could you tell me where my fiancée is?" Warren asked. "And how she's doing?"

Bankston shook his head. "I don't know, and even if I did, I couldn't tell you. Privacy rules. Sorry, our hands are tied. We're strictly prohibited from giving out patient information to anyone without prior authorization."

Warren thought he saw the nurse roll her eyes. He looked at her hospital badge. Micah Rollins.

Bankston left the room, while the nurse prepared Warren to leave.

"Can you take me up to six? I want—"

"My orders were to get you ready to be discharged. You're going home," Micah said, ignoring his request.

He picked up his phone and called Becky. "Are you picking me up? Looks like I'm going home."

Becky told him she was on her way and would be out front.

"See if you can get Gordo and find out what's going on with Alex. Nobody will tell me a damn thing around here," he said, glaring at Micah.

Another woman, this one dressed in street clothes, came in pushing a wheelchair. Micah introduced the newcomer as she finished her tasks.

"This is Mona Edwards, the discharge coordinator. She'll go over your discharge instructions and take you downstairs. Take care of yourself, Mr. Thompson," Micah said as she turned and walked out.

"What do I need a wheelchair for? I can walk," he said.

Mona shook her head. "As long as you're in here," she said, spreading her arms, "you're my responsibility and you have to be in a wheelchair."

He grumbled, but listened patiently as Mona went over the list of instructions, which seemed to be mainly another cover-your-ass step for the hospital. As she wheeled him downstairs, he appealed to her for information on Alex, but got the same response as he'd received from Bankston.

Gordo caught up with him downstairs as he was waiting on Becky. "Hey, buddy. Going home, huh?"

Warren nodded, glad to see his friend. "Can you tell me what the hell's going on with Alex? Nobody will tell me anything."

Dr. Pollock looked at the discharge coordinator and asked her to give them a minute. She walked over to the reception desk and started talking to the two volunteers seated there.

Satisfied she was not listening, Gordo looked back at Warren. He had a serious look on his face. "I ran into Kevin this morning. She's not doing well. The infection has spread—"

"What the hell you mean it's spread? I thought they were going to try another antibiotic?"

Gordo shook his head. "I don't know any of the details. All I know is what I told you."

Warren grabbed Gordo's arm. "Do I need to get her another doctor? What would you do?"

His friend shook his head. "Relax. Kevin's good. I'd recommend him to anyone."

He nodded and released Gordo's arm. "Alright, if you say so. But let me know if I need to do anything."

"Sometimes infections can be tricky. Kevin will stay on top of it—don't worry. She's in good hands."

Gordo motioned the discharge coordinator over as Becky walked up.

"Dr. Pollock, good morning. Mr. Thompson, are you ready to go?" Becky said, walking over to the wheelchair.

Gordo chuckled. "Good morning, Becky. I think he's beyond ready. I've got to run. Warren, I'll call you as soon as I hear anything."

"Thanks," Warren said as he watched his friend walk away.

Becky introduced herself to Mona, and said she was there to take Mr. Thompson home.

"Great," Mona said. "I'll help you get him in the car."

"That won't be necessary," Warren said.

Mona hesitated. "We're supposed to make sure—"

"I understand, Mona, but Becky is very capable of helping me get in the car. I am officially discharged, right? You're done?"

The coordinator looked perplexed. "Well, yes, but—"

Warren stuck his hand out. "Good. Thank you for your help. I'm sure you've got plenty of other things to do."

Mona nodded, shaking his hand, and conceding. "Thank you, and give us a call if we can do anything." She spun and walked away, her heels clicking on the tile floor of the waiting area.

Becky unlocked the brakes on the wheelchair, took the handles, and started toward the main entrance.

"No, Becky."

She stopped. "Did you forget something?"

"Take me up to the sixth floor. I want to see Alex."

When they got to the pod, the curtains were pulled back and there was a cadre of caregivers around Alex's bed, working frantically. A tall man in a white lab coat was bent over her bed, hands busy doing something, and shouting instructions. One of the nurses was handing him things from a wheeled cart parked at the foot of her bed.

"We need to get her to the OR—stat," Warren heard him say. One of the nurses fiddled with the bed, releasing the wheel brakes. As Warren watched helplessly from his wheelchair, a nurse from the unit came up and stood between him and Alex.

"I'm sorry, but you're going to have to leave. It's an emergency, and we need to keep the halls clear," she said.

Warren strained to look around her, which was a challenge with her girth. He started to get out of the wheelchair. "That's my fiancée, and I'm not going anywhere," he said.

She moved a step closer, blocking his path. "If you don't leave right this minute, I'm calling security."

He leaned around her and could see the man he thought was a doctor at the head of Alex's bed. Before the nurse could speak again, he saw the doctor turn to a nurse and shake his head. The team of caregivers slowed their pace and then stopped, heads lowered. The sense of urgency was gone.

Warren had a clear view of the man's face, and he didn't have to have medical training to know what the doctor's expression meant.

Alexis Sutton was no longer in this world.

Chapter 4

It was a bright, sunny day in southwest Florida, the kind the Chamber of Commerce and tourists loved. There were a few, small, white clouds scattered against the backdrop of a brilliant blue sky. The temperature was comfortable, and with such a setting, it seemed surrealistic to be going to a funeral.

Warren had flown Alex's mother down from Chicago, along with an aunt, her only family left. Her father had died some years ago, and her mother had never remarried. She lived in the same house on the south side of Chicago where Alex had grown up.

Becky arranged for a limo to pick them up at the airport and bring them over to his house, where he insisted they spend the night. Carmela, Warren's housekeeper, had come in the next morning to prepare breakfast. He had invited Becky over for moral support, to join them for breakfast, and the ride to the church.

Warren had arranged for the funeral home to pick up the family at his house. He and Becky rode in the car with the family. As far as he was concerned, they were family and it never occurred to him to think otherwise.

The car stopped in front of the church, and a young man from the funeral home, dressed in a dark suit, white shirt, and tie, opened the door to the stretch limousine. They were escorted to a family room outside the main chapel, where the priest met with them privately.

Alex and Warren had never discussed this phase of life and the required decisions. Forties were not the age those kinds of determinations were usually made. He made the choices he thought Alex would've wanted, like a closed casket. Alex had expressed an aversion to the custom of viewing the dead—something Warren agreed with—so that much was easy.

When the funeral home representatives escorted the family in, Warren was surprised at how crowded the church was. Although it was a large church, few empty seats could be seen as they processed down the aisle to the front pews reserved for family. Tim and Tabby were already seated in the second row. When Warren slipped into the pew, both of his friends reached up and put their hands on his shoulders, giving him a squeeze.

The priest, a good speaker, waxed eloquently about Alex, even though he barely knew her. Warren knew it was part of the show, and his eyes remained dry. When they left the church, the funeral party moved to the graveyard across the street, where a tent had been set up to house the deceased and family.

The funeral coach arrived at the gravesite and the pallbearers transported the casket to the rack over the grave. That was when it hit Warren. As much as he tried to halt them, the tears began rolling out from under his sunglasses down his cheeks. He willed them to stop, yet onward they came, as if marching to orders from outside his body.

The priest recited a bible verse and a short prayer, then thanked those in attendance and dismissed the group. In the distance, Warren saw the cemetery employees by their truck, waiting for the group to disperse so they could finish their work for the day.

Part of Warren wanted to watch. He wanted to see Alex being lowered into the ground and the dirt shoveled in over her. He wanted to hear the sound of earth falling on the casket. He needed that closure, but didn't think he could bear it.

As the crowd thinned, the last of the mourners hugged him or shook his hand as they made to leave. He glanced over once more at the crew of gravediggers. They were polite enough to appear as inconspicuous as possible, but he knew they were anxious to get started.

Becky escorted Alex's family back toward the limousine, giving Warren a chance to say his goodbyes in private. He walked over to the casket and stood there. The mahogany surface was covered with beautiful flowers in all the colors of a rainbow, but it still looked as lifeless and cold as its contents.

He heard footsteps, and turned to see a petite blonde in a plain black dress approach him and extend her hand. She wore sunglasses, and her hair was cut short, complimenting her round face.

"I'm so sorry, Mr. Thompson," she said, clasping his hand. Her voice was clear and strong, belying her stature, commanding your attention in a non-threatening way.

Something about her looked familiar, but he couldn't place her. "Thank you," he said, holding on to her hand.

"I'm sorry, were you a friend of Alex's?" he asked, still wondering who she was.

She shook her head. "No, I work at the hospital."

As soon as she said that, he remembered. She looked very different, dressed in something besides scrubs. She was the nurse from his floor.

"I just wanted to express my condolences," she said, as she withdrew her hand and turned to leave.

"Wait," Warren said. "Please."

She stopped and turned around, glancing around the now-empty cemetery, before settling her eyes on Warren.

Warren took a step toward her and reached his hand out for hers. Reluctantly, she put her tiny hand in his. Her grasp was surprisingly firm, and he could feel her strength.

"Thank you for coming," he said. "I just didn't recognize you. I apologize."

Her face flushed, and her eyes darted around again. "It's understandable, given your situation. I'm sorry, I shouldn't have come. I—"

""No, no. I'm glad you did. I remember you rolling your eyes when Dr. Bankston said he couldn't tell me anything about Alex. Micah, right?"

She nodded.

"You were refreshingly genuine. Especially compared to that unctuous Dr. Bankston."

A nervous laugh escaped her lips and she put her free hand over her mouth. "I'm sorry," she said.

"Don't be. It was kind of you to take the time to come. I really appreciate it. Thank you."

She pulled her hand from his. "I really must be going. Again, I'm so sorry about what happened." She turned and walked away.

Warren stared as he watched her get into a compact sedan of some sort, Honda or Toyota, and drive away. He remembered the confrontation when he'd first met the nurse, and was surprised that she'd come.

He turned his eyes toward the limousine, the engine running, parked at the edge of the pavement. The driver stood next to the rear door, waiting for him.

Warren looked down at the casket and gathered his thoughts. He brought his fingers to his lips, then reached over and touched the cold wood of the casket. He let his hand rest there for a moment, bidding Alex a last farewell.

He raised his head and looked over at the cemetery workers, nodded, then turned and walked to the car.

Chapter 5

Warren stood at the front door of his house, watching as the last of the steady stream of guests drove off. It was almost dark, and he was exhausted. He gave a final wave, and turned to shuffle through the house. His left arm ached inside the cast, and he was ready to crawl into bed. He still couldn't believe she was gone.

He passed by the fish-shaped key rack hanging next to the desk in the breakfast room and paused. Alex had hung it there. He smiled as he remembered when she bought it on one of their trips to Key West. She'd found it at a shop on the upper end of Duval Street and insisted that it belonged in this spot. As with all things involving décor, she was right. It was perfect.

His heart ached. There were so many things he had wanted to tell her. He didn't even tell her he loved her the last night in the hospital, when he called and left a message.

He went upstairs, took off his clothes and washed his face. Looking at the large, walk-in shower, he wished he could go in and stand there for hours, letting the hot water pound the muscles in his bruised body and wash away the memories. He looked down at the cast on his left arm and realized that wouldn't happen for weeks. He hunched over the sink, his tears mixing with the water from the faucet and swirling down the drain.

When he got out of the bathroom, he checked his answering machine and had thirty-seven messages. He listened to none of them. He unplugged the phone and went to bed, falling asleep within minutes.

The next morning, he was awakened by the buzzing of his cell phone. He ignored it and looked at the clock on the nightstand. It was six o'clock. He'd slept for twelve hours.

He went to the bathroom, then made his way downstairs. Doing everything with one arm was a pain in the ass—even walking up and down stairs. He was glad the architect had talked him into installing an elevator when he'd built the house.

He fixed a small pot of coffee, and sat at the bar in the kitchen in silence, not switching on the television as usual. He took his time, staring out the window at the river. The only sound was the tick-tock of the grandfather clock in the living room. When he poured the last of the coffee, he put on another pot and fished a bagel off the platter he spied in the kitchen.

He wanted to go outside, but realized a cup of coffee, bagel, and cream cheese exceeded his carrying capacity with only one good arm. He sliced the piece of bread, spread the cream cheese on each half, and put it back together. Searching the cabinet over the coffeemaker, he found an insulated mug with a top. After he transferred the coffee to the mug, he opened his mouth and stuffed the bagel in as far as he could. Mug in hand, he managed to hobble out to the table on the deck, overlooking the river.

It was a nice morning out, still and pleasant. He eased down into the chair and took the bagel out of his mouth.

He tore off a piece, and set the rest on the table. On the weekends, he and Alex loved to come out and have their morning coffee at this table. A tear rolled down his cheek, and he wondered how there could be any left.

After refilling his mug several times, he decided he'd go into the office. Sitting at home by himself was driving him crazy. He made himself go upstairs to get dressed. Realizing he couldn't wear a long-sleeve shirt, he managed to get his right arm in and just left the other arm in the sling underneath. He looked into the mirror.

A scruffy, one-armed man in an ill-fitting shirt and grey slacks stared at him. His face was bruised and swollen, and he needed a shave. No *GQ* fashion shoot today. He took the electric razor and gave his face a quick trim. Checking the mirror again, he decided it would have to do.

Downstairs at the key rack, he reached for the keys to Alex's white BMW 435i. The tears ambushed him, streaming down his face, and he stood there sobbing. Damn, he hated this, worse than anything he'd ever felt. When they finally subsided, he stumbled into the kitchen. He found a towel and dried his face before going out to the garage.

He looked over at his motorcycle, a Jesse James original that he'd purchased two years ago at a charity auction. It'd be a while before he'd be riding again. He turned back to the BMW. Good thing it was an automatic, he thought, as he got in the car and headed to the office.

He ignored the one-finger salutes and honking horns he received for not giving turn signals. In the parking garage, he took the back way into his office, not ready to face the gauntlet of people he knew would be waiting with condolences. Taking the freight elevator upstairs, he limped down the hall to the back, unmarked entrance to his suite, and unlocked the door. Becky, sitting at her desk, looked up and saw him.

"Mr. Thompson," she said, rising to greet him. "What are you doing here? You should've stayed home." She walked over and hugged him as if he were a child. "Why didn't you call me to come get you if you were determined to come in?"

The older woman's arms comforted him, and he hugged her with his one good arm, not wanting to let go.

"I couldn't stand sitting at home by myself. Need to get my mind off of things, anyway. Thanks for everything. I know it's been crazy."

"How're you feeling?" she asked, then caught herself and said, "Other than the obvious."

He tried to smile and nodded. "Sore, and realizing how much you need two arms, but other than that—okay."

She nodded. "Good. Let me get you a cup of coffee, and I'll come in and get you caught up."

He was staring out the window when she came back and set the steaming cup of coffee in front of him.

"You sure you're up for this?" she asked, a worried look on her face. "You should probably take some time off. Go somewhere. It would do you good."

He shook his head. "No. Work gets my mind off of things." *For a little while,* he thought.

Becky went through the day's agenda, slower than she usually did. She also went through the dozens of messages, most of them condolences.

"I've already started on Thank You notes, so don't worry about that. You need to take it easy for a few days.

I'll do my best to keep everyone at bay," she said, standing to leave.

He nodded, and she walked out, closing his office door behind her. He tried handling some routine paperwork, then realized he wasn't mentally ready and quit, not trusting his state of mind. He skimmed through the financial news, but his heart wasn't in it.

Alex was the first woman he'd been serious about in a long time, maybe the only one if he was honest with himself. And now, she was gone. *How could this have happened?* he asked himself over and over. According to Gordo, his injuries had been more serious than hers, with none life-threatening.

In the shadows of his mind, he felt responsible. If only he hadn't been in such a hurry, maybe he would've seen the car running the stop sign in time to avoid the collision. Still, she shouldn't have died.

By early afternoon, he'd muddled his way through some of the less taxing items on his desk, putting aside anything that required his usual concentration. His lunch that Becky had brought him sat untouched on his desk. He reached over and punched the intercom button on his desk set.

"Can you get me the name of Alex's doctor?" he asked, as soon as Becky answered.

"Her doctor?" she repeated.

"Yes, the doctor who treated her at the hospital. I can't recall his name."

Thirty minutes later, Becky walked in and handed him a piece of paper. The name *Kevin Vann, MD,* was written on it. She had included an address and phone number.

"Can you call Dr. Vann, give him my cell number, and ask him to call me as soon as convenient?"

An hour later, his cell phone buzzed. He recognized the number as the one Becky had given him, and he answered.

"Warren Thompson."

"Mr. Thompson, Dr. Vann here." The voice on the line hesitated. "I'm so sorry for your loss. You'd asked that I call you?"

"Yes, and thank you for returning my call. I was wondering when would be a good time to grab a cup of coffee. I just need a few minutes."

There was a pause on the other end. "May I ask in regard to what?"

Warren had been expecting this. "Just a personal issue. Something I'd rather not discuss on the phone. I promise it won't take more than ten minutes of your time."

There was another pause, then, "How about the hospital cafeteria in the morning? I usually make rounds around seven, so six thirty—if that's not too early?"

"Great. Thank you. I'll see you in the morning."

Warren hung up the phone and asked Becky to find him a photo of Dr. Vann so he'd recognize him.

Chapter 6

For once, Warren was early. He didn't want to give Dr. Vann any excuse, so at twenty minutes past six, he was sitting at a table where he could see the entrance to the cafeteria. Steam rose from a large cup of Seattle's Best Coffee sitting in front of him, the aroma drifting in front of his face.

Like most institutional cafeterias, Rivers had transitioned to name brands to prop up sales. After standing behind a long line of people ordering ventis, double grande skinny lattes, pretentious iced coffee drinks, and everything else under the sun, he asked the thick, brown-skinned lady behind the counter if he could just get a large black coffee. She threw back her head, laughing out loud, replying that she was so glad to hear that for a change.

He handed her a ten and told her to keep the change. She smiled, thanked him, and said she'd bring it out to his table if he wanted to grab a seat. He started to protest, but then figured he had better get used to not being able to do everything for himself. He found a table nearby and plopped down into the seat, not very gracefully. The barista brought his coffee over and set it on the table in front of him.

In a few minutes, a short, pudgy man, balding on top, walked in to get a cup of coffee. Warren recognized him from the picture. The doctor looked around the uncrowded cafeteria and saw Warren, who waved. The doctor acknowledged him, ordered his coffee and as soon as he had it, walked over.

"Mr. Thompson? Kevin Vann." He extended his hand, shook Warren's, and sat.

"What're you drinking?" Warren asked, curious.

"Grande, double shot, skinny mocha," Vann answered. "My favorite. You?"

Warren smiled. "Just coffee," he said. He took a sip, then continued. "Thanks for agreeing to meet with me."

"Not sure what I can do for you, but glad to try," Vann said, his voice and expression guarded. "How is your arm?" he asked, looking over at Warren's cast.

"Fine." Warren noticed that Vann didn't ask what happened, and he was sure Vann had done his homework. For once, Warren was going to take advantage of his connections at the hospital.

"You're in Gordon's group, right?" Warren asked, invoking the first name of the senior partner in the physician group that included Vann.

Vann took a sip of his grande, double shot, skinny mocha, and nodded.

"Good friend of mine. I've known Gordo for years. Nice guy," Warren said.

"Yes, he is. I have a lot of respect for Dr. Pollock."

Vann was trying to maintain an air of formality. Warren looked around to make sure no one was listening, and leaned across the table. He lowered his voice. "Look, I know with all the privacy stuff, you're not supposed to say anything to me about another patient. But, I'd consider it a personal favor—to me and to Gordo—if you'd tell me what exactly happened with Alexis Sutton."

Vann started shaking his head.

Warren held up his hands. "I'm not blaming you, so this conversation doesn't go any further, okay? It's just me and you, so you can deny it ever took place. From what I understand, she wasn't hurt that bad in the accident. I was in worse shape than she was, so you can imagine how shocked I was when I learned she . . . she didn't make it." He choked on the words, and wondered how long it would be before he could say the D word.

Vann took a long sip of his coffee, glanced around, and then leaned across the table. "Mr. Thompson, I am very sorry for your loss. Believe me when I say we did everything we possibly could. But she had injuries that didn't show up on the initial evaluation by the EMTs and she got an infection.

"That's not uncommon. Those guys do a great job, but they don't have the resources or time on site to do what we can do here. They did everything by the book, but medicine is not a perfect science. Sometimes, bad things just happen. I wish I could tell you more, but there's just nothing else to tell. Again, I'm very sorry."

Warren composed himself and spoke. "I understand. Medicine is part art, and I realize that. But, may I be candid here? What I don't understand is why she wasn't given Zena. She wasn't responding to the cheap shit, so my question is 'why wasn't she given the good stuff?'"

Vann's face flushed and his eyes darted around. He was clearly uncomfortable with the direction of the conversation, and not accustomed to having his medical opinion challenged, especially by a layman.

"I realize you're upset, and again, I sympathize with you," Vann said. "However, I am not at liberty to discuss a patient's care with you, including the type of medications they may have received. In fact, I'm curious as to how you think you know what antibiotic she was receiving?"

Warren struggled to control his emotions and not get angry, but he was not going to let Vann redirect the conversation. He didn't take the bait.

"Doctor Vann. I'm not questioning your medical judgment. I'm simply trying to understand what happened to my fiancée. It makes no sense whatsoever. They were pumping me full of one of the most expensive antibiotics available when I had no infection. Yet, for Alex—"

"Mr. Thompson. As caregivers, we are bound by the care guidelines that accompany each patient. We don't have the latitude that you're implying. I can assure you we followed her care guidelines to the letter."

"What do you mean 'you don't have the latitude?' Aren't you the doctor? Don't you make the final decision on the patient's care?"

Vann took a deep breath. "Our health care system is extremely complex. Dr. Pollock could probably do a better job of explaining it to you, but the bottom line is that when patients are admitted, they have care guidelines that indicate the level and type of care they are to receive. Deviations are rare, and must be approved in advance."

He finished his coffee and looked at his watch. "I apologize—I wish I could tell you more, but I've got to make my morning rounds. Again, I'm sorry about Ms. Sutton." It was clear that Vann was retreating behind the textbook reply and not going to say any more. He stood, shook hands with Warren, and walked out.

Warren sat there, staring at his coffee. He was angry with himself for losing his patience with the doctor. Vann had told him the same story that Gordo had the day Alex died, almost verbatim. For some reason, it sounded even less plausible today than it had before.

He knew medicine wasn't an exact science, but he still had trouble believing the story. If he'd done something, Alex would still be here. He couldn't get her face out of his mind.

He didn't have a clinical background, and realized sometimes "bad things just happen," as Vann said. But as a businessman, he was logical and rational. The question of what happened still nagged him and he wasn't satisfied with the answers he had received. He'd just have to talk to a clinician he could trust.

On his way back to the office, he called Gordon.

Chapter 7

Warren and Gordo were having dinner at Jimmy's, a Fort Myers institution that had relocated to a renovated block downtown near Harborside. Warren had requested a table in a secluded alcove at the restaurant where they could dine uninterrupted.

"So, how're you doing?" Gordo asked, taking a sip of his wine.

"Okay, I guess. Trying to get back in the saddle." He swallowed. "It's hard. I miss her."

He'd known Gordo for ten years, since he'd moved back to Fort Myers. Besides being close personal friends, Gordo the physician had poked and prodded him every year at physical time, and knew the workings of his body better than he. Warren found it relatively easy to open up to him, as much as he could with anyone.

Gordo nodded. "I know you do. It'll take time. Not something you can speed up or control. You sleeping okay? I can give you something, you know?"

Warren lied and told him he was sleeping fine. He knew his friend would be happy to give him a prescription for something to help him sleep, but he didn't want it. He wanted to feel the pain and not have it dulled. Escape was not an option.

They ordered, then talked about investments. Gordo had long since turned over his investments to Warren to manage, and had done well over the years. Gordo asked him about several of the specific investments and any changes that needed to be made.

"Are you still holding that parcel out near the airport?" Warren asked.

Gordo nodded. "Why?"

"I had lunch with the mayor yesterday. There's talk about a new shopping center further south. You should sell the airport land and buy something down there."

"I thought I'd hold on to it for a few more years. It's bound to keep going up."

Warren shook his head. "You paid six for it. You can sell it for eight, eight and a half, which is a forty percent profit. Not shabby, but you get in now on that mall parcel, you can easily triple your money in a couple of years."

Warren was offering him the chance to make millions. That was the problem with Gordo, he was too conservative. Warren had given him other tips over the years, tips that could've made the doctor some real money, but he was too timid to stretch.

"I'll give it some thought," Gordo said, but Warren knew that was his friend's way of saying *no*.

When the entrees arrived, they both dug in. Warren had ordered Florida lobster—a misnomer, since it was a different species—and Gordo had ordered a shrimp dish.

After the first mouthful, Warren, pointing his fork at Gordo, said, "I need to ask you something."

Gordo finished chewing his first bite and said, "Sure, what?"

"Explain to me, in layman terms, what happened to Alex," Warren said.

Gordo put his fork down and shook his head. "Warren . . ."

"Don't give me that song and dance routine about how medicine's not an exact science and sometimes things just don't go the way we think. I've heard all that. As a friend, I'm asking you to explain what happened. I can deal with it, but I just need to know the truth."

Gordo took a deep breath as he looked at Warren, seeming to consider his request. "Kevin told me you talked to him. I know you didn't like the answer, but the reality is that she got an infection and couldn't shake it. Unfortunately, sometimes that happens and there's nothing we can do."

He took a drink of wine before continuing. "We don't know as much as we like to think we do. Kevin's a good doctor, but even the best of us don't always succeed. You've got to turn this loose, my friend. I know you're hurting, but believe me when I say there's nothing anyone could've done. Period."

Warren thought back to that day in the hospital when he watched Alex die. His face flushed, and he felt his blood pressure rise.

"Nothing, huh? So tell me why didn't they give her Zena? They were pumping that shit into me by the gallon and I didn't even have a damn infection. The cheap crap wasn't working for Alex, so why didn't they give her the good stuff before it was too late? That's what I really want to know, Gordo. And that's what no one will tell me."

Gordo shook his head, taking another nervous drink. "It's not that simple, Warren. Everything is controlled by the insurance companies. There are treatment protocols—care guidelines—which determine who gets what. Physicians don't have nearly the flexibility we once had. It's what you'd recognize as the Golden Rule—he who has the gold, makes the rules."

"So you're telling me that the insurance company wouldn't let her doctor give her the good stuff? Is that what you're saying?"

Gordo glanced around the restaurant. "I'm saying they wouldn't pay for it."

"That's the same thing."

"The system sucks, Warren. I'm sorry, but it's the system we're stuck with. It's a complicated, expensive system that doesn't always work."

"For Christ's sake, Gordo. I'm your friend. I need to know what happened."

Gordo looked across the table, locked eyes with his friend, and lowered his voice. "Listen to me, and listen carefully—one friend to another. Just drop it. This will not bring Alex back and it will result in nothing good—nothing, okay? I know you're grieving. And I feel for you, but there was nothing that could've been done."

They ordered coffee, and drank it quickly, a cloud hanging over the table. Warren realized he wasn't going to get anything else from Gordo, friend or not. As they walked to their cars, Warren thanked the doctor for dinner, the words sticking in his throat.

When he got home, he went upstairs and got ready for bed. There was an emptiness in the big house that was depressing. For the first time since he'd moved back to Fort

Myers, he thought about selling and moving somewhere else. Maybe he needed to leave Fort Myers, make a new start. With his business, he could locate anywhere with access to a decent airport and good Internet service.

He turned on the wireless speaker next to his bed, then picked up his iPhone and thumbed through the music he had loaded, deciding on Otis Redding—one of his favorites. He pressed shuffle, and got in bed.

He picked up a novel by Michael Connelly, looking for an escape. Then the disconsolate words of the Big O came tumbling out of the speaker, singing "Pain in My Heart." The words to the song cut through him like a knife and he cried himself to sleep.

Chapter 8

Two days later, Warren made himself go to the hospital for the monthly foundation meeting. Since he was early, he stopped by the cafeteria for a cup of coffee. The same lady was behind the counter and remembered him.

"You the one likes real coffee," she said, in a pleasant Caribbean lilt, not even giving him a chance to order. She was already filling a large cup with steaming coffee. "Your arm doing okay?" she asked, cocking her head and looking at him.

Warren had just gotten the full cast off but was still wearing a sling. "Better, thank you. I'll be glad to be rid of this contraption." He took the cup she slid toward him and said, "Now, what if I wanted a fat mocha or something else?" He laughed as he handed her a ten and told her to keep the change.

She smiled, her white teeth contrasting against her dark skin, and slowly shook her head. "Then I'm leaving to go prepare for the end times. 'Cause you ain't ever ordering no such thing."

He was still laughing as he made his way over to a table in the corner. She was right, and he was impressed at how perceptive she was. He made a mental note to give her his card next time he came in and tell her to call him if she ever needed a job. She had the kind of smarts that couldn't be taught, which was exactly the kind of person he liked to hire.

He sipped his coffee, perplexed that he was early. This had happened with alarming frequency since the accident, and he had no explanation for it. Maybe his internal clock had gotten shaken up in the accident.

He looked to his right, and saw the petite nurse from the cemetery walking by, a tray in her hands. This time she was dressed in familiar blue scrubs.

"Micah?" he called.

Not sure where the voice originated, she looked around before recognizing him seated at a table in the corner.

"Micah, right?" he repeated.

She nodded, and he asked her over to his table. He saw the nametag that he remembered from before. Micah Rollins.

"Please, sit down. I was early for a meeting and just having a cup of coffee."

She set her tray on the table and pulled out a chair. "Mr. Thompson. How are you? How's the arm?"

"Please, call me Warren. I'm doing well, thank you." He grabbed the sling with his good hand and shook it. "I'll be glad when I'm done with this. And you?"

"Fine," she said. He watched her pour cream and one pack of sugar in her coffee, then open the yogurt container on the tray.

"You're eating healthy," he said, nodding toward her food.

She smiled and shrugged. "I try. What are you doing getting hospital coffee—Starbucks closed?"

He grinned at her sense of humor and quick wit.

"Too many people in the drive-through," he answered. "Plus the coffee's cheaper here."

She put the napkin in her lap. "I wouldn't think that'd be a problem for someone like you," she said, watching him with a twinkle in her eyes.

He nodded, wondering how much she knew about him. They talked about the hospital, and she disclosed she'd worked there for four years. She loved nursing, and couldn't imagine doing anything else.

"So, how are you doing?" she asked.

Before he could launch into his usual reply, her eyes bore into him.

"Really doing," she said.

Once again, he was struck by her sense of caring and genuineness.

He exhaled. "Not sleeping well. I have some good days, but more bad ones."

"Are you taking anything to help you sleep?"

As he started shaking his head, she said, "It's okay, you know. You strike me as the type who doesn't like to take anything."

He smiled, but kept quiet.

"But, during periods of extreme stress, sometimes it can help," she said.

"I miss her. And I still wonder what happened. I can't let it go until I understand 'why.'" He was surprised at his reply. He saw the muscles in her neck tighten at his remark.

"What do you think happened?" she said, her voice softer now.

He shrugged and told her the same story he'd been told by everyone. He could repeat it almost as well as the people who told it to him.

"Why don't you believe it?" she asked.

He was surprised at her question. He hadn't said that he didn't believe it, but she seemed to be as perceptive as the lady behind the counter. He thought for a minute before answering.

"Do you know what I do for a living?" he asked.

"You're a hedge fund manager, and a good one, from what little I know."

He nodded, astounded that she knew that much. "A lot of what I do is based on math and science, but part of it is based on gut feeling. There's no other way to put it. I can't explain it, and I've given up trying. But I learned long ago to pay attention to that little voice inside my head. That same voice is telling me there's more to Alex's death. And I believe that voice."

She finished her yogurt and stood. "Good seeing you again. I've got to get to work." As she picked up her tray, she said in a hushed tone, "Trust the voice," and walked away.

He watched the nurse leave, and was intrigued. There was more truth in what she said than he realized. Since Alex's death, he had been disoriented, not trusting himself. Micah's comment had been like a wake-up call, a shock to his mental state. She was right, he thought, he had always been able to trust his inner voice. Now was not the time to stop.

Warren went up to the tenth floor, where the hospital administration offices were located. Kenneth Taylor was the CEO, and Warren was going straight to the top.

He walked in the door and was greeted by Cheryl, Taylor's assistant. She occasionally attended the foundation meetings with Taylor. He flashed her a disarming smile.

"Mr. Thompson. How are you doing? I'm so sorry about . . . Alexis," she said. She glanced at her computer screen. "I wasn't expecting you today."

"Thank you, Cheryl. I'm doing as well as can be expected. I wasn't planning to be up here today, either. I had a few minutes before the foundation meeting, and thought I'd stop by and see Ken. Is he in, by any chance?"

Cheryl shook her head. "No, I'm afraid he's out of town and won't be back until tomorrow evening. Is there something I could help you with?"

He looked around and leaned over her desk, talking in a lowered voice. "Actually, there is. I need to speak to someone about . . . about Alex. I'm struggling to understand, and am having trouble finding out anything. No one will tell me a thing, citing all of this privacy mumbo-jumbo."

He stepped back and raised his hands, palms facing her. "I'm not asking anyone to say anything out of school, but I just . . . I just need to talk to someone. That's why I wanted to see Ken. Is there someone else who I can talk to?"

Cheryl gulped and cleared her throat, looking around the office, hoping for someone to come in and rescue her. "Mr. Thompson, I . . . I don't know what to say. I could lose—"

Warren shook his head. "I don't want to get you into any trouble, even though I wouldn't breathe a word." He looked at her hopefully, but could see she wasn't budging. "Is there anyone here who I can discuss this with? Please?"

She nodded as if struck by a way out. She held up her index finger, picked up her phone and punched in a number. "Joan? Hi, it's Cheryl. Are you busy?"

She waited for a reply, and said, "Warren Thompson is here, asking about Ms. Sutton. Could you please talk to him?" She nodded, and said, "Thank you. I'll bring him to your office."

Cheryl took him over to the office of Joan Frazier, the COO of Rivers. As the number two person at the hospital, Warren had worked with her before. She was sharp and known for her directness.

Joan stood and shook Warren's hand, her grip firm and her eyes looking directly into his. Cheryl, glad to be able to pass the buck, bade him goodbye, and closed Joan's office door on her way out.

"Warren, I'm so sorry about Alex. How are you doing?"

He nodded. "Alright. I appreciate you coming to the funeral. That meant a lot. I'm still a little sore, but glad to be home."

She didn't offer him a seat. Still standing, she said, "I've only got a few minutes. What could I do for you?"

"Joan," he said, pausing for emphasis while collecting his thoughts. "I've always appreciated the fact that you're a straight shooter. For the past week, I've tried to get a number of people to tell me what happened with Alex. I've spoken with her doctor, Kevin Vann, and nobody, including my best friend Gordon Pollock, will tell me anything."

The woman took a deep breath and held Warren's gaze. "I know this is difficult for you. It's difficult for me, too. I knew Alex well. I won't insult you by repeating all of the privacy warnings and corporate bullshit that I'm sure you're sick of hearing by now."

Warren nodded. "Thank you."

"No one will discuss her case with you because there are significant penalties involved with violating patient privacy. I'll tell you what I know, but I'll deny this conversation ever took place."

"I understand."

"The initial evaluation didn't reveal the full extent of her injuries. When she got here, there were some issues that weren't apparent at the scene of the accident. Then, after her arrival, she acquired an infection. They did everything they could."

Warren started to interrupt, but she held up her hand.

"Anytime a patient is admitted to a hospital, the diagnosis and insurance coverage mandate care guidelines that dictate most aspects of a patient's treatment. This includes obvious things, like type of accommodation. For example, you get a private room. Some coverage's don't pay for that."

"I understand that, but—"

"Hear me out. The care guidelines also dictate diagnostic tests, treatments, and medicines. There are significant potential penalties for the hospital and the physicians if they don't adhere to these guidelines. There are appeal processes in place, but unfortunately, they can take time."

"My God, Joan. You're telling me Alex was dying, and you couldn't get approval—" His voice rose several decibels, and he realized he'd inched closer to Joan.

She paused, this time holding up both hands. Increasing the space between them, then lowering one hand to her desk, she lowered her voice. "All I'm saying is that in Alex's case, by the time they got approval to deviate from the care guidelines, it was too late."

He stood there, shaking his head in disbelief, not trusting himself to say anything at first. His temples were throbbing, and he realized he was leaning toward her in a threatening posture, but he didn't care.

"That is pure bullshit."

She moved back another inch or so. "I'm sorry, Warren. I wish there was more to tell you, but unfortunately, it's that simple."

"Thanks, Joan. For nothing," he said, in a hoarse whisper as he turned to leave. She didn't bother to walk him to the door of her office.

Seething, he skipped the foundation meeting and went back to his office, ignoring Becky, and slamming the office door when he walked in. He threw his leather notebook on the desk and paced behind it.

Although Joan had told him a more elaborate version, it was the essentially the same story he'd heard from Gordo and Dr. Vann. They were all hiding behind these damn care guidelines, and pointing the blame at the insurance companies.

He punched the intercom button and asked Becky to get a phone number for Micah Rollins. He wasn't sure how she came up with such information, and not sure he wanted to know. She was a creative assistant, and when he asked her to get information, she succeeded more often than not.

She was also discreet, a quality Warren had long since learned to rely on. While she never hesitated to tell him what she thought when asked, she didn't intrude. So, several hours later, he was not surprised when she came into his office bearing a handwritten note with Micah's name, address, and phone number.

He recognized the name of the condo complex. It was an older, upscale building overlooking the Caloosahatchee River near downtown Fort Myers. Not the most exclusive address, but nothing shabby, either.

He pulled out his phone and entered the number. The call went straight to voice mail. Frustrated, he left her a brief message, asking her to please call him back.

He hoped he didn't sound as angry as he felt.

Before lunch, his phone buzzed. He looked at the caller ID, and it said *M Rollins*.

"Hello," he said when he answered the phone.

"Mr. Thompson. Micah Rollins, returning your call." Her voice was formal and businesslike.

"Warren, remember? I'm not that much older than you."

He heard a faint chuckle on the line. "Fine, Warren. You called?"

"Yes, and thank you for returning my call so promptly. I was wondering if I could meet you for lunch sometime this week?"

There was a pause, and for a moment, he thought the connection had been lost.

"May I ask why?" she said.

He knew better than to lie. "I want to talk with you about what happened to Alex."

Another hesitation.

"I'm not really sure I can tell you anything. I didn't work on her floor, and I'm not familiar with her case. Even if I was—"

"I know—because of the privacy rules—blah, blah, blah."

He heard a stifled snicker and continued, "Look, I'm not asking you to say anything you're not comfortable with. I've talked to her doctor, my doctor, the hospital COO, and I just get stonewalled. I just want to talk to someone with a clinical background, and you seem like the most direct and straightforward person I've talked to recently."

"I'm not sure how much I can help you." She paused, and he thought she was going to refuse him.

"How's Thursday?" she asked. Before he could answer, she continued. "Say 11:45 at Ray's on the River?"

Ray's was an old Fort Myers restaurant downtown on the Caloosahatchee River—a casual spot. At one time, it had been a place that he frequented, though he hadn't been there in years. He liked the fact that she took the initiative.

"Ray's is fine. I'll see you then," he said.

Before he could say anything else, he heard a click, and realized she'd disconnected.

Chapter 9

He got to Ray's five minutes late. Walking out to the dining room, he saw Micah sitting at a table next to the window overlooking the water. She was wearing jeans and a peasant top, which told him she wasn't working.

"I'm sorry I'm late," he said, pulling out a chair and sitting.

"No problem. I'd have given you another five minutes before I left," she said. She was smiling, but her look told him that she was dead serious.

They ordered water to drink and made small talk for a few minutes as they waited for their server to return.

"Thanks for meeting me," he said.

"You're welcome," she said, watching him and waiting for him to continue.

Their server returned with water, and they ordered lunch. She ordered the grilled grouper sandwich with a side salad, while he ordered a burger and fries.

"I'm not sure where to start, so I'll jump in. I'm usually pretty direct, so I hope that doesn't offend you," he said.

She shook her head. He told her about the accident, talking in more detail than he'd discussed with anyone else. She listened intently, not interrupting until he got to the point where the hospital COO told him about the care guidelines.

Micah fidgeted and rearranged her silverware. After taking a quick glance around the nearly empty restaurant, she looked at him, appearing to study his eyes. "How much do you know about the health care system?"

"Here in Fort Myers?"

She shook her head. "No, the U.S. health care system."

"A fair amount," he said, nodding. "Learning more each day. Plus, I invest in several health care companies and I'm on the foundation board at the hospital. One of my best friends is Dr. Pollock."

"So, you don't know shit, is what you're telling me?"

He was surprised at her language—not that he was surprised at cursing—he just had not expected it from her.

"And I thought I was blunt," he said.

She laughed. "You'll see that I also call things like I see them—for the most part." She shrugged. "If that offends you, then . . ."

"Tough shit," he answered for her.

"Exactly. But you're not alone, Warren. Most people don't have a clue as to how our health care system works."

"So, enlighten me."

For the next hour, she gave him a basic primer on the fundamental mechanics of the largest segment of the U.S. economy, pointing out aspects of it he'd never considered. She was intelligent and sharp, able to distill her comments down to the essence required to communicate what was behind them without obfuscating the important parts.

One of his favorite sayings was *follow the money*. And that was precisely what she was telling him about health care.

"You have health insurance, right?" she asked him.

"Of course. Everyone does, now."

With the passage of universal health care several years ago, health insurance had been extended to everyone. Unlike socialized medicine, common in other developed countries, the United States had decided on a commercial model, preserving the capitalist components of the American system. The result was that everyone now had a Care Card, signifying their coverage through the USCare program, as it was called.

She looked around to make sure no one was near, and leaned across the table. "But . . . not really."

"Of course they do—that was the whole idea behind it. That much I do know."

"All coverages are far from the same."

He snorted. "I realize that. I know there are different levels, depending on cost and benefits. Some plans have higher deductibles, some have higher co-pays, and some don't pay for private rooms. Tell me something I don't know."

She looked at him. "And you have the highest level, I presume?"

He nodded.

"What did your fiancée have?"

"I'm not sure. Why? What difference would that make in the type of care she received?"

"You might want to investigate. There's more to it than you realize."

She made ready to leave. "I've said enough, maybe too much. Thank you for lunch."

As she pulled away from the table, he put his hand on her arm. "Wait," he said. "You can't just leave me hanging like that. What are you trying to tell me?"

"You don't have a clue how our health care system really works. Do your homework, because I'm not saying any more."

He shook his head, frustrated. "Okay, but tell me you'll see me again."

"I'm not sure that's a good idea, for you or for me." She stared at him, and said, "We'll see." She rose and walked away, leaving him sitting there with his mind racing.

When he got back to the office, Becky was waiting on him, frowning.

"Why didn't you answer your phone?" she said.

He reached into his pocket, pulled the phone out, and punched the Home button. Four missed calls from Becky.

He looked up at her, puzzled.

"You missed your one o'clock conference call with the bond desk. I tried to call you."

"Shit," he said out loud, staring at his phone as if it had betrayed him. "Why the hell didn't I—" He looked at the icons across the top of the display, and realized he'd put it in silent mode, something he almost never did. He'd done it when he arrived at Ray's, not wanting to be interrupted.

Becky's face softened. "Are you okay? That's the second appointment you've missed this week."

He nodded. "Just distracted. Sorry. I'd put it in silent mode."

She raised an eyebrow, obviously surprised at the admission, then shrugged. "I covered for you, told them you were tied up with a client. I asked them to send a transcript of the call."

"Thanks."

He asked her to get him a profile on Micah Rollins. That wasn't unusual. From time to time, he would ask

Becky to compile a profile of someone who he was negotiating with or considering hiring. He never asked for specific information and never asked how she obtained it. These days, more information was available on the Internet than most people realized.

He'd also asked Becky to put together reading material on USCare and the health care system. When she asked him for more specific information, he told her he just wanted to educate himself on how the whole system worked.

The next day, she handed him a thick folder. "That was like asking 'how gravity works,'" she said, laughing. "I'm not sure it's what you wanted, but it's a start."

He read all of the information Becky had compiled. He'd also downloaded four books she'd included as references, and he read or skimmed most of those. After his cram course, he realized that Micah was right—he didn't know shit about health care. The finance business was complex, but health care was bigger and even more complicated.

Three days later, he came in and another folder was on his desk, labeled *Micah Rollins*. He opened it and read the information Becky had put together. Two facts stood out.

First, she was the only child of Gabriel Rollins, III, a name that Warren and most American businessmen recognized. He was the former CEO of Forte Health Insurance Company, the largest health care insurance company in the country. At the time of his death two years ago, he had been one of the richest people in the country, up there with the likes of Clay Fortson and Bill Gates.

Second, was that Micah had a son. *Interesting*, he thought. He didn't remember seeing a wedding ring.

He pulled out his cell phone and entered her number. He was surprised when she answered.

"Hello, teacher," he said. "I've done my homework. How about lunch this week?"

"No."

That was quick, he thought.

"Okay, when?"

"I told you, I don't think that's a good idea for either of us."

"Why not?"

"Are you always this persistent?"

He laughed. "Pretty much. You don't get anywhere in my world by being shy or taking *no* for an answer. I've just got some questions, not like I'm asking you to give away state secrets."

There was silence on the line.

"You're the only one who's been willing to even talk to me about it," Warren said.

"I think I've said enough."

"Please."

He heard her exhale. "There's someone you should meet—a friend. Maybe he can help."

"Okay."

"He's a physician."

Warren wasn't sure where this was headed. He wondered if this was someone she was involved with.

"Do you think I need to see a doctor?" he asked.

This time she laughed, and it made him smile.

"I wouldn't know, but I think you'll find the conversation stimulating, and it may help you in your quest."

His ears perked up at her reference to their last discussion.

"Sure. Should I give him a call?"

"No, I'll ask him to call you and set up a meeting."

"Alright."

"Give me a call after you've talked to him."

"Okay, thanks."

He put his phone down. She didn't even give him a name.

The next day at the office, Warren's cell phone buzzed. He picked it up and looked. It was an unknown number, but a 239 area code. A Fort Myers number.

"Hello?" he answered.

"Is this Warren Thompson?" the voice asked. It was a male voice, maybe a trace of New York, but no real discernible accent.

"Yes. May I ask who's calling?"

"Hi. This is Samuel Abrams. I believe Micah Rollins spoke to you about me, at least I'm hoping she did."

Warren relaxed. "If you're the doctor, yes, she did. Although she neglected to give me a name before we hung up."

Abrams laughed. "I'm not surprised. Anyway, she suggested that you might want to get together and chat."

Interesting, Warren thought. Micah told him that *I* wanted to talk. Abrams didn't mention anything about being a doctor. "Uh, yes, she thought we might have something in common, I suppose."

"How does tomorrow afternoon sound? Say around three? At Café Nation?"

Café Nation was a bohemian coffee shop downtown in the same block as Jimmy's restaurant, which is the only reason Warren knew about it. He looked at his calendar, still fairly open, thanks to Becky's continued enforcement of his light schedule.

"Sure, sounds good. I'll see you there at three."

Warren was seated outside on the patio of Café Nation, electing to wait on Dr. Abrams before ordering. He had no idea who he was looking for as he scanned the sparse crowd at the coffee house. He saw no one he thought would be Dr. Abrams.

About that time, a man approached his table. He was not a big man, and appeared to be about Warren's age. He wore shorts, sandals, and a faded blue T-shirt that sported the washed out remains of the logo of The Bull and Whistle Bar in Key West. His brown eyes were clear, even though the beard and shoulder-length hair looked like someone lost in the sixties. He stopped opposite him and said, "Warren?"

Warren nodded, and stood to shake his hand. Abrams's handshake was firm and he met Warren's eyes without flinching.

"Dr. Abrams. Thanks for meeting me."

Abrams said nothing, taking a seat on the other side of the small table. The waitress came over and took their order. When he ordered a coffee—black—Abrams nodded and said, "Make it two."

"What kind of doctor are you? Micah didn't say."

"Unemployed, on probation after being sanctioned by the medical review board," Abrams said, meeting Warren's stare.

Warren raised his eyebrows. Micah hadn't told him that. "Why?" he asked.

"Does it matter?"

Warren detected an attitude, one that he didn't appreciate. He wondered if the person sitting across from him was a quack.

"It might. I'm beginning to question why you agreed to talk to me, if this is all I'm going to get."

The waitress brought their coffees, and Abrams took a sip before speaking. "I did it as a favor to Micah. According to her, you're the one who wanted to talk to me. I'm not wasting my time establishing my credentials—I know what they are. If you were concerned about that, you should've done your homework before meeting me."

Warren's face reddened. Another reference to homework. Dr. Abrams was right, and it perturbed him to admit it. He was also more than a little miffed that Micah told this prick that it was Warren who suggested the meeting. He took a deep breath, and decided to give it another chance.

"Look, Dr. Abrams, my fiancée died, and I'm convinced she didn't have to. From what little I can gather—which hasn't been much—she acquired a fairly routine infection. When the cheap antibiotics they were giving her didn't work, they waited too late to give her the expensive stuff. I want to know why."

"I'm sorry about your fiancée." A thin smile crossed Abrams's face. "It's the money. You, of all people, should understand that."

Warren felt his blood pressure rise. "I don't apologize for being successful. I worked hard to get what I have, and none of it was handed to me.

"I can understand that everyone doesn't get a private suite on the VIP floor, just like everyone doesn't drive a Lexus. But you want me to believe that Alex got substandard health care because she didn't have money? In a country with the best health care system in the world? That's preposterous."

Abrams leaned forward, clasped his hands together and rested them on the table. He met Warren's glare without retreating. When he spoke, his voice was calm and collected. "Ignorance I can forgive. Consciously ignoring the facts is *preposterous.*

"Fact number one is that the standard of care you get in this country correlates directly to your tax bracket. Higher income—better care. Fact number two is that our health care system is nowhere close to being the best in the world. That's a common misconception, based on the fact that we spend the most per capita of any country in the world by a considerable margin. The dual myths of equal care and the best system are perpetuated by the players who have the most to gain from doing so."

Warren reached for his wallet and pulled out a twenty dollar bill, laying it on the table. "My treat. I don't need some washed-out, has-been flower-child preaching to me because I've been successful." He pushed his chair back, and rose to leave.

As he walked away, Abrams called out, "Come back when you're ready for the truth."

Chapter 10

The next morning in his office, Warren pushed the intercom button and asked Becky to get Tim McLaughlin on the phone.

A few minutes later, his intercom buzzed and Becky indicated Tim was on line one.

"I need your help," Warren said as soon as he picked up the phone.

"Oh God, what have you done now? Please tell me it doesn't involve small animals or the Mafia."

"You know, I have got to find a decent attorney—one who respects his clients and doesn't dish out so much bullshit."

Tim laughed. "I don't think anyone in Fort Myers would take you as a client, especially if they know you. Guess you're stuck with me, pal."

Warren cleared his throat. "Tim, who's the best medical malpractice attorney in the state?"

Tim's voice turned sober. "Whoa, Warren. What's going on here? Talk to me."

Warren told Tim what he was planning and why. He'd made the decision this morning at the gym while he was on the treadmill. Since he was getting nowhere being a nice guy, it was time to turn up the heat.

"You need to think this through, buddy. This is going to piss off a lot of people," Tim said.

"I have thought it through, and I don't care. I want answers, Tim, and it looks like this is the only way I'm going to get them."

"Maybe you should try other avenues first."

"I've tried other avenues, and all I get is people hiding behind this privacy crap."

"The reason they're doing that is to avoid what you're proposing to do—a lawsuit."

"They had their chance. You got a name, or not?"

"There's one name that comes to mind. He's the best, but . . ."

"But, what?"

"You're unleashing the dogs of hell."

"Good. That's what I want."

Lawrence Dalton, Esquire, was a successful attorney practicing in Tallahassee. He was beyond successful, to the point of being feared and despised by many in the health care industry. He specialized in medical malpractice and was good at what he did.

Several years ago, he'd stumbled on a client who ended up winning a two hundred million dollar judgment against a who's who of defendants in the state of Florida. With his cut of forty percent, he was set for life.

He was a big man, and used his physical size to his advantage. He knew how to play to a jury and excelled in the courtroom. The largest and most prestigious law firm in the state had tried to hire him, but Dalton was big enough on his own and elected to stay that way.

He insisted on being called Lawrence, and any who referred to him as Larry, did so at their own risk. Warren had scoffed at this, but Tim had told Warren that even Dalton's mother had called him Lawrence.

Armed with this knowledge, Warren was careful to ask to speak to Lawrence when he called. The cheerful assistant took his name and information, stating that Mr. Dalton was busy and would return his call within the day.

Later that afternoon, Warren's cell phone buzzed. It was Lawrence Dalton.

"Mr. Dalton. Thanks for returning my call."

"Rhonda tells me that Tim McLaughlin referred you. How's Tim doing?" The voice was deep, with a pronounced southern drawl.

"He's doing well, thanks," Warren said.

"I suppose he told you we suffered through law school together."

Warren laughed. "Yes, he did. He also said you were the best medical malpractice attorney in the state."

"Only Florida?" Dalton said, laughing. "I'd like to think my reputation reaches a little farther than that."

"I want you to handle a malpractice case for me," Warren said.

"That's what I do, Mr. Thompson. And please, call me Lawrence. Briefly, tell me what's on your mind."

Warren gave him a concise version of what happened to Alex. He concluded by saying what he wanted was an explanation, not money.

"So, you weren't married?"

"No, why?"

"Since the patient . . . didn't make it, this would be considered a wrongful death suit. In Florida, only the executor of the deceased's estate can file suit, and it must be on behalf of an immediate relative, such as spouse, parent, child, etc. Does she have any relatives alive?"

"Yes, her mother is still alive, and I'm the executor of her estate."

"Good, then we can make that work. Now, you say you're not interested in money?"

"Correct."

"Well, I'm afraid we have a problem, then, Warren. Money, or the threat of losing a chunk of it, is the only thing that motivates these people. To be honest, it's what motivates me as well. I'm not interested in a 'warm puppy' kind of case."

Warren chuckled. At least this guy was honest. "I just wanted you to know what my motivation was. For once, it's not money. That said, I don't care how much you go after. Whatever it takes to get me results. I think there's a case here, and it's probably worth a lot of money."

"As long as we're clear," Dalton said. "I require a retainer in advance of one hundred thousand dollars, to be applied to expenses incurred. I'll file a notice of intent and records request. I'll look through everything to determine if there's enough to go forward. Should I decide there is no case, I'll refund any remaining balance to you. Should you get cold feet, I'll bill you for my time as well to be charged against the retainer. My rate is $2,000 an hour."

Damn, Warren thought. Maybe I should've gone to law school with Tim.

"That's acceptable. I'll have my assistant, Becky, contact your office to work out the details."

"Excellent. I'll be in touch." The line was disconnected, and Warren sat back in his chair, feeling strangely calm about what he'd started.

He wasn't concerned about the cost, but Tim's comment on unleashing the dogs stuck in his head. But he had to find out what happened, and if this is what it took, then so be it.

He picked up his phone and called Micah's number. Voice mail. He left her a message, asking her to call him.

Later that afternoon, she returned his call.

"I met with Dr. Abrams yesterday," he said.

"Great. I'm sure it was helpful. He's brilliant, and—"

"I didn't particularly care for him. I know he's your friend, but I found him arrogant and condescending," he said. "It was a short meeting."

"What do you mean?"

"After a couple of minutes of his Haight-Ashbury routine, I walked out. Didn't even get a chance to finish my coffee."

There was silence on the line. "Are you still there?" he asked.

"You're a fool," she said. "Do you know anything about him? Other than what you so keenly observed in a few minutes?"

"No, but—"

"*Doctor* Samuel Abrams graduated at the top of his medical school class from Harvard. He was one of the top neurosurgeons in the country."

She went on to tell him how, five years ago, shortly after the passage of USCare, he saw a patient—a child—who could have greatly benefited from a simple, but costly procedure. When the patient's insurance company refused, he did the surgery anyway, taking an expensive medication from the hospital and giving it to her himself.

The patient walked out of the hospital, completely healed, but Dr. Abrams was sanctioned by the medical review board. No hospital would give him full privileges, and no insurance company would admit him to their panel. His brilliant career was effectively over.

Warren was astonished and embarrassed. "What is he doing now?"

"He works as a patient advocate. There are a few physicians who let him consult, informally, since he can no longer officially practice medicine. But they have to pay him out of their pocket, so his income is negligible. He's a voice in the wilderness. And, he has a clear picture of what is happening in the U.S. health care system.

"I was hoping he would be of help to you. But, it seems you are such a pretentious asshole, you didn't even give him a chance."

"Micah, I'm sorry. I didn't—"

The line went dead.

He sat there, shaking his head. Somehow, he'd managed to piss off the two people in town who were able and willing to help him.

Chapter 11

Warren punched the intercom button and asked Becky to get him a phone number for Dr. Samuel Abrams. A few minutes later, she walked into his office and handed him a slip of paper.

He called the number. When his call went to voice mail, he left a detailed message, apologizing for his behavior, and asking Dr. Abrams to please meet with him at the doctor's convenience. Although he was tempted to call Micah again, he figured it would be better to talk with Abrams first before groveling to Micah.

He was surprised when the doctor called him back in less than an hour. Before Warren could say anything, Abrams said, "How about Café Nation at three?"

Warren looked at his calendar. That was only forty-five minutes away, and he had a conference call with New York scheduled at three thirty. He tapped his pen on the desk. New York would have to wait.

"Okay, I'll be there. Thanks," he said, hanging up the phone.

They met at the same spot as before. Dr. Abrams wore sandals, and a linen shirt instead of denim, but it was like déjà vu. Abrams was seated, and didn't bother to rise when Warren approached.

Warren said, as he sat, "Doctor Abrams, I owe you an apology. I'm sorry, and I appreciate you agreeing to meet with me again, especially after I was so rude."

"Apology accepted," Abrams said. "And call me Sam."

A humbled Warren nodded. "I want to know why she died. My gut tells me she didn't have to."

"Tell me what happened to your fiancée."

Warren spent the next hour going through Alex's case, at least all he knew about it. Sam took no notes, but listened intently. He occasionally interrupted with questions, or wanting clarification.

When Warren was done, Sam said, "Take out your Care Card."

Warren got out his wallet, pulled out his insurance card, and held it in his hand, staring at it. It was plastic, like a credit card, and red, white, and blue. It was embossed with a variety of codes.

"Look at the Member ID Number."

It was the longest one on the card, a dozen or so letters and numbers strung together, no separation or hyphens, and no apparent logic.

Warren looked up at the doctor, awaiting further instructions.

"Third digit from the right. It's a two or a three," Sam said, his eyes on Warren the entire time and never glancing at the card.

Warren looked back at the card. It was a three. He looked up at Sam, a question forming on his lips.

"Do you have Alex's card?" Sam asked.

Warren shook his head. "Not with me. It may be in her things."

"If you find it, take a look. That digit is probably a seven."

"What does all this mean?"

Sam spent the next two hours explaining the hidden details of how the health care insurance system worked in this country, going into more detail than Micah had. Warren was impressed at how knowledgeable Sam was, and embarrassed by how little he knew about the largest segment of the country's Gross Domestic Product.

USCare had been the successor to the Affordable Care Act. Once the Republicans accepted that health care reform was not going away, they wanted to put their imprint on it. Democrats insisted on maintaining universal coverage and Republicans wanted private sector control. The result was USCare, a typical Washington compromise.

The three largest health insurance companies were appointed to manage the entire program. In order to achieve the spending goals, major changes had to occur. The Big Three, as Sam called them, insisted that they could wring out huge inefficiencies in the system in order to pay for it.

The public had been sold on the four levels of coverage—Platinum, Gold, Silver, and Bronze. Everyone knew that the higher level plans were more expensive and covered a greater percentage of charges and different services. That much was easy to understand, and transparent.

What Sam told him was that another rating system existed, invisible to the public.

This system, driven by the financial resources of the insured as measured by their credit score, determined the actual care provided. This was accomplished by care guidelines formulated by the insurance companies and triggered by the insurance code that Sam had pointed out.

Lower tier insurance plans meant bare bones accommodations, which was obvious. Less obvious were more subtle differences in the standard of care. Lower staffing ratios and less qualified providers were assigned to those levels. These levels used the cheapest, generic drugs—if they used any at all, and an absolute minimum of diagnostic tests. Patients were kicked out earlier and told there was nothing else that could be done.

Warren thought back to Alex's bed in the hospital, and remembered how there were no IV's or monitoring equipment.

"Let me get this straight. You're saying that patients with essentially the same diagnosis but different insurance not only get cheaper accommodations, they don't get the same tests, the same drugs, the—"

Sam took a sip of his coffee. "That's exactly what I'm saying."

"But that's—"

"Rationing? Absolutely."

Sam went on to say that in return, providers and insurance companies were rewarded with strict caps on malpractice awards. In reality, what they had done was ration care. Since the care guidelines dictated those standards, caregivers could rationalize their actions without consciously withholding resources.

Warren was enraged. "You're telling me that the insurance companies control this, not the government?"

Sam nodded. "Publicly, everyone wants to blame the government, but privately, the insurance companies pull the strings."

Warren picked up his card, stared at it, then turned it around for Sam to see. "So a Platinum plan is not always a Platinum plan?"

"I'm telling you that there are different levels of *care* that have nothing to do with the published plan levels. The published plan levels refer to the items covered and the reimbursement levels.

"That third digit represents the level of care you actually get, with one being the highest, and nine almost nothing. One's are for the President, members of Congress, Supreme Court Justices, and military leaders. Top tier plans are twenty-fours—two through four. The wealthy are usually twos and threes. Fours are caregivers. Second tier plans are fifty-nines, or five through nine.

"You're a twenty-four. She was probably a fifty-nine. That's why you got Zena and she didn't. Zena is $3,000 a dose. A cheaper, less-effective generic is probably fifty dollars. My guess is she got that if she got anything at all."

Warren laid the card down on the table as if it were radioactive. Questions were racing through his mind, overwhelming him. "Who determines this?"

Sam shrugged. "The insurance companies. Whenever you send in your application for coverage, their underwriting department ranks you."

"Does your number ever change?"

"Of course. Say you're a five, and Aunt Rebecca remembers you in her will, leaving you a fortune. Once your insurance company gets your new credit report, you may move up to a three."

Warren was shaking his head. "How did you find this out? Surely, other people know about this?"

"A lot of people know, actually. More than you realize. Your doctor probably knows."

"My doctor? Here in Fort Myers? How do you know that?"

"I don't know specifically. I don't even know who your doctor is, but I'd be surprised if he didn't."

This was too much for Warren to absorb. Gordo knew this, and he didn't say anything? How could he do that?

"You're thinking, 'how could he not tell me,' right?" Sam said.

Warren nodded, in a daze.

"You know the answer. It's right in front of you," Sam said.

He studied the hippy-looking doctor and thought back to his story. His life, his career had been ruined. A Harvard-educated physician. How? He stared at Dr. Abrams, looking for an explanation, then it hit him.

"The number can go down, too," Warren guessed.

Sam smiled, and nodded, snapping his fingers. "Just like that, you can go from a three to a nine."

Unbelievable, Warren thought. "So, you and your family lose health coverage."

Sam shook his head. "No, you still have coverage, if you can call it that. They don't literally leave you in the gutter, only figuratively. But you and yours don't get Zena, you don't get the latest diagnostic tests, and you don't get the top-ranked caregivers. You'd get better care at a Days Inn with a bottle of aspirin.

"And, as the game show host says, 'that's not all.' If you're a clinician, your contracts get cancelled. If you're not a plan member, patients go somewhere else, where they're covered. And hospitals won't hire you. Your career is over. Finished."

"Why couldn't you hang out your shingle and take patients who can afford to pay?"

Sam laughed. "You forget. It's a closed system. Say you still have a license—at least until they come up with some trumped-up excuse to write you up. So you hang out your shingle and take patients who can afford to pay out-of-pocket. Do you realize what percentage of the population that is?"

Warren shook his head.

Sam held his thumb and forefinger together. "About that much. And, where do I go for surgery? For diagnostic tests? Pharmacies aren't required to fill prescriptions that I write. I think the Puritans called it 'shunning.' You are a pariah."

"I don't understand. Why isn't this all over the news? Why doesn't someone do something?"

"Not that easy. It trickles all the way down the line. If you work in a hospital, you keep your mouth shut if you want to keep your job. You say something, then you're blackballed—no one will hire you. Plus, insurance for you and your family is downgraded. Other doctors suddenly aren't accepting new patients.

"For the few like me who do say something, you're ostracized. The powers that be orchestrate a vigorous campaign to totally discredit you. Sanctions are imposed on your license."

"You realize how unbelievable this all sounds?"

Sam nodded. "You saw what happened with your fiancée. Why don't you believe it?"

"I know—or think I know—that she didn't receive Zena when she should. I do know I received Zena when I didn't need it."

"Have you seen her medical record?"

He laughed. "You're kidding, right? With all that patient privacy crap. Believe me, I've tried."

"You hire an attorney, he or she can get a copy."

"Really?" He remembered Dalton saying something about a records request, but didn't think about that including Alex's medical record.

"Sure. How else could an attorney evaluate whether or not they had a viable malpractice case?"

Warren left the café, angry and in a daze. Although Sam couldn't say for certain that Zena would've saved Alex, it would've been the best shot at doing so. Warren wanted to believe Sam, but he still wasn't convinced.

He had to get a copy of Alex's medical record.

When Warren got home, he went to his closet and pulled out a cardboard box. It was unlabeled, but he knew it was the box containing Alex's personal effects from the accident. He hadn't opened it since Becky brought it over to the house.

He set the box on his dresser and studied it. It was a plain cardboard box, nothing remarkable about its appearance. Yet, his hand was shaking as he reached out to open it.

The first thing he saw was her purse. He smiled. It was her favorite, and she had it with her regardless of whether she was wearing jeans or a dress. It was stylish, a classic design, made of maroon leather by some designer he didn't recognize. He'd bought it for her in New York.

They'd gone up in December, her first trip to the city. He'd wanted her to see the Big Apple at Christmas, in all of its holiday finery. She was fascinated with the city. At that time of year, no one was immune, even someone as jaded as him. His eyes welled up as he thought about seeing it through her eyes as though it was his first visit.

He opened the purse and pulled out her wallet, unsnapping it to reveal the collection of cards along the inside. A slip of paper fell out. He picked it up and as he placed it back in the wallet he recognized Alex's handwriting.

The number didn't look familiar. He shook his head, placed the piece of paper back in her wallet and thumbed through the plastic cards.

Her driver's license was first. He pulled it out and looked at the picture. A typical, low-quality mug shot. He didn't remember ever seeing her license. Her hair was shorter than he'd ever seen it, and lighter than he remembered. Was it the poor photo, or had she really looked that different?

Next was her VISA card. He smiled as he remembered her insisting on keeping the credit card, even after she'd practically moved in with him. *It took me too long to get it,* she claimed. *And I don't ever want to be totally dependent on someone else again.*

He spotted the red, white, and blue card with the USCare logo on it, a blue caduceus on a white background. He'd always thought the symbol of two snakes winding around a winged staff was a universal symbol of medicine. He'd since learned that's an American interpretation.

Most of the world recognizes the rod of Asclepius as the symbol of health care. It was a rod entwined by a single serpent, associated with the Greek god Asclepius, the god of healing and medicine.

The caduceus, the symbol he looked at, represented the staff carried by Hermes. It symbolized commerce and protection of thieves. How appropriate, he thought, that the United States symbol has ancient ties to commerce and trickery.

He stared at the Member ID Number, printed across the middle of the card. Thinking back to Sam's description of the numbering scheme and key digit, he looked at the third number from the end.

It was a seven.

Chapter 12

The next day, Becky came into Warren's office and said that Lawrence Dalton wanted to fly in for dinner to discuss his case. Warren's schedule was open, she said, so she accepted. He nodded. For years, he'd trusted Becky to make those kinds of decisions.

She handed him a note with a West Gulf Drive address for a residence on Sanibel Island. The exact address was unfamiliar, but he knew the street ran parallel to the Gulf, and was home to some of the most spectacular houses on the island.

That evening, he drove out there. The barrier island was oriented west to east and was a popular tourist destination. At the west end, a small, two lane bridge spanned Blind Pass and connected Sanibel to Captiva, the last island that could be reached by car. The commercial center of Sanibel—what little that existed—was located on the east end of the island.

He wound his way over to the west end of the two lane street, came to the address, and turned left through the wrought iron gates. The crushed shell drive opened up into a courtyard of a spacious home overlooking the Gulf. The only car in the courtyard was a black Lincoln Continental.

The driver was standing outside, leaning against the front fender and reading a newspaper.

A porch surrounded the contemporary home, which sat on pilings and fit well on the lot. It was mostly concrete and glass. The railings were strands of stainless steel cables, giving the appearance of no barrier.

Warren parked, nodded to the young man reading the paper, and walked up the whitewashed steps to the house. When he got to the porch, he was greeted by a large, barrel-chested man wearing khakis and a green golf shirt. The man extended his hand.

"Mr. Thompson, I'm Lawrence Dalton. Thank you for coming out. I don't like meeting in public places when discussing sensitive information. Too many prying eyes and ears."

"Nice place you have," Warren said.

"A friend's," Dalton said, giving no further explanation. He led Warren into a large library, with a glass wall facing the Gulf. The sun was low on the horizon, and twilight was creeping over the expanse of water toward the house. "Would you like something to drink?" he asked, walking over to a large, well-stocked bar.

"A Macallan, neat." Warren watched as the big man poured two healthy tumblers of Scotch and handed one to Warren.

"To your health," Dalton said, raising his glass.

They sat on the huge leather couch. Dalton had several folders in front of him on the square bamboo coffee table. He picked up the first one and opened it.

"I need an entire chronology of the case, including the names of everyone you discussed it with. Dates, times, and your recollection of the discussion."

"I've only talked with a few people about it," Warren said.

"Good. Then this shouldn't take long."

Several hours later, Dalton suggested they take a break for dinner.

Warren was impressed with Dalton's thoroughness. He had made meticulous notes, and was quick to grasp the significance of seemingly trivial items.

They retired to the dining room, where Dalton assured him the staff was completely reliable and had been thoroughly vetted, so they could continue their discussion over dinner. A competent but silent staff of two proceeded to serve them a wonderful dinner of stone crab claws and fresh grouper.

Over dinner, Warren told him about his meeting with Abrams.

"The hippie doc," Dalton said. "Smart guy, but he got screwed by the system."

"Is what he said true? I mean, about the insurance companies stratifying the plans?"

"I've heard that, but I don't have any proof. I wish I did, but nobody will talk about it."

"But, how can they get away with that? Isn't that discrimination?"

"No, they only have to have the same apparent coverage for people in the same covered group. It's a carefully crafted illusion. For example, if you and I are in the same group, we have to have the same deductibles and spending caps. But nothing says that we have to get the same treatments, meds, tests, etc. That's driven by—wait a minute, what did you just say?"

Warren shook his head. "When? Just a minute ago?"

"You said something about discrimination?"

Warren thought about it, and said, "I just asked how the insurance companies could do that? Isn't that discrimination?"

Dalton picked up a pad and jotted down half a page of notes as Warren watched.

When he finished, Warren said, "But, I think that's what killed Alex."

"I understand what you're saying. But we have to prove it in a court of law. My guess is you've never seen a copy of her care guideline. And, you won't."

"It's not in her medical record?"

"No. What is done to the patient is in the record, but not the care guideline driving it."

Warren was incredulous. "You're telling me there's this 'invisible' hand dictating our treatment, and we can't even get a fucking copy of it? Can't you subpoena it or get a copy from her physician?"

"Nope. That is the proprietary information of the insurance companies and protected by statutes enacted as part of USCare. Sweetheart deal, eh? I can get a copy of her medical record, but I can't get a copy of the care guideline."

"You already have a copy of her medical record?"

"Of course. How else could I evaluate the substance of a potential lawsuit?"

"Can I see it?"

Dalton picked up another folder, withdrew a small sheaf of papers, and passed them over to him.

He flipped through the papers, unfamiliar with the medical jargon. Even so, he was struck by the paucity of information.

"Can I get a copy of my medical record?"

"Sure. As the patient, all you have to do is request it from the provider—provider being doctor, hospital, etc. Each provider has their own medical record."

"Can I get a copy of hers?"

Dalton stroked his chin. "Officially—no. I'm responsible for protecting the privacy of it. Why?"

"I want someone to look at it."

"Who?"

"Not sure. I just want someone with a clinical background to review it."

"I've already done it. That's part of my evaluation."

"I'd still like a copy. Please."

Dalton sat back, then took the papers from him. "Hold on a sec." He walked out of the room, and a few minutes later, returned with what appeared to be a duplicate set of pages.

Warren watched as the attorney went through every page with a black marker, seeming to randomly mark things. He went through the stack a second time, nodded, then handed it to Warren. "I've redacted any patient identifiers. So, technically I'm not giving you any PHI-protected health information. It could be any patient's information."

Afterwards, they went back to the library for dessert and coffee. They settled on the couch as the staff brought out Key Lime pie and coffee.

Dalton picked up another folder, opened it, and told Warren that he thought the suit was worth fifty million dollars. The defendants would be the health insurance company, Rivers Community Hospital, and Dr. Kevin Vann, Alex's physician. Dalton assured him they all had pockets deep enough to withstand that kind of assault. The physician group alone had malpractice coverage for twenty million.

"Physician group? Why would you go after the entire group?" Warren asked.

"As the saying goes, falsely attributed to Willie Sutton, 'that's where the money is.' Plus, by naming lots of well-heeled defendants, you encourage dissension in the ranks. One party is willing to throw another under the bus to get off the hook. It's like sending a bunch of cannibals to an all-you-can-eat buffet."

Warren shifted in his seat. He would be going after Gordon Pollock, his best friend.

"I sense reluctance on your part," Dalton said, sipping his coffee.

"Dr. Gordon Pollock, the senior partner of the physician group, is a close personal friend of mine. I'd rather not involve him if we don't have to."

Dalton closed the folder, put it on the table, rose and walked over to the bar. He poured a couple of snifters of port and brought them over to the sofa, handing one to Warren before he spoke.

"Let me explain something, Mr. Thompson. Filing a malpractice suit is like starting a war. You can't manage this like the U.S. tried to do with Vietnam, cordoning off certain targets and placing limits. We're either all in or not in. There's no middle ground. I'm successful, because when I go to court, I do everything legally and ethically permissible to win, nothing less. That's the only way I work."

He took a sip of his port, and continued. "You're the client, and it's your choice. But, and this is a deal-breaking *but*, if you don't have the stomach for this, then now is the time to face that. I would assume that in your business, you don't take on clients who try to second-guess you. Neither do I."

Dalton finished his drink. "Either way, we've done what I wanted to accomplish this trip. I suggest you think about it overnight, and let me know how you want to proceed. It's been a pleasure."

On the drive home, Warren thought about what Dalton had said. He couldn't find fault with the lawyer's philosophy, as it mirrored his own. Warren had had those kinds of conversations with his own clients. Some capitulated, some left.

He called Tim and asked if he could drop by for a nightcap.

When he got there, Tim met him at the front door. They went to Tim's study, which was his man cave. Warren filled him in on the evening's discussion with Lawrence Dalton. "I see what you mean about unleashing the dogs of hell," he said.

Tim laughed. "Hey, I tried to warn you. What could I get you to drink?"

Warren shook his head. "Water for me, Pellegrino if you've got it."

Tim took a small bottle of water out of the refrigerator and then pulled a glass off the shelf over the bar.

"Bottle is fine," Warren said.

Tim handed him the bottle, then poured a healthy splash of Scotch into the glass for himself. "Lawrence didn't get his reputation by playing nice. He is one of the most ruthless people I know, and I know a lot of lawyers. Ethical—barely—and vicious. He takes no prisoners."

"How's this going to affect Gordo and me?" Warren asked. Tim knew Gordo almost as well as Warren. The three had been close friends for a long time.

Tim shrugged. "That's why we don't do those kinds of cases in our backyard. Even if Dalton doesn't prevail, it still takes a lot of energy and money to defend against a suit like this. There's a lot of negative publicity generated as well. And, in Florida, there's the three strikes law."

Warren shook his head. "Three strikes law?"

"In Florida, if a physician has three malpractice judgments against him, he automatically loses his license to practice. Three strikes, and you're out."

"Within a certain time frame?"

"No, they're on your record forever. And it also affects your malpractice insurance rate."

Warren hadn't realized any of this. Even though Gordo had nothing to do with Alex's death, he was going to be impacted.

"You're the only friend who hasn't told me to walk away from all of this. Is it because you don't think I should, or because you know how stubborn I am?" Warren asked.

Tim chuckled and shook his head. "Probably a little of both. I know how much Alex meant to you, and I know you need closure. I probably understand that better than Gordo, since I'm more objective in this instance." He glanced at the clock over the bar and continued.

"You've tried to get answers, but from what you've told me, they haven't been forthcoming. I know that you're cranking up the pressure. I also know how stubborn you are, and in the end, you're going to do what you're going to do, regardless of what I say." Tim stifled a yawn.

Warren shifted in his chair and checked his watch. "It's more than just closure. It may have started out that way, but now . . . when I saw all of those patients up there on Alex's floor. Damn, Tim, they were stacked in there like cattle. I thought everyone had access to health care, but they don't—not like the care you and I get."

Tim shrugged. "Not everyone gets a private room—you should know that. But everyone gets the best care in the world."

Warren snorted. "I used to think that, too. But, now I'm not sure."

"All I'm saying is that you need to think about this. The impact on your friends, your clients." His voice softened. "I know you miss her, but this is not going to bring her back."

Warren rose to leave. "Thanks, Tim. For listening, and being a friend."

As Tim walked him out, Warren noted that his friend didn't ask what he was going to do. Either he thought he knew the answer, or he thought Warren had not made his decision.

The truth was that Warren wanted to sleep on it. He was leaning toward dropping the entire thing. The number of people affected by his move was climbing, and they were just getting started.

Over the years, he'd found that the old adage of sleeping on it was good advice. The subconscious seemed to be more objective in considering complex and difficult decisions. He'd seldom regretted taking the additional time to allow it to work for him.

When he got in bed, he reached over to turn out the light, and saw the picture of him and Alex. He paused, picked it up, and brought it close to him. God, he missed her. As much as he wanted to know what happened, he realized Tim was right. Nothing was going to bring her back.

Chapter 13

The next morning, Warren called Sam and asked if they could meet at Café Nation. On the way, he stopped by Dr. Pollock's office.

"Hello, Mr. Thompson," the receptionist asked as he walked up to the window. "Did you have an appointment today?"

"No, Wendy. I just wanted to stop by and get a copy of my medical record."

A slight frown crossed her face. "Is there a problem?"

"No. I just wanted a copy for my information."

She nodded and handed him a release form to sign. "We should have that ready for you in a couple of days."

"Any way I could get that while I wait? I'd appreciate it."

She hesitated a minute, then said, "Of course. I'll see if we have someone available to print a copy."

After he got a copy of his record from Gordo's office, he went next door to the hospital and asked the volunteer at the front desk where he needed to go to get a copy of his medical record. She directed him to the medical records department on the fourth floor.

When he told the receptionist on the fourth floor he wanted a copy of his medical record, she handed him an Authorization for Disclosure of Health Information release form, indicating he should complete it and sign at the bottom.

"I'll also need to see some identification. Is this for personal use?" she asked.

"Yes."

"Since it is for personal use, there will be a charge of one dollar per page."

He rolled his eyes, nodded, and completed the form. After Gordo's office, he was familiar with the drill. It still seemed ridiculous that he had to pay to get a copy of his own damn record.

He handed the form to her and she entered the information, the keyboard clicking away.

"How many pages is it?" he asked out of curiosity.

When she was done, she looked up and told him approximately one hundred-eight pages.

One hundred eight dollars for a copy of his own medical record. On top of the thirty-six dollars he paid at Gordo's office that came to a grand total of $144. *How do poor people afford this*, he thought.

He was still seething when he arrived at Café Nation. Sam was at the counter ordering.

"Thanks for meeting me on such short notice," Warren said, as they ordered their coffee.

"No problem. You sounded like a man on a mission. What's up?"

They went outside and sat at a table underneath an umbrella. He handed Sam the copy of Alex's medical record and the copy of his. "The one with all the identifiers redacted is Alex's."

Sam thumbed through each of them, then looked up. "Okay, now what?"

"Based on her diagnosis, could you 'back into' her care guideline?"

Sam winced, and shook his head.

Warren continued. "I'm not asking for it to be precise. Just give me a rough idea of the kind of care guideline that would drive that sort of medical record. And compared to your opinion of what should've been done, given the diagnosis."

"You still don't believe me, do you?"

"Let's just say 'I'm doing my homework.'"

"It'll be rough. Looking at a piece of paper is not the same as examining a patient."

"I understand."

"I'm assuming you want this now."

Warren nodded.

"Give me a little while."

He watched as Sam flipped through the pages, making notes on the pad he pulled from his backpack. From time to time, he would shake his head and frown.

As soon as Sam finished his coffee, Warren went inside to get refills. He sat and resumed his vigil as they consumed another cup. He was contemplating one more refill when Sam put his pen down, rubbed his temples and said, "I'm finished."

"What do you think?"

"As I said, it is difficult to second-guess someone else's treatment approach, especially without being able to examine the patient. What little they did do points to a very bare bones care guideline. A third-world country would've done more. Based on the diagnosis and the limited test results in her chart, what they did was nowhere close to what any reputable physician operating without restraints would've done."

"So, she didn't get Zena?"

"Nope. A cheap, generic that in many countries you can get over-the-counter. But it goes deeper than that."

"What do you mean?"

"They did a totally inadequate job of diagnosis at the hospital. There's no evidence they did any of the basic diagnostic tests that should've been done."

Warren shook his head. "I'm not sure I follow you."

"Think of it as two different paths. In a perfect world, when a doctor first sees a patient, there's a fairly standard process that includes taking a patient history, routine tests, etc., based on where the answers lead. The physician then determines the appropriate treatment plan.

"With the current system, that process is dictated by the care guideline, which is driven by the patient's insurance number. The first track is like a pilot climbing into the cockpit of a plane and manually flying it from the time the door is closed until the time the plane pulls up to the gate.

"The second track is where the pilot gets into the cockpit, enters a bunch of numbers in the flight computer, and then sits back and reads a book while the computer flies the plane."

He struggled to understand what Sam was telling him. "So you're saying in my case, the physician controlled the process?"

Sam shook his head. "No, the process was still controlled by the care guideline. I'm just saying the care guideline in your case was far more comprehensive. In fact, yours appeared to be classic overtreatment. It implies a super-conservative, no-cost-spared approach. In my professional opinion, much of what they did in your case was totally unnecessary."

Now it was dawning on him what Sam was saying. The insurance companies were manipulating the system to control what was done, which allowed them to control costs and therefore profit margins.

"So you're saying that you would've done more diagnostic tests and would have given her Zena?"

Sam hesitated for what seemed like a long time before he answered. "Based on what I see here—yes. For example, they should've run a CTA and they didn't. I don't think the infection was what killed her."

"What's a CTA? I thought you said you would've given her Zena?"

"Computed Tomography Angiography—a specialized type of X-ray with a dye to highlight blood vessels. And yes, I would've prescribed Zena. But the CTA was more important. That would've picked up the aortic trauma, which was the ultimate reason for her crashing in the hospital."

Warren crushed the coffee cup in his hand. "In other words, they killed her."

Sam shook his head. "I didn't say that. In all fairness, medicine is sometimes as much art as science. Bad things happen. Even if she had the best treatment in the world, that's no guarantee. But—in my professional opinion—she didn't have the best treatment. Nowhere near it."

He tightened his hands into fists. "How could you people do that? I thought you guys took an oath to heal?

You're telling me that doctors and hospitals turn a blind eye to doing what is best for the patient?"

Sam shrugged. "I'm not defending it, Warren. But I told you how it happens. Like soldiers, you start out with the best of intentions. It's a gradual progression. The entire system is designed to mold you into a compliant soldier. You start fudging a little here and a little there. Eventually, you end up convincing yourself that there's nothing you can do. The pressure is enormous, and comes from all sides. It's amazing how the human mind can rationalize."

He slammed his fist on the table. "But it's wrong."

"Of course it is. And many doctors try to do the right thing. But, we're handcuffed and the penalties for bending the rules are pretty severe."

"Damn right, they're severe. It cost Alex her life."

"I'm sorry, Warren. I didn't mean to trivialize what happened. I'm just trying to explain."

Warren shook his head. He was disgusted with the health care system and its shortcomings. Now, more than ever, he was determined to bring this out into the light of day. He couldn't bring Alex back, but maybe he could prevent it happening to someone else.

"I know, Sam, you're trying to help. And you've paid a tremendous personal price for trying to do the right thing. I've got to run. I appreciate your time."

Sam handed him the records as they both rose to leave. "Give me a call if you have any more questions," he said.

Warren shoved the door open leaving the coffee shop, almost hitting a customer entering. "Excuse me," he mumbled, still replaying the conversation with Sam as he left the coffee shop and headed to the hospital for a foundation meeting. Since he was a few minutes early, he decided to stop by hospital cafeteria, grab a cup of coffee, and try to calm down.

As he stood in line, he noticed the barista's smile and positive attitude were absent. She was taking orders robotically, not engaging the customers as she'd done before.

"How's my favorite coffee lady?" he asked, when his turn to order came.

She gave him a forced smile. "Fine. What will you have today?"

Warren shook his head. This couldn't be the same lady who greeted him with a jovial smile and hearty laugh. The lady who roared in laughter, and last time, had automatically begun preparing him a plain, black coffee. He looked at her name tag. *Ciel.*

"Ciel, what's wrong?"

She looked up at him with bloodshot eyes, eyes that spoke of tears and little sleep. She shook her head, and stared at him, waiting for him to order.

"Just a large black coffee, please," he said.

She acknowledged his order and filled the cup, putting it on the counter and sliding it toward him.

"$4.75"

He took a ten out of his wallet and handed it to her. As she took it, he put his other hand over hers.

"What's the matter? You're not yourself."

A tear formed in the corner of her eye and rolled down her cheek. She clutched his hand as though she were drowning. "My baby girl, Leta. She's here in the hospital. She's sick, and she's not getting better."

"What happened?"

"She's running a fever. Yesterday, her doctor said she needed to be in the hospital. This morning, he said they were sending her home, that she could take whatever she needed at home." Ciel sniffled, trying to hold up. "She's only ten. She's up on the sixth floor, and I've got to be down here, working."

Warren stiffened. That was the same floor Alex had been on.

"I'm sorry, Ciel. They'll take good care of her here, I know. Be strong, okay?"

Ciel nodded, a thin smile creasing her face. "Thank you," she said, patting his hand.

Instead of sitting down in the cafeteria, he walked outside and pulled his phone out. He pressed the number and listened to Gordo's message.

"Gordo, it's Warren. I need you to call me, please. It's urgent. Thanks."

He ended the call and paced around the outside of the lobby, drinking his coffee.

In a few minutes, his phone buzzed. It was Gordon.

"Thanks, Gordo—"

"I'm really busy, Warren. What is it?" The chill in Gordo's voice was unmistakable.

"There's a ten-year old girl named Leta here in the hospital. She's on the sixth floor. Could you check—"

"I don't have a ten-year old female patient on six."

"I need to speak to her doctor."

"What's this about? Or do I even want to know?"

"I just need to speak to her doctor."

"You'll have to check with the reception desk. They can tell you."

The call was disconnected. He went to the reception desk and stated his request.

"I'm sorry, sir. We're not allowed to give out that—"

"I understand." He held up his hands, frustrated. "All I'm asking is that you have her doctor call me," he said, handing her one of his business cards. "It's very important."

He walked back into the cafeteria and sat. As he drank his coffee he watched Ciel go through the motions of working, her heart and soul not in it.

His mind drifted back to thoughts of his mother. She worked two jobs most of the time while he was growing up, determined that he would have a better life. He remembered the times when she came in from work when he was still awake. She'd be exhausted. He'd come into the living room of the tiny apartment and find her sitting there, her head back and eyes closed. Her feet would be propped up on the coffee table.

He'd walk over to her, take her shoes off, and rub her swollen feet. The smile on her face was one of pure pleasure.

He smiled as he remembered her face and what she'd sacrificed for him. He finished his coffee, and walked down to the business office.

The clerk at the desk asked how she could help him, and he told her he needed to talk to somebody about his account. She asked him to be seated, and told him someone would be with him in a few minutes.

A middle-aged woman came out to the waiting area and called his name. He rose and followed her back to a cubicle containing a small desk and two chairs.

As he sat, she smiled and said, "Mr. Thompson, I'm Judy. The receptionist said you wanted to discuss your account? What could I help you with today?"

Warren explained that there was no problem with his account. He wanted to make sure a patient currently in the hospital was getting the highest level of care possible.

The smile disappeared. "All of our patients receive the best care possible," she said.

He started to take exception to that, but tried to control his emotions. "I don't know what kind of insurance she has—"

"Is she a relative?"

He shook his head. "A friend."

"I'm sorry, Mr. Thompson. That's privileged information, and without written authorization, we're not allowed to—"

He held up his hand. "I realize that, and I'm not asking you to divulge anything." He pulled out his black credit card and handed it to her. "This credit card has a million dollar limit. Do whatever you need to do to attach this number to her account. I want to make sure she receives anything, everything, she needs."

She looked at the card, but didn't take it. "This is, uh, highly unusual, Mr. Thompson. I need to speak to my manager."

He dropped the card on her desk and sat back in his chair. "Fine. Please do that, and I'll wait." He crossed his arms.

Judy left the cubicle and disappeared. Five minutes later, she returned with a stocky, older man, with thinning brown hair.

"Mr. Thompson. Lee Roberts. I'm the Patient Accounts Manager." Lee extended his hand. Warren shook it, not bothering to get up. "Judy explained to me that you're wanting to . . . guarantee a patient's bill? Something to that effect?"

"More than that, Lee. I want to make sure she gets the *highest* level of care possible."

"All of our patients—"

"I know, everybody here gets great care." He started to add, *like my fiancée,* but bit his tongue. "But, I understand that the care you get is directly related to your particular insurance plan."

Lee glanced at Judy and their eyes met for a second before he recovered and looked back at him.

Warren continued. "What I want is for this little girl to get the Mercedes plan. Charge the balance to me."

"We're not allowed to—"

Warren leaned across the desk. "I'm the chairman of the Rivers Foundation, which last year raised fifty million dollars for this hospital. If you'd like, we'll call Ken Taylor's office and run it by him."

Lee blushed at the mention of the CEO's name. He glanced at Judy before turning his attention back to Warren. "Mr. Thompson, this could be very expensive. And we would need a deposit, in advance, to do what you're suggesting."

Warren picked up his credit card still lying on the desk and handed it to Lee. "Here's my card. Charge whatever deposit you need."

Lee nodded, and this time, Judy took the card. "It'll take a few minutes to determine the deposit amount and make the necessary changes," Lee said. "We'll need to look up the patient's name and account number."

"Thank you, Lee. Her mother, Ciel, works in the cafeteria, and her daughter's name is Leta. She's on the sixth floor. That's all I know. I'll wait here while you do whatever you need to do."

"I'll be right back," Judy said, as she and Lee walked away.

While he was waiting, his phone buzzed. He didn't recognize the number, but answered anyway, since he was sitting in the cubicle by himself.

"This is Dr. Hughes. Is this the person who requested to be called regarding a patient of mine in the hospital?"

"Yes, Dr. Hughes. This is Warren Thompson. Thanks for calling me. I was calling about a patient, a ten-year old girl named Leta—sorry, I don't know her last name, but her mother works here in the hospital. Leta is on the sixth floor."

"Mr. Thompson, I'm sure you understand I'm not at liberty to discuss a patient with anyone not having proper authorization."

Warren lost what little patience he had left. "I realize that, Dr. Hughes. What I want you to understand is that I'm sitting here in the business office and have just authorized, and paid for, Leta's care to be upgraded. I don't give a rat's ass what her current care guideline says. It's being changed even as we speak. Make sure you respond accordingly." He punched End and slammed the phone down on the desk.

He was still angry when Judy returned with his card, an authorization for him to sign, and a copy of the receipt. The authorization was for $100,000, and the description on the bill was simply *Additional Charges*.

"How soon before she's moved from the sixth floor?" Warren asked.

Judy looked flustered. "I'm not sure. It will have to be processed and that make take some time."

Warren looked at his watch. "It's twenty minutes after nine. If I haven't heard from you before noon, I'll be calling you back. For a hundred thousand dollars, I expect her to be moved by then."

As soon as he walked out of the business office, he called Lawrence Dalton's cell phone. The attorney answered the phone on the second ring.

"Lawrence Dalton."

"Wide open is my answer. I promise not to tell you how to do your job. If you need to go after the entire city of Fort Myers, that's fine," Warren said, skipping the usual pleasantries.

"Excellent. I'll be in touch." The line went dead.

Chapter 14

The next day, Becky brought in a laptop computer that had been delivered by courier. When Warren gave her a questioning look, she handed him the letter that accompanied it. It was from Lawrence Dalton.

The letter instructed him to use the computer for all correspondence regarding their case. It was fully encrypted and protected. Under no circumstance was Warren to use any other computer except this one. The master password would be arriving under separate cover. Warren shook his head, and placed the computer on the corner of his desk.

Later that afternoon, Becky walked in, accompanied by a burly, heavy-set man wearing a FedEx shirt. He had a small, letter-size envelope with him.

"Mr. Thompson, I'm sorry, but this gentleman insists that you sign for the package and show him some identification," Becky said.

Warren started to complain, but she continued and stated that the package was from Lawrence Dalton.

The FedEx guy shrugged, and said, "Sorry. Just following the rules."

Warren pulled out his wallet, removed his driver's license, and handed it to the delivery man. He scanned it through his device, punched a few keys, and handed his scanner to Warren for a signature. After confirming the signature matched the license, he handed it and the package to Warren.

"Have a nice day," he said, as he turned and walked out.

"Are you working for the CIA, now?" Becky asked.

Warren laughed. "No, just a paranoid attorney." He filled her in on Lawrence Dalton and gave her a brief explanation. "He's a bit eccentric, but supposedly the best at what he does."

Apparently satisfied for the moment, Becky walked out of his office. He opened the package and removed the pages.

The instructions were explicit. He had a password that would be valid for two attempts and only for twelve hours. When first signing in, he would be required to enter a new password that met a host of criteria. The computer would also require a fingerprint that matched Warren's. He was instructed not to write the password down anywhere, and several tips were included on password do's and don'ts. Only if the correct password and fingerprint were accepted would the computer work. All communication would be sent to and received from only this computer. Communications from other channels would not be accepted.

Warren turned on the MacBook Air and entered the password. It took him several tries to come up with an acceptable password, and using a combination of Alex's birth month and day, along with her grandmother's nickname of Nayme, he completed the process and got access.

The suit would be filed in two days, on a Friday. Warren was instructed to discuss it with no one and direct all inquiries to Lawrence's office. Lawrence had also attached a detailed transcription of their conversation on Sanibel, and he wanted Warren to review it and make any necessary changes.

He was surprised at the level of detail. He knew Lawrence had been taking notes, but didn't realize the depth and completeness of Lawrence's record. He had very few changes to the document.

The letter also contained information regarding an encryption app for Warren to install on his iPhone. This would allow him to have secure conversations with Lawrence. The details for the app were included. He was to call Lawrence as soon as everything was set up and installed.

An hour later, he called Lawrence, verifying the encryption icon was visible on his phone. Lawrence answered. "It looks like you've got everything set up properly. Any questions?"

Warren started to ask if all this was really necessary, but he knew the answer and decided to keep quiet. Lawrence gave him the name of a junior associate who would be working on the case with him. These were the only two individuals who he could discuss the case with—no exceptions.

The attorney told him the level of activity would increase dramatically once they filed. "We're going to be making waves in Fort Myers."

"What do you mean?" Warren asked.

"We're going to be making a lot of people very uncomfortable. Most people don't like getting subpoenas and don't like giving depositions. It's going to be unpleasant. Just warning you."

He thought about asking Lawrence for a list of people getting subpoenas, then decided he didn't want to know.

Lawrence asked him again about anybody he'd tried to get information from regarding Alex. When he mentioned Micah Rollins, Lawrence interrupted. "Gabriel Rollins's daughter?" he asked.

"Yes, but she won't cooperate. I've tried." Warren heard pages flipping.

"Did you tell me about talking to her?" Lawrence asked.

"I'm not sure. I told you about talking to Dr. Abrams, right?"

"Yes, yes. I've got that. But I have no notes regarding Micah Rollins."

For the next thirty minutes, Warren told Lawrence about meeting Micah in the hospital and having lunch with her. "She's the one who introduced me to Abrams."

"Interesting," Lawrence said. "Why is she working at the hospital?"

"I don't know. You'd have to ask her. But, as I said, don't expect her to cooperate."

"I haven't talked to her yet. Anything else related to her? Anyone else you neglected to mention?" There was a chastising tone in his voice.

"I've tried to remember everything, but it's been a stressful period."

"I realize that, but it's important that you tell me everything. Even things you think may be irrelevant could be important to the case. I don't like surprises, especially from my clients. Understood?"

Warren wondered if he should mention his conversation with Tim, and decided not. "I hear you."

Lawrence ended the call. Warren didn't like the attorney's tone. He was tempted to call him back and say something, but remembered his earlier promise to let the attorney handle things his way. This was going to be trickier than he realized.

Friday evening, Warren was working late. He'd finally gotten the lawsuit out of his head and been busy working on several new complex investment packages. His phone buzzed and he saw it was Gordo.

He figured his friend wanted to go out for drinks or dinner. He couldn't have been more wrong.

"Hey, Gordo? Getting thirsty?" Warren said.

"What the hell are you doing?" his friend answered. "Have you lost your fucking mind?"

Warren shook his head. *The dogs were loose,* he thought. "I assume you're—"

"I'm talking about the papers that were just served on me by some goon while I'm trying to have a drink with my wife and another couple at Jimmy's, that's what. A lawsuit that's being filed by you, as executor of Alex's estate. I'm hoping you're going to tell me it's a big mistake."

Warren took a deep breath. *The shit had hit the fan.* "Gordo, we need to talk. Can I meet you somewhere?"

"Is it true?"

"Let me explain, Gordo. Why don't I meet you over there? I'll even pick up the tab for dinner."

When he didn't hear a response, Warren repeated himself. Still getting no answer, he looked at the phone and realized that Gordon had hung up on him. He called

Gordon back, and it went to voice mail. He left his friend a message, asking him to please call him back.

He put the phone on his desk, then glanced at the clock. 7:15. He'd forgotten that the lawsuit would be filed today. Maybe he should call Micah and warn her. His phone buzzed as he reached for it, and he answered without looking, figuring it was Gordon returning his call.

"Hey Gordo, give me a chance—"

"This isn't Gordo and you've got ten seconds to explain." It was a female voice.

"Micah? I was just about to call you."

"I'll bet you were. It would've been nice if you'd warned me *before* sending some Neanderthal to serve papers on me while I'm picking up my son at school. Do you realize how that looks? No, and you probably don't care."

"Micah, wait, please—" This time he heard an audible click as she disconnected the call.

He called Tim, half-expecting him to be mad as well.

"Tim? It's Warren." He held the phone away from his ear, and paused to see if Tim was going to lash out or hang up.

"Warren? You still there?"

"Sorry. On my last two phone calls I was cursed out, then hung up on. Just holding my breath to see which way you were going. Want to grab a beer? Assuming you're still speaking to me."

His friend chuckled. "Sounds like you've had a bad day. I'm easy, especially when it comes to someone else buying. Meet you at Barney's in fifteen?"

Barney's was a local downtown bar that Warren and Tim had been frequenting for years. Not much to look at, but the beer was cold and it was reasonably quiet.

"Who said I was buying? I'll meet you there." He hung up before Tim could respond.

On the way to Barney's, Warren called Lawrence Dalton. "Got a minute?" he said when Dalton answered.

"Glad you called. I needed to talk to you. Do you know a Dr. Robert Michaels?" Dalton asked, not even bothering to ask Warren why he called.

Robert Michaels, MD, was a local cardiologist. Now at the peak of his game, he'd been practicing medicine in Fort Myers for almost twenty years. He and his wife, Ann, had everything. Everything, that is, except children. After much testing and numerous visits to specialists all around the country, the conclusion had been that Ann was unable to conceive.

They were the toast of the town. Well-known, and well-liked by everyone, they made a handsome couple. Robert had done well over the years. They lived a comfortable life, not ostentatious. But Dr. Michaels had invested wisely and was one of Warren's clients.

"Sure. Michaels is a client of mine. He's a well-known cardiologist here in Fort Myers. Why?"

"Not sure, yet. I'll let you know. Have you ever heard of a physician nicknamed 'Benefactor?'"

"Benefactor? No. What kind of nickname is that?"

Ignoring his question, Dalton asked, "Rumored to be a Good Samaritan, diverts extra meds from wealthy patients to needy ones. Did you need something?"

Warren shook his head. This guy was something else. "Look, I know I said I wouldn't interfere—"

"Good, then don't. I told you it was going to get nasty. And we're just getting started."

Great, Warren thought. At this rate, I won't have to worry about moving out of town. I'll be tarred and feathered.

"I expected Dr. Pollack, but I didn't expect Micah Rollins," Warren said.

Before he could say more, Dalton interrupted. "She's important to our case."

"I realize that, but I don't want to see her hurt by this."

"*Hurt?*" Dalton said. "I thought I made my position very clear to you out on Sanibel."

"You did," Warren said. He was trying to maintain his composure, which was difficult with someone like Lawrence Dalton. "I'm just sharing my concern. She has a lot to lose. Much more than me."

"Anything else?"

"No. Thanks," Warren said and ended the call. This was going to get worse, he had a sickening feeling.

He parked a block away from Barney's. On his short walk to the bar, he kept glancing around. After the calls from Gordo and Micah, he wasn't in the mood to run into anyone else.

At the entrance, Warren recognized the chopper parked out front. There was only one like it in Fort Myers. It belonged to Terry Harris, also known as Paco, a long-time member of the Split Aces and an old friend.

He stepped into Barney's and stopped, letting his eyes adjust to the darkness. The place had not changed in twenty years. Dingy, just this side of grungy, it was a local hangout, off the radar of the hordes of tourists. Barney Odom, the proprietor, liked it that way.

A burly guy with long hair sat at the bar, his back to Warren. He wore a vest displaying the Split Aces colors. Warren walked up next to him.

"Paco. How's it going?" Warren said. Paco had acquired his nickname after eating a dozen tacos on a poker run years ago.

The biker turned his head a few degrees. Recognizing Warren, he nodded. "Not bad, Double T. You?"

Warren smiled. His middle initial was T, hence the Double T nickname. "Can't complain. Everybody doing okay?" Warren asked, referring to the other members of the motorcycle club.

Paco nodded. "Slick's taking a little vacation at Union," referring to the prison in the little north Florida town of Raiford, near Jacksonville.

Must be serious, Warren thought. Union Correctional Institution was usually reserved for the more dangerous criminals. Warren spotted Tim sitting in their usual booth on the right

"Tell everyone 'Hello.' Keep the shiny side up," he said, leaving Paco to join Tim.

Barney was standing at the table talking to Tim and saw Warren approach.

"Mr. Popularity, I see," Barney said, eyeing Warren suspiciously.

"I suppose that means my money's no good in here, then," Warren said, as he slid into the booth opposite Tim.

"Nope, just means you have to pay in advance," the big man said. "Cash."

"Are there no secrets in Fort Myers?" Warren asked Tim as Barney walked over to the bar to grab the two frosty mugs of Newcastle for them. Barney knew everything about everyone in town, usually before they did.

"He was just telling me about Gordo," Tim said, as Barney sat the beers down between them.

"I hadn't got to the nurse, yet," Barney said, as he turned and walked back to the bar.

"Nurse?" Tim asked, as he looked at Warren and took a swig of his beer.

Warren just shook his head. Barney needed to work for the CIA or FBI or one of those alphabet agencies. There were no secrets from Barney in this town.

He nodded toward Paco, still sitting at the bar. "He said Slick's in Raiford."

Tim nodded. "Yeah. Paco said someone parked too close to his bike, so Slick took a bat to the guy's car, then gave him a few licks as well."

Warren shook his head. "Slick always did have an anger management problem."

Changing the subject, he told Tim about his day and the phone calls from Gordo and Micah. "And this is just day one," he said.

Warren looked up and saw Tabby, who was having a brief chat with Paco. He heard Paco laugh, and then Tabby headed toward their table. He was wearing jeans and a golf shirt stretched across his torso. The shirt appeared to be two sizes too small.

"As usual, I see my friends started without me," Tabby said, as he slid his massive frame into the booth next to Tim. He looked over at the biker, then said, "That could be us."

"I know. I'm beginning to wonder if I made a mistake not going that way," Warren said.

Barney brought Tabby a beer. "Food?" he asked. When they nodded, he said, "The usual?" More nods and Barney went back to the kitchen.

The usual meant grilled grouper sandwiches and homemade onion rings. Barney's had the best in Fort Myers.

"Glad you're still speaking to me, Tabby. You and Tim are about the only ones left in Fort Myers willing to be seen with me," Warren said, taking a long drink from his mug.

Tabby looked puzzled. "Maybe I shouldn't be. What did I miss?"

They brought Tabby up to speed on the day's events.

"You sure know how to piss people off," Tabby said. "Good news is I guess that means you're buying."

Tim laughed. "We should ride this as long as we can." He turned to Warren and said, "I warned you."

"I know, you and Lawrence both did. I guess I didn't expect this strong of a reaction. But, I don't want to tell him how to do his job. I did ask for this."

"Now you see why we don't do malpractice cases locally. Makes for very uncomfortable neighbors. Fort Myers is still a small town in a lot of ways. Estate planning is safer. Then, you're just limited to the abuse of warring factions of the deceased's estate."

"Maybe I need to send a marked car over to park outside your house," Tabby said.

Warren eyed his friends as he drained his beer. "If I've got to listen to you two bust my balls all evening, I'm going to need another."

Chapter 15

Sunday morning, Warren put on a pot of coffee and went out to the street to get the Sunday edition of the *News-Press*, the only daily newspaper in Fort Myers. Several times, he had threatened to cancel his subscription, but always reneged, wanting to support the paper and keep up on any local news that escaped his ears. There wasn't much to it anymore, but it served as an appetizer before launching into *The New York Times*, also waiting in his driveway.

He unfolded the *News-Press* on the way to the house, and was greeted with the headline.

Local Financier Sues Hospital and Doctors

Shaking his head, he put both papers out on the lanai table and went inside to grab his coffee.

Reading the lengthy article twice, he finished his first cup of coffee and refilled it from the carafe on the table. The article wasn't half bad in terms of accuracy. There were guarded quotes from several of the deposed parties, clearly muzzled by their legal counsel. Considerable column space, including a picture, was devoted to the scourge of Tallahassee, also known as Lawrence Dalton. The attorney spoke of noble motives, and a grieving fiancé wanting answers.

He wondered why no one had contacted him for comment, not that it mattered, since he realized he hadn't bothered to check his house phone for messages.

Wanting to cleanse his palate, he put the local paper aside, and started in on the *Times*. Several hours later, he retrieved his cell phone and called Sam Abrams.

"I stepped into a huge pile of shit with this lawsuit, didn't I?" Warren said, when the doctor answered.

Sam laughed. "So it seems. Front page, no less."

"I'd like to chat about it, if you can come over to the house. I've got plenty of good coffee, and can probably scrounge up something to eat. You probably don't want to be seen in public with me, and I'd rather not go out this morning."

"Sure," Sam said, laughing. "Don't worry about food. I'll stop and pick up some breakfast for us."

An hour later, the doorbell rang. "Thanks for coming, Sam," Warren said, opening the front door as the doctor walked up the steps.

"I brought comfort food," he said, holding up a bag from Café Nation. "Bagels. They have the best ones in town."

He and Sam sat outside. Sam produced two whole wheat bagels, each layered with a poached egg, spinach, and cheese, putting one on Warren's plate as Warren poured two fresh cups of coffee.

"Who's that?" Sam asked, referring to the music playing in the background.

"Otis Redding. 'These Arms of Mine.' His first single."

"I like it."

"He was one of the best. I've got everything he ever recorded, at least what was released. Never get tired of him."

Sam pointed to the *News-Press,* still setting on the table. "Lawrence Dalton. I'm impressed," he said.

"Glad someone is. I don't think I'm going to have many friends left in Fort Myers by the time he's done. I'm not sure how to control this now that I've sicced him on the entire city of Fort Myers."

"You talk to Micah?"

He shook his head. "She's not speaking to me at the moment. She did manage to tell me she was one of the ones deposed before she hung up on me."

Sam arched his eyebrows and winced. "I'm sure that didn't go over well. She does her best to stay out of the limelight."

"Did you get a subpoena?" Warren asked.

Sam shook his head. "Not yet. I'd be surprised to get one, though. I'm sure Lawrence Dalton would rather have people with more . . . stellar reputations." He said it with no trace of bitterness or anger. "It makes no difference to me. If I do, I do." He laughed. "I'll still speak to you. There's not a lot they can do to hurt me."

Warren smiled. "Thanks. By the way, did you ever hear of a local doctor nicknamed 'Benefactor?'"

Sam paused for a moment before taking another forkful of bagel, then shook his head. "Benefactor? No, why do you ask?"

Warren shrugged. "Dalton asked me. He said he'd heard about a local doctor with that nickname. A Good Samaritan type. Supposedly, he diverts meds from wealthy patients to less fortunate ones. Sounded like you."

"Not me. I'm on probation, remember?"

"I know, but it sounds like something you'd do. Probably an urban legend, but Dalton's convinced he's on to something."

"What else did he say?"

"Nothing more than that, but he's determined to find out who this doctor is."

They talked about the case, Warren telling Sam more than Dalton would've approved, but he needed to talk to someone. Sam was a good listener, and he figured Sam was as safe as anyone.

Sam was curious about Dalton's strategy, especially concerning the insurance company.

"Not sure," Warren said.

"Dalton's good, but Forte has a lot of resources in that department. It's going to be hard to beat them at their game."

"You sound as if you've had some experience going up against them?"

Sam nodded. "Several times. Like any big corporation, they just wear you down. It goes on and on—never stops. They have cases lasting for years. The other side either runs out of money, or gets tired—which is what they count on."

Warren thought he was committed for the long haul, but wasn't sure. Time would tell.

"What do you know about Micah Rollins?" Warren asked.

Sam smiled. "I've known Micah for ten years. She's a good friend." He studied Warren's face. "She's not my type, if that's what you're asking."

Warren blushed at being called out. "None of my business," he said, trying to recover. "Just curious as to what happened with her and her father."

"Short story is she and her father had a disagreement. They didn't speak for ten years. When he was diagnosed with pancreatic cancer, he reached out to her and her son Gabe. Three months later, he was gone. For the unabridged version, you'll have to ask Micah."

He wondered what the disagreement was about. With Gabe being ten years old, it appeared that it could've had something to do with the boy.

"Why are you so willing to talk to me about all of this? No one else will," Warren asked.

Sam shrugged. "I'm just a wacko, washed-up doctor. There's nothing they can do to me that they haven't already done. I'm like the guy on the corner with aluminum foil on his head and holding a cardboard sign saying 'The End is Near.'"

Warren smiled at the visual. "But you keep trying. Why?"

"Somebody has to. There are a lot of fifty-nines out there. They need a voice, too." He topped off Warren's coffee cup, then refilled his. "I heard about what you did the other day at the hospital."

"What?"

"Ciel's daughter."

Warren blushed. "How'd you find out? I'd asked for that to be kept confidential."

"I still have a lot of contacts in the medical community. That was a good thing you did."

"No big deal. I just wrote a check. Doesn't take a lot to do that. Unlike what you've done." He hesitated. "Do you miss it?"

Sam nodded and didn't take long to answer. "Of course. It's what I wanted to do with my life, and I spent years training. And, to have that taken from me because of someone else's greed . . ."

There was a pained look on the doctor's face, and Warren could sense his frustration.

"The worst part is not my loss—it's that I have the capacity to help others. People who could benefit from my years of training and experience. That's what really hurts."

Warren thought about what that must feel like. All he'd ever done was to focus on making money. There would be no loss in the world if he disappeared, and he felt small sitting across from Sam Abrams.

Sam rose to leave. "I've got to run. A meeting on a new clinic for the farm workers in Immokalee. Whenever I start to feel sorry for myself, I go out there. You should try it. Makes you thankful for what you have."

Warren stood and walked him out. "Thank you for your time—and the bagel. I appreciate it." At the front door, he said, "Will you give Micah a message for me?"

Sam nodded.

"Tell her I'm sorry, and I'd like to apologize in person."

After Sam left, he got his laptop and took it outside, spending a couple of hours researching health care companies.

He was surprised to see that only eight companies controlled the lion's share of health care. Two were pharmaceutical companies, three were insurance companies, and two were what was called provider companies. Health care comprised eighteen percent of the Gross Domestic Product and represented a three *trillion* dollar industry. If the health industry in the U.S. were a country, it would be the fifth largest economy in the world.

He whistled out loud. These eight companies controlled over a trillion dollars, or over a third of total health care expenditures. By comparison, last year Apple had revenue of around 150 billion dollars. Warren discovered that the other two trillion was spread out over thousands of companies. This meant that the eight companies in reality had even more control that one would think at first glance.

He also suspected that these companies, which he dubbed the Big Eight, probably had more influence with many of the other smaller companies than anyone realized. Many were probably suppliers to the Big Eight and had various degrees of overlap and ownership that would take years to unravel. These eight companies, and their respective leaders, probably controlled a bigger slice of the U.S. economy than anyone on the planet. Doing the rough math in his head, he figured these eight CEOs managed ten percent of the entire U.S. economy—a staggering amount of influence for such a small group.

When he researched the companies, even *he* didn't recognize the names of six of the eight chief executives, and he was in finance. He only recognized two of them because Everglades Investment Fund had substantial investments in those two companies. These were not household names or names that showed up in *People* magazine.

He sat back, overwhelmed by the amount of power these eight people wielded. He would've never guessed that so much influence was concentrated in such a small group of relatively unknown people. He was David versus Goliath; never in his life had he felt so powerless.

Chapter 16

Few people outside of Forte Health Insurance Company knew the name Blaine Harris. Even fewer would recognize a picture of the man. Blaine's official title was Press Secretary for Pete Manning, the CEO of Forte. However, those in the know recognized that Blaine Harris was more than just a press secretary.

Forte, like most Fortune 100 companies, had adopted the Washington model, where staffers with boring titles exercised enormous clout. In an environment where corporate officers were subject to incredible scrutiny and reporting requirements, staffers operated in the fringes, which made them very influential and efficient weapons wielded by those at the top.

Blaine had worked for Pete for six years, rising through the ranks with him. He was content to operate in the shadows of obscurity, shunning the spotlight. Yet, his cell phone contained a virtual platinum Rolodex of who's who in health care and insurance. Along with Pete's personal secretary, Blaine was the gatekeeper to the king.

Although he was about the same age as Pete, he didn't have the external political skills that his boss did. But, he was compensated handsomely. He had a reputation for getting things done and that was more important to him than appearing on the cover of *Forbes.*

He was headed to a meeting upstairs with Pete. Earlier that morning, Blaine had met with Tully Boone, the senior partner of Boone, Martin and Griffin, Forte's principal law firm.

The news was not good. Apparently, Lawrence Dalton, a perennial pain-in-the-ass malpractice attorney, had filed a lawsuit against Forte. That in itself was not cause for alarm. Forte, like most insurance companies, had legions of attorneys to handle litigation, which was a constant threat. The difference was the fact that Dalton was taking the lead, and the plaintiff happened to be a wealthy hedge fund manager in southwest Florida—well-known and well-respected.

Blaine nodded to Sally when he got off the elevator, and she motioned him into Pete's inner office. He shut the door and walked over to the CEO's desk. He sat in one of the chairs facing Pete and made himself comfortable.

"Blaine. What's going on? Sally said you needed to see me ASAP."

Blaine threw a folder down on Pete's desk. "Trouble." He wasted no time getting to the heart of the matter, disclosing a concise summary of his conversation with Boone. Pete listened attentively, jotting down a few notes on a yellow legal pad in front of him. He didn't speak until Blaine wrapped it up.

"We can't afford the negative publicity right now. As you know, I'm scheduled to testify on the Hill next month, and we have a bond issue coming up. Timing's not good."

Pete leaned forward in his chair and continued, "We have an obligation to the shareholders of this company.

Can't Tully drag his ass out in court? That's why we pay him the big bucks. Tell him to work his legal magic."

"Don't worry—I've got it under control."

"We've got to stall this thing, or better yet—settle it. Offer—what's the guy's name?"

"Thompson. Warren Thompson."

"Make him a settlement offer—sooner rather than later. Put pressure on him. Does he work with anybody we know?"

"He used to work with Jenkins-Gilmore."

"Really? Call Mason Gilmore. Better yet, I'll call."

"It might be better if you stayed out of it, Pete."

Pete thought, then nodded. "You're probably right. You know Mason. Give him a call. Don't let me down, Blaine. We need to make this go away."

Blaine went downstairs to his office, only one floor down from Pete's office. Lately, he was beginning to regret not retiring two years ago.

He'd turned in his notice, intending to spend more time with Kay, his wife, while she still remembered him. She'd been diagnosed with early onset dementia. At the time, her symptoms weren't that severe, so he let Pete talk him into staying four more years, dangling lucrative stock options as a carrot.

Unfortunately, her condition deteriorated rapidly. Now, she was in a long-term care facility, not recognizing him or anyone else. Physically, there wasn't anything wrong with her. She was healthier than he.

Her care was costing $100,000 a year, and who knew how long it would go on. With Forte's current stock price already double the exercise price of his yet-to-be vested stock options, he could ill afford to walk away from the millions he stood to make if he worked out his contract.

Back in his office, he slammed the door and sat at his desk, massaging his temples. He had lots of phone calls to make.

His first call was to Tully Boone. The syrupy sweet voice of his secretary answered. "Mr. Boone's office, this is—"

"This is Blaine Harris. I don't care where he is or what he's doing, as long as he's not in a courtroom—which I know for a fact he's not. I need to talk to him. Now."

She responded in a perturbed, but restrained voice. "Yes, Mr. Harris. If you'll hold, please."

He drummed his fingers on the desk. A few minutes later, Tully answered.

"I was in with—"

"I just got my ass reamed out by Pete, so I'm not in a real sympathetic mood right now, Tully. I need to know what we—you specifically—are going to do to derail this case down in Florida."

"We're studying it right now. Lawrence seems to be taking a different strategy. There are pretty strict malpractice limits under USCare, but his filing complained not only of malpractice, but also discrimination. That's a new one, and we're going to have to do some research."

Blaine shook his head. "You're telling me you weren't expecting this?"

"What I'm telling you is this is an unusual approach in a complaint like this. As such, we're going to have to do some additional research in order to formulate our response."

"Shit," Blaine muttered under his breath, loud enough for Tully to hear. "When? How soon will you have a response?"

"We'll probably have something in a couple of days—"

"Call me this time tomorrow and let me know what the hell you've got." He slammed the phone down in the cradle.

This wasn't a good sign. If they were depending on Tully's legal magic to make this go away quickly, they were out of luck. Obviously, Blaine couldn't afford to depend on that coming through.

He punched the intercom button on his phone. "Peggy. Hold my calls and clear my calendar this afternoon."

"Mr. Harris, you've got—"

"I don't care. Make it happen." He punched the button to disconnect, then reached for his Rolodex. It was going to be a long afternoon. His new priority was to make life miserable for one Warren Thompson.

Chapter 17

Monday after the article came out in the *News-Press*, Warren had decided to work from home for a couple of days, not wanting to deal with the aftermath. Wednesday morning, Warren had just sat at his desk when his cell phone rang. Lawrence Dalton. He wondered what the attorney wanted now.

"Lawrence. Good morning," he said, answering the phone.

Dalton ignored his greeting and asked, "Didn't you tell me you spoke with . . . Joan Frazier, the COO at Rivers?"

Warren winced. He could hear the sound of papers shuffling on the attorney's end. "Yes, but I told you she said our conversation was off the record."

"There is no such thing. We'll see what she says under oath," Dalton said, chuckling.

Warren put his hand up to his forehead. This was going from bad to worse. Joan would be livid.

"Are you sure you have to—"

"Uh-uh. Remember our conversation, Warren," Dalton said, chiding his client.

Warren bit his tongue, once again regretting this entire idea.

"Did you find out if anyone has heard of Benefactor?" Dalton asked, changing the subject.

"No, but you've got to remember—not too many people in the medical community in Fort Myers are speaking to me these days. Thanks to you."

Dalton ignored the dig and continued, "He keeps a low profile, working within the system. We got the information from a reliable source. I haven't been able to find out his name—yet."

He wondered if Micah knew about this. For some reason, he believed she would. She still hadn't spoken to him, and that was driving him crazy.

"Sorry, Lawrence. No help here." He hung up the phone and his thoughts returned to Micah. He'd called several times since Friday, but she'd let the call go to voice mail. Maybe he could catch her at the hospital.

Becky came into his office. "Ken Taylor is here. He didn't have an appointment, but said he needed a few minutes of your time if possible."

"Sure. Send him in."

Becky left, and the CEO of Rivers Hospital strode into Warren's office, closing the door as he walked over to Warren's desk. He was not a big man, but stayed in shape, looking younger than the number of birthdays he'd celebrated. He was dressed in a suit and tie, as always.

"Warren. Thanks for seeing me on such short notice. I won't take much of your time."

He stood and shook Ken's hand, then motioned for him to take a seat. "You know you're always welcome. What could I do for you?"

Ken settled in his chair, then shifted in his seat. Warren let him squirm. Ken had never just dropped by his office, unannounced.

Clearing his throat, Ken crossed his legs, and said, "I'll get right to the point of my visit. I'm getting a lot of pressure from the board, as you can imagine. You've done a lot for the hospital, but . . ."

Warren cocked his head. A college professor once told him that whenever someone uses the word *but* in a conversation, discard anything said before the word, and pay close attention to everything said after.

Ken stroked his chin as if trying to conjure up the words. "They want to remove you as Chair of the Foundation." He paused to let the words sink in.

Warren stared at him. "Who's *they?*"

Ken looked surprised at the challenge. "Well, the Foundation Board, of course."

"I thought you appointed the board?"

"Well, technically, I do," Ken stammered. "But they function independently of the hospital."

Warren smiled, letting him know that he wasn't buying the explanation.

Ken ploughed ahead, trying to put a smiley face on the news and dodging the blame. "As you can imagine, the foundation Chairperson suing the hospital isn't going over well with them." He paused to regroup. "I convinced them to let you resign."

I bet you did, Warren thought, still eyeing Ken as he fidgeted in his seat. He steepled his hands under his chin, while he appeared to be considering the request.

Shaking his head, he said, "Sorry, Ken. I'm not resigning." He stood, indicating the meeting was over.

Ken hesitated, then stood, a stunned look on his face. "I wish you'd reconsider. That would be best for everyone."

Warren stuck out his hand. "Best for you or for me? My answer is final. They want me out, they'll have to kick me out."

"I hate for things to end like this. You're putting me in an untenable position." Ken shook his hand, nodding. He turned and walked away.

Later that afternoon, Becky walked in, holding a letter. "A courier just delivered this. I thought you'd want to read it immediately." She handed him the letter.

It was on Rivers Community Hospital letterhead, from the office of Kenneth R. Taylor, CEO. It didn't take long for him to read the two short paragraphs.

Dear Mr. Thompson,

I regret to inform you that the Rivers Foundation Board has met and terminated your association with the Foundation, effective immediately.

We appreciate your service and dedication, and hope you will continue to support the mission of this organization.

Sincerely,

Kenneth J. Taylor, CEO

Not only was he being demoted, he was being kicked out. Warren arched his eyebrows and handed the piece of paper back to Becky.

"Thanks."

"What a jerk," she said, shaking her head. "After all you've done for that place." She spun and walked out, not waiting for a response.

He sat back in his chair, stroking his chin. *What next,* he wondered. At this rate, he was going to have to move to another city.

He turned his attention back to the pile of mail on his desk. Halfway through the stack, he paused when he saw the familiar red, white, and blue USCare card, clipped to a note from Becky.

This is your new health insurance card. According to the instructions, you should start using it immediately and destroy the old one.

He stared at the card. Forte Health Insurance Company was emblazoned across the top. His gaze shifted down to the Member ID. He looked at the third number from the right. It was a seven.

The bastards didn't waste much time, Warren thought. According to Sam, he'd just gone from the haves to the have-nots.

He yelled for Becky, but realized she'd left for lunch and wasn't at her desk.

When she returned, he asked, "Becky, how did we end up with Forte for our health insurance?"

"Carl Knight," she replied. "That's who he recommended. Why, is there a problem?"

He knew Carl handled their liability and property insurance, but wasn't sure if he did their health insurance, too.

"Did you get a new insurance card?" he asked her.

"Sure. Everyone did."

"Did anything change?"

"Not that I noticed. Why?"

"Would you bring your card in here for a minute? I just wanted to check something."

She walked out and returned in a few minutes, handing her card to him.

He looked at the Member ID number. Her third digit was still a three.

"Everything okay?"

He handed her card back. "Yes, just checking, is all. Thanks."

After she left, he called Carl. A deep voice with a Midwest accent answered on the second ring.

"Hi, Warren. How are you?"

"Not bad, considering the headlines this weekend."

Carl cleared his throat. "Yeah, I read that. Hope I'm not on your list."

"Don't think so, but my attorney's running the show." They chatted for a few minutes, then Warren asked him if he would stop by the office.

"I'll be happy to. I'll set up an appointment with Becky. Is there a problem?"

"Any chance you can stop by this afternoon? No need to set up an appointment."

"I can be there in thirty minutes."

"Great. See you in a bit."

Twenty minutes later, Warren's intercom buzzed. "Carl's here," Becky said.

"Give me five minutes, then send him in," Warren said. He was trying to finish up a trade with the bond desk in New York.

Most people thought that assets had to go up in value in order to make money. Warren was the new breed, which saw just as much opportunity, if not more, in falling stocks. What people like Warren realized is there was profit potential in movement—up or down, as long as you were out front.

Old-school investing said to buy low, sell high, and hold for long-term appreciation. In some quarters, that still held true, but for the most part, the name of the game was to be nimble, moving in and out at the right times. Timing and not being greedy were the two rules that governed Warren's market activity. He tried his best to never violate those rules.

He finished up the transaction, just as Carl walked in. Warren had known the tall, slim black man for several years. He was easygoing, but knowledgeable, and had won Warren's trust a few years ago when he promised an insurance review at no cost to Warren. If he couldn't save him anything at the end of the day, he'd walk away and not bother him again. Otherwise, he expected to be rewarded with Warren's business.

The previous insurance agent had taken Warren for granted and not kept pace. When Carl's review showed Warren that he could save over six thousand dollars a year *and* have better coverage, Warren switched. That was six years ago, and every year, Carl had updated his review.

"Tell me about Forte. Why did you recommend them and what other choices do we have?" Warren asked.

"Bottom line is that you have only two viable options in Fort Myers—Forte and All Care. Forte has better contracts in this area, so they're my choice. It's who I have my insurance with," Carl said.

Warren recognized the name of the other company. They were also in the Big Three. He wondered if it really made any difference.

"Who does the rating on people covered?" Warren asked.

"Rating?"

"You know, the level of insurance coverage. I understand there are different tiers of benefits."

Carl nodded. "The underwriters with the carriers do that. When I submit an application, they gather the information and come back with the levels available and rates. The client chooses what they're willing to pay for. Like picking out furniture."

"What if I wanted to upgrade? Move up a level?"

Carl shrugged. "We submit a new application, the companies review it and let us know if it's available, and if so, what the cost is."

"If it's available?" Warren asked.

"Coverage isn't always available. All levels aren't offered by every company in each location. They look at things like experience, health issues—I'm not sure what else, but they're pretty thorough."

"People ever get downgraded?"

"You're asking a lot of detailed questions about the underwriting process. Are you thinking about making a change?"

"Maybe."

"Sure, glad to help. You were starting to worry me there for a bit. Just want to make sure you're happy with my service."

"So, back to my question. Do people get—"

"Downgraded? Sometimes, but not often. Insurance companies can't change your coverage until the policy expires, which is typically twelve months." Carl looked out the window and reflected for a minute. "I've probably had a couple of clients get downgraded in the past few years."

"What about specific employees? Do they get changed?"

Carl shook his head. "I don't know of any case where one employee was changed. I can check if you want?"

He laid his new health insurance card on the desk, along with his old one. "You want to explain this?"

Carl picked up the two cards and studied them for a minute. He broke out into a grin, then set them back on the desk.

"You still have the Platinum level of coverage—the best—same as I do. Covers ninety percent of charges and—"

"So why did I get a new insurance card?"

Carl threw up his hands. "They do that from time to time. Internal reviews, accounting changes, that sort of thing. Besides, cards wear out."

He nodded. "They changed my Member ID, Carl."

Carl frowned and leaned forward. "You sure?"

He pointed to the cards on the desk

Carl studied one, then the other, still puzzled. "I've seen that a few times, but I have to admit, it's a little unusual. Maybe they changed something in their policy admin group."

"What determines the kind of drugs you get or which tests are done?"

Carl smiled. "Oh, the doctors control that. They have to order the tests, and they prescribe the drugs."

He couldn't figure out whether Carl was playing dumb or was avoiding the question. He tried a different tack.

"Maybe I'm phrasing it the wrong way. I thought that the care guidelines determined that sort of thing. It's my understanding that the care guidelines are dictated by the insurance companies?"

"Okay, I think I understand what you're asking. It's true that insurance companies use patient care guidelines in order to insure the consistent and efficient use of resources. But, the physicians have the ability to override those guidelines if they determine, in their professional judgment, that a different approach is indicated. Insurance companies don't tell physicians how to practice. Doctors wouldn't stand for that."

Watching Carl's face, he was convinced that Carl was just regurgitating the corporate line and didn't know any better. That or he was in complete denial. Either way, this was getting nowhere.

"Carl, how long have you been doing our insurance?"

Carl looked up at the ceiling for a moment, then back at him. "Six years this summer."

"And, you remember why I switched my business to you?"

Carl smiled. "Of course. You got tired of the previous company not being straight with you."

Warren sat back and nodded. "So. We have a problem." He leaned forward, speaking in measured tones. "I have reason to believe that my insurance has been downgraded."

Carl shook his head. "No, no." He pulled a sheet of paper out of the folder he was carrying and placed it on the desk facing Warren.

"See," he said, pointing to the two columns. "Your deductible remains at $10,000. Your lifetime cap remains at—"

"Bullshit. My plan has been downgraded."

Carl started to protest, but Warren raised his hand and continued.

"I know what the third digit from the right means, and I understand the significance of being downgraded from a three to a seven. I may have the same deductibles and all the other stuff, but the bottom line is I won't get the same level of care. I'll get not only cheaper accommodations, but the generic drugs, fewer diagnostic tests, and lower-rated physicians."

Carl laughed a nervous laugh. "That's an urban legend, Warren. There's no truth to that. It's like the one saying you can type your pin number in backward at an ATM to summon the police. It's not true."

Warren shook his head. He was convinced that Carl believed the pablum he was fed by the insurance companies he represented. Otherwise, he would've kicked him out of his office.

"Maybe, maybe not. But I believe it. Your insurance company fucked me—not you—and I don't appreciate it. What I want you to do is call your boss's boss or the highest ranking person you know in that company. Tell them about this conversation. Understood?"

He watched as Carl, visibly shaken, left his office in a hurry.

Warren went back to his trading desk screen, watching a series of trades in a hot stock he'd taken a major position in. Satisfied with the return, he clicked on a couple of keys, selling half of the stock he'd just purchased a week earlier.

His cell phone buzzed, but he ignored it. A few minutes later, it chimed, indicating a text message. It was Lawrence Dalton, wanting him to call.

"Damn, and I thought *I* had a knack for pissing people off," Lawrence said, when he answered.

"As you told me, 'we're just getting started.'" Warren was enjoying throwing Dalton's platitudes back at him. Life in Fort Myers had been miserable since initiating the lawsuit, and he figured that Lawrence might as well share the fun.

"I thought that was a pretty good article."

"Maybe for you," Warren said, unable to hide the bitterness in his voice.

Lawrence either missed it or chose to ignore it. "I can honestly say I've never seen this forceful a reaction."

"What are you talking about?" Warren asked.

"I got a call today from Boone, Martin, and Griffin. T-Bone himself called."

"T-Bone?"

Lawrence laughed. "That's what I call Tully Boone when I want to get under his skin."

"Who the hell is Tully Boone? And why do I care?"

Lawrence Dalton let out a big, belly laugh. "T-bone is me if I'd gone into corporate law. He's the managing partner of one of the largest corporate law firms in the world. And apparently, you have pissed off one of his clients—Forte Health."

"I know the name. And what, exactly, have *I* done?"

"You have libeled and disparaged his client's reputation. As we speak, someone out there is on their way to present you with a subpoena."

"A subpoena?"

"No big deal, just send it to me. They're firing back by deposing our witnesses."

Shit, Warren thought. *This is just starting.* "You're not getting cold feet, are you?" he asked Lawrence.

There was a throaty chuckle on the line. "This is what I live for. It tells me they're concerned, which is good news for us. What we need is a copy of those damn patient care guidelines. You know anyone there at the hospital who would be willing to give you access?"

Now it was Warren's turn to laugh. "You're kidding, right? Nobody there is speaking to me. I can barely get a cup of coffee in the cafeteria. Maybe you should've thought of that before you papered Fort Myers in subpoenas."

"I'll be in touch." Lawrence ended the call.

Warren set his phone down on the desk, returning to his client list. There were Xs by three of the first ten names. Three of his biggest clients in Fort Myers had sent him letters, asking that their position be liquidated and the balance transferred to Jenkins-Gilmore, the same firm he used to work for. Though he couldn't prove it, he suspected that Forte was behind the selection of that firm.

The intercom on his desk phone buzzed.

"Yes?" he answered.

"Garrett Thomas is on line three," Becky said. "I figured you wanted to talk to him."

Garrett Thomas was one of the wealthiest men in southwest Florida, and the second name on Warren's client list. His family had owned huge tracts of land in Collier County and Lee County. The first was home to Naples, one of the richest zip codes in the country. The second was home to Fort Myers, at one time one of the fastest growing areas.

Thomas had a reputation for questionable business deals. It seemed like most big development projects in this area almost always involved land held by him. Some of the land was acquired in what could be described as a fortuitous manner.

Warren didn't know if the rumors were true, but wouldn't be surprised if they were. He picked up the phone and punched the blinking button marked Three.

"Garrett. How are you?"

"Not bad—for an old man."

Warren laughed. "Most days, you look younger than me."

"Not sure about that." Garrett was not one to beat around the bush. "Warren, you've always been straight with me, and you know that's the way I do business. That's why I wanted to call you."

Warren held his breath, waiting for the shoe to drop.

"I'm closing my account. Everglades's returns haven't been that good this year. But, that's not why I'm moving my money. I wanted you to hear it from me."

He cursed under his breath.

"This lawsuit of yours has a lot of people riled up. I've always liked the fact that you operated out of the limelight. You know I don't like that sort of thing."

Warren was biting his tongue, wanting to interrupt, but knowing he needed to listen.

"I've already got reporters calling me, asking about our relationship."

How the hell? "Garrett, you know I haven't said anything to anyone about my clients. I'd never do that."

"I know, I know. I'm not saying you did. All I'm saying is that I don't want that kind of publicity. So, I think it's best we part ways as friends. Again, that's why I thought it was important to tell you straight up. No bullshit, no flimsy excuses."

He knew it was no need to argue with someone like Garrett. His mind was made up, and there would be no reversal, regardless of what Warren said or did.

"Garrett, I appreciate your call. I'm sorry, and hope that in the future you'll consider coming back."

"I will, Warren. You get off the front page, you give me a call."

He replaced the handset, careful not to slam it down. *Fuck.* Garrett Thomas was his second largest client, behind Clay Fortson. A few more losses like that, and he'd be out of business. Forte was turning the screws tighter and tighter.

Blaine hung up the phone. He'd just talked to the Southern Region Vice President, who had fielded a call from one of his agents in Fort Myers. Apparently, Mr. Thompson was not happy with his new insurance card, implying that his coverage had changed for the worse.

Blaine smiled. *That's just the first round, Thompson. I'm just getting started.* He picked up the phone and called the head of underwriting with further instructions.

Chapter 18

Warren tapped his pen on his desk. Becky had received a call from Clay Fortson's assistant that morning. The old man was flying in next weekend and wanted to meet with Warren. As usual, he didn't say what the meeting was about, but when your largest client wanted a meeting, it didn't matter.

He figured it had to do with Clay's previous comment about moving his business. In consideration of Alex's untimely death, Clay had put his decision on hold out of respect for Warren, but Warren knew that wouldn't last indefinitely.

Losing Clay's account, on top of the other losses, would be disastrous. Lawrence Dalton didn't come cheap, and Warren was already trying to figure out how to stem the outflow of cash.

That afternoon, he drove out to Clay's house on Sanibel. It was a huge, two-story house with a commanding view of the Gulf at the upper end of West Gulf Drive past Rabbit Road, not too far past the house where he'd met with Lawrence Dalton. Nice neighborhood, but it was a long drive from downtown Fort Myers. He was glad he didn't have to come out here often.

The entrance to the house belied what couldn't be seen from the road. It was well-manicured, with a simple mailbox next to a driveway of orange brick payers that curved out of sight. The house was hidden behind an artful planting of various shrubs and palm trees, effectively disguising the grandeur of what was behind. There were no gates, nor any indication that one of the wealthiest men in the world was in residence there.

Despite this apparent ordinary entrance, Warren knew that there were closed-circuit cameras throughout the grounds, and a full-time security staff. Clay wasn't the type to surround himself with such trappings, but at the insistence of his insurance company, he felt obligated to comply.

Warren turned in the driveway. He was still driving Alex's white BMW. Although the insurance company had written him a check for the Porsche, which was totaled in the accident, he couldn't part with Alex's car just yet.

He parked out front on the circular drive and walked up the steps to the house. There was movement to his right, and he saw one of the security guards approaching. The man was stocky with a crew cut and not an ounce of fat showing anywhere. He wore a green golf shirt that looked painted on, a blue blazer, and a pair of khakis. Warren was willing to bet that the man was ex-military and had a shoulder holster on underneath the blazer with a loaded weapon.

"Mr. Thompson," he said. "Mr. Fortson is waiting for you on the back deck. You know the way, I believe."

Warren couldn't remember his name, but recognized him and thanked him as he walked around the porch. As always, he was blown away by the view when he rounded the corner of the house. The Gulf of Mexico stretched out in the distance, framed only by palm trees. The sun was low on the horizon and the sky was already turning shades of orange and pink. A sailboat was visible several miles away, only the mast showing. It was calm, and not enough wind to power the sails.

Clay was sitting at a table on the far end of the deck, reading a magazine. He looked up when he heard movement.

"Warren, come on back and have a seat. Curtis met you out front, I trust?"

Warren nodded. *Curtis.* He'd remember that on the way out. "Of course. He recognized me and told me to come around back."

"Good, good. After all, you are family. Would you like a drink?"

A server had materialized out of thin air, and was standing quietly a few steps away.

"Jacob here will be glad to bring you something," Clay said.

"A Macallan, neat, please," Warren said to the young man.

"Is the twenty-five satisfactory?" he asked Warren, referring to the 25-year old version of the single-malt Scotch.

Warren smiled and nodded. The last time he priced it, it had climbed to over a thousand dollars a bottle. *Better enjoy it while you can.*

Jacob turned and picked up Clay's empty glass. "Another, sir?"

Clay nodded, and the young man disappeared as quietly as he had come. "Have a seat," he said, motioning to the chair next to his, facing the water. "Should be another magnificent sunset."

Warren tried to get comfortable as Clay made small talk. He was having to bite his tongue to keep from asking Clay what he'd decided.

After the drinks arrived, they raised their glasses and took a sip. He noticed the darker liquid in Clay's glass.

"Still drinking bourbon, I see," Warren said.

Clay smiled. "The only thing I drink besides water."

"Jeb wants to transfer our account to a New York firm," Clay said.

Warren swallowed, hard. He'd had a tumultuous relationship with Jeb Fortson, Clay's oldest son. Jeb was a brash, Ivy-League educated, spoiled brat—Clay's words, not his. Warren knew the account was safe as long as Clay was around. This shed a different light on things.

"With the returns we've been getting this past year, I'm hard-pressed to argue with him," Clay said.

Warren couldn't stand it any longer. "Clay, I know this has been a tough year—in a lot of ways. But look at the run we've had." He quoted the returns from the last five years. He'd memorized them prior to driving out. "Taken in the longer-term view, we've done well. You know that." He tried to hide the desperation in his voice.

"I realize that, Warren. And my decision is not solely driven by the less-than-stellar returns this past year. The bigger issue is my retirement."

He took a long drink of bourbon, letting it rest in his mouth for a moment before swallowing and then continuing. "Once I step down, I'm out. I'm not going to interfere. I'm an old man, and I'm tired. I'm set financially—I have more money than Martha and I can ever spend. And you know, I'm leaving a big chunk to charity. The rest is Jeb's, to do what he will with it, including pissing it all away."

The old man drained his glass, and set it on the table. Warren followed suit. Jacob appeared and collected the empty glasses, thankfully returning in a few minutes with fresh ones. Neither Clay nor Warren said a word until the young man left again.

"Reaction?" Clay asked.

"Please don't take offense at my question, Clay, but has anyone pressured you to do this?"

"None taken, and no, you know me better than that. Why do you ask?"

"Well, I've heard through the grapevine that some of my clients are getting subtle hints to move their business."

Clay took a sip of his bourbon. "Jeb has gotten a few calls. Nobody's got the balls to call me. I'm assuming you're talking about the lawsuit. But, no, I don't give a rat's ass about that. That's your business."

Warren shrugged, not ready to concede. "I'm surprised you're leaving. I guess I always figured you for a 'die with your boots on' type."

Clay chuckled. "Well, that's what I always thought. I'm eighty-two, Warren. Me and Martha don't have many years left, and that's a fact. We're in pretty good health, but God knows how long that will last at this point. There's still a few things we want to do in this world, and I don't want to be bothered with running a business."

"I understand completely. And, I also know you're the kind of person who won't meddle, and I think that's smart. But do you really think it's wise to dump that much on Jeb at once? Don't you think it'd be better to ease him into the top position over a period of time?"

The old man nodded and took a sip of his whiskey. "I've thought about that. But it's not fair for me to hang around. You know we butt heads enough as it is. You'll still have mine and Martha's account, and whatever we're leaving to charity. That's not a small chunk. But, the rest of it is up to Jeb, and . . ."

"*And*, pardon me for saying, which will be transferred before the ink is dry." Warren couldn't hide the bitterness in his voice.

Clay nodded. "Probably."

Warren took a swallow of the Scotch, letting it warm him on the way down while he considered how to respond. Losing Fortson Holdings, LLC was going to be a major blow. He shook his head. There was nothing he could do.

"Clay, you're a good friend, and that's the most important thing. At the end of the day, it's your money and your decision. I have to respect that."

Clay looked at him and smiled. "I know you don't like it, Warren, but I told Martha you'd understand."

On the way back to Fort Myers, Warren was running the calculations through his head. Even with retaining Clay and Martha's account, the loss of the business account was huge. Coupled with Garrett Thomas and the few other big clients he knew were leaving, he was looking at a significant cutback.

The next morning, he was still thinking about the decline in business when he got off the elevator on his floor. A short, older man in a cheap sports coat was standing there as if waiting on the elevator, but he didn't move. He looked at Warren as if he knew him.

As soon as the elevator doors closed, the man asked, "Are you Warren Thompson?"

He hesitated, unsure as to why the man would be asking. "Yes, can I help you?"

The man reached into the inside of his jacket and removed an envelope, handing it to Warren. He saw his named typed on the outside and reached out to take it.

As soon as he did, the man smiled, and said, "You've been served. Have a nice day."

He stood there speechless as the man punched the elevator button, still grinning. The elevator arrived, and when the doors opened, he got on, turning around to give Warren a little wave as the doors closed.

Warren walked in and threw the envelope on Becky's desk, not bothering to open it.

"What's this?"

"My subpoena. Send it to Lawrence," he said, walking into his office.

Chapter 19

The alarm clock sounded, but Warren was wide awake. He'd had a fitful night: bad dreams and restlessness. He pulled on a T-shirt and shorts, then made his way downstairs where he turned on the coffee maker. He sat at the bar, staring out at the river, waiting for the machine to dispense the first shot of the caffeine-laced brown nectar.

Warren was a fixer, a doer, a man of action. But for once, he didn't know what to do. He'd started out wanting to know what happened to Alex. Now he knew, but he was obsessed with the bigger picture. The incident with Ciel and her daughter had made him realize how pervasive the problem was. Untold numbers of patients were victims of health care rationing, and they didn't even know it.

He walked out on the lanai, sipping his coffee, looking toward the river. Several boats passed by, and he heard seagulls cawing down by the water. A mullet launched itself completely out of the water like a missile. The aroma of fresh coffee filled his nostrils.

He needed to talk to Micah, to tell her he understood. He wanted to apologize, but in person. Since Micah wouldn't return his calls or answer her phone, he decided to surprise her in the hospital cafeteria.

At the hospital, when he entered, he half expected the security guard next to the main entrance to bar him admission, but the man only acknowledged him with a slight nod as he walked past.

At the door to the cafeteria, he ran into Joan Frazier, walking out with a co-worker. She stopped in front of him, arms folded across her chest, and green eyes boring into him. Warren was reminded of the saying *if looks could kill.*

"What brings you here, Warren, now that you're no longer on the Foundation?" She spoke loud enough that people passing around them turned to see what was going on.

"Hello, Joan. Last time I checked, this was a public place. I like the coffee here." He was determined to hold her stare.

She sneered, put her hand up to her lips and turned to her companion. "What a jerk," she said in a mock whisper, shaking her head. "She should've dumped him." She turned and they walked away, each glancing over their shoulder for a parting look at the bewildered Warren.

Anger rose within, and he took a step toward her path of retreat, determined to get clarification. He stopped as he watched her and the other woman disappear around the corner, heels clicking on the tile floor. He realized she was baiting him.

He shook his head and turned back toward the cafeteria. Once inside, he walked over to the coffee counter. His arm was still stiff, which didn't go unnoticed by Ciel, the barista.

"You looking a lot better. No sling, I see," she said, as she filled a large cup with coffee.

"I am. You still have the best coffee in town. How's your daughter?"

A broad grin spread across her face. "She's much better. Home now, and starting back to school next week."

"That's great news. I keep waiting for you to call me. I was serious about my job offer."

She smiled as she put a lid on the coffee and slid it over to him. "I hadn't forgot. I just can't afford to lose my health insurance here. When the time comes—and it will—I'll be calling. I just hope you remember."

He had to force a smile, not wanting to rain on her enthusiasm. *Can't afford to lose my health insurance,* he thought. *My God, they've got everyone completely snowed.*

Warren handed her a twenty. "That's yours," he said. "And, don't worry. I'll remember."

He turned and went over to a table where he could see the entrance. About halfway through his coffee, he was beginning to think Micah wouldn't come in. Maybe she wasn't working today. He could've found out, but he didn't want to do that.

Joan's words kept ringing in his ears. He almost missed Micah, coming in the door with a male co-worker. She looked at him and stared for a moment. Then, she turned and said something to her companion as they walked the other direction and sat at a table on the far side of the cafeteria.

Now he knew what a leper must have felt like in days of old. The barista was the only one who treated him with any kindness. To everyone else, he felt like he wore an L branded on his forehead.

He gave it a few minutes, finished his coffee, and walked over to Micah's table. Her co-worker saw him coming, looked at her, and gave a slight nod in Warren's direction.

"Hello, Micah," Warren said.

She looked up at him with a penetrating stare, not saying a word.

"I was hoping I could have a few minutes to speak with you."

The male, a doctor, Warren guessed, based on his white lab coat and stethoscope around his neck, started to leave. Micah reached out and put her hand on his arm to stop him. She continued to stare at Warren.

"I'm sorry. As you can see, I'm busy," she said.

"Look, I'm sorry—"

"What part of that did you not understand?" she said, her voice dripping with a poisonous mix of anger and sarcasm.

Warren noticed the people at the next table watching the exchange. It was turning into a scene, one he had hoped to avoid. He felt his face flush as he looked at the doctor sitting at her table. Warren looked back at Micah, but there was no sympathy in her stare. "I apologize for interrupting," he said to them both, turned, and walked away. He felt the stares of the people at the adjacent table as he stormed out of the cafeteria.

On his way to the car, he called Micah's number and left a terse voice mail. He didn't bother hiding his embarrassment and anger.

He was still fuming when he got back to the office. As he walked past Becky's desk, not even stopping, he barked, "Becky, do you still have Micah Rollins's address? And, find out when she gets off work." Halfway to his office, and over his shoulder, he said, "And what she drives."

Two steps later, he added, "Please," before closing his door.

Twenty minutes later, she handed him a piece of paper with the information requested, in her familiar handwriting.

The Palms of McGregor
Building C, Unit 1218
4114 McGregor Boulevard

3:00 p.m.

Silver Toyota Camry

He knew where the condominiums were, only fifteen minutes from the hospital and twenty minutes from his office.

At five minutes before three, he walked out of his office, his only comment to Becky that he'd be back in an hour.

When he got to the entrance of The Palms of McGregor, the driveway split. A sign directed residents to a gated drive on the right and visitors to a drive next to the guard house. Both gates were closed. At the guard house, a uniformed security guard stood outside, wearing sunglasses and holding a clip board.

He eased the BMW up next to the guard and pressed the button to let the window down. "Good afternoon," he said, hoping to soften up the gatekeeper with a pleasant attitude.

"May I help you?"

"I'm here to see Micah Rollins," Warren said, smiling.

"Your name, please." All business.

"Warren Thompson."

The guard looked at the clipboard, scanning the list attached, then back at Warren. "I'm sorry, there's no 'Warren Thompson' on the list."

Warren kept the grin pasted on his face. "I'm her investment advisor. Everglades Investments, here in town. I had an appointment with her this afternoon. I'm sure she just neglected to leave my name with you."

Warren heard another vehicle pull up behind him.

The guard looked at the other car, then back to Warren and pointed. "Drive through and park over on the right in the visitor spot. I'll give Ms. Rollins a call to confirm your appointment."

Shit, Warren thought. The guard raised the gate, and Warren pulled through, parking where directed. He left the engine running and the window down, watching the guard give the car that had been behind him a pass.

After that car cleared the gate, Warren drummed his fingers on the door as he watched the guard pick up the phone in the guardhouse, presumably to call Micah.

As he watched, a silver Toyota Camry pulled up to the resident gate. An arm covered in blue reached out and inserted a card. The barricade opened, and the car drove through. As it passed, he recognized the driver. It was Micah.

He slammed his car in reverse, and backed out of the parking spot, squealing the tires. Slamming on brakes, he threw the gearshift knob into drive and started after the Camry. He glanced in his rearview mirror and saw the security guard standing in the middle of the entrance, his radio up to his mouth.

The Camry pulled up under a covered parking shelter, and the driver's door opened just as Warren screeched to a stop behind her. As she got out, he did also, and strode toward her. Surprise registered on her face as she saw it was him.

Before he got to her, another security guard in a golf cart roared to a stop between them, the overweight man getting out and ordering Warren to leave.

"I apologize, Ms. Rollins," he said, blocking Warren from getting to Micah. "The police are on their way."

Warren shook his head. "You've got to be kidding me," he said. That was when he noticed Micah with a tight grin on her face, standing there with her arms folded, enjoying the show. He looked at her with a pleading look on his face, begging her to intervene.

After what seemed like forever, she turned to the security guard and said, "It's okay, Frank. I forgot I had an appointment with Mr. Thompson this afternoon. I'm sorry."

Frank looked at him, then back at Micah. "Alright. But he'll still need a parking pass and have to park in the visitor area," he said, determined to save face.

"I understand, and he will," she said, giving Warren a stern don't-open-your-mouth look.

Frank went to his golf cart and retrieved a visitor pass. After recording Warren's license plate number, he handed the pass to Warren, giving him a smug look. "You need to put this in your dash, and park your vehicle over there," he said, pointing to a row of exposed parking spots thirty yards away.

"Thank you," Warren mumbled, as much to Micah as to Frank.

"I'll wait," Micah said, the grin still creasing her face.

Warren parked his car and walked back over to Micah.

"You are one persistent pain-in-the-ass," she said, arms folded across her chest.

He gave her a thin smile. "Thank you," he said. "I mean for not having me arrested, not for the term of endearment."

"What do you want?" she said, her slight smile disappearing.

"First, to apologize. Ten minutes of your time. I've had several meetings with Sam Abrams, who accepted my apology. I'd like to talk to you about it. Please," he added.

Arms still folded, she leaned back against her car and said, "Ten minutes. The clock starts now."

He explained that he didn't realize she was going to be subpoenaed, and for that, he was truly sorry. He also told her about Sam educating him on health insurance levels.

"My attorney is very aggressive, and subpoenaed everyone who I had mentioned talking to. I even got one from the other guys," he said, hoping she'd take pity.

"You don't have a clue what you've done, do you?" she asked.

He took a deep breath. "I'm starting to figure that out. What can I do to get back in your good graces?"

"Call your damn Doberman off—now."

He started to protest, and she shook her head. "Non-negotiable. You asked."

"I don't understand. What can they do to you?"

She stared at him in disbelief. "You said Sam explained to you how the health insurance levels work?"

He nodded.

"Did he explain to you about my son, Gabe?"

"No, he wouldn't tell me anything personal. He said I'd have to get that from you."

She put her hands up to her face, shaking her head. She looked at him with those piercing blue eyes as if deciding how much to tell him.

"Gabe has a rare form of epilepsy. He's had it since birth. After trying every drug in the formulary, with no success, his doctor put him on a brand new drug. It's worked."

"That's wonderful."

She smiled and nodded. "You don't know how great that is. He can lead a normal life, and has, as long as he's on that drug. *But,* it costs $3,000 a month. Three thousand dollars. Every month. Forever."

Warren realized what she was saying.

"You're on the hospital insurance plan. They can't—"

"They can, and they will. Did you not listen to anything that Sam told you?"

He thought about the disgraced, brilliant Harvard-trained surgeon, and what had happened to him. Remembering his own new insurance card, he understood why she was so upset.

"I'll call Dalton as soon as I leave. I'd like to try and make it up to you. Dinner?"

"Make the call, first. Then, I'll think about it." She got her bag out of the car. "Time's up. I have to go."

Looking at his watch, he started to say that he had a minute left, but thought better of it and said, "Thanks."

He watched her walk to her building, then went to his car. He started it so the air conditioning would work, and pulled out his phone to call Dalton. His mind wandered back to Joan's comment at the hospital. *She should've dumped him*. Joan wanted to hurt him, and she'd succeeded.

He shifted his attention back to Dalton, and placed the call. It rang once before answering.

"Dalton. Leave a message." *Beep*.

"Lawrence, Warren. Give me a call when you get a chance."

He ended the call, and placed the phone in the console. The attorney was not going to be happy, but too bad. Dalton was going to have to find a way to make his case without Micah Rollins.

Chapter 20

Warren's cell phone buzzed, and he picked it up to see who was calling. It was Lawrence Dalton, returning his call. He verified that the little Secure icon was displayed in the bottom corner of the screen, then answered.

"Lawrence, thanks for returning my call."

"There's been a development. We need to talk."

The attorney sounded ominous and business-like, without bothering to ask why Warren had called.

"We're talking on a secure line. I'm in my office—alone. Go ahead," Warren said.

"Tully Boone called. I just got off the phone with him. Nothing official, one of your 'off-the-record' conversations."

"Tully Boone? The attorney for Forte?"

"The one and only. According to him, the Big Three are joining forces on this. They consider it that important."

"That's good news, right?"

"Damn right, it is—great news. This is bigger than we thought. In the twenty years I've gone against T-Bone, he's never done this. He said that the three companies are prepared to take this all the way to the mat, whatever the costs. He tried to intimidate me into dropping the case or settling."

Warren couldn't believe what he was hearing. "Settling? What's the offer?"

"No, no, no, no. We've got them on the run. This means—"

"What's the offer, Lawrence? I told you, I want answers, not money."

"The offer is bullshit, Warren, bullshit. Normally, in these cases, they hide behind the fact that all they're doing is following accepted practice, or care guidelines, if you will. But what we've done is find a seam. They're discriminating based on economic status, which is illegal.

"Think about it. If giving you the answers you're looking for was all there was to it, do you think they'd join forces and write a blank check? No way, my friend. Give it some thought, and call me tomorrow." Lawrence hung up before Warren could tell him about Micah.

Frustrated, Warren punched in Lawrence's number. It went to voice mail. "Lawrence, dammit. Call me back. *I* had something to talk to *you* about." He hung up the phone.

Looking out the window at the sunlight reflecting off the Caloosahatchee a few blocks away, he thought about the lawsuit. He wanted to settle. As Lawrence had warned him, it was getting more uncomfortable. Plus, a settlement would be an out for Micah. Although he questioned the attorney's agenda, he had to agree that Lawrence had a point. Why would the three largest health insurers go to such extremes to quash the suit?

Warren picked up the phone and called Tim.

"Hey, you up for some racquetball this afternoon? I need to beat the shit out of something," Warren said, when his friend answered.

Tim laughed. "I hope you're talking about the ball and not me." There was a pause. "You sure you should be playing this soon?"

"Hey, it was my left arm. I'm right-handed, remember?"

"I realize that, but are you sure you should—"

"Do you want to play or not? I can find someone else."

"You are in a shit mood, aren't you?"

Warren heard keys clicking in the background.

"How about five?"

"See you there."

As soon as he hung up, the phone rang again.

"What is it?" he said, thinking it was Tim calling back.

"I don't know. You called me. I was returning your call." It was Lawrence Dalton.

"Sorry, I thought it was someone else." Warren told him about talking with Micah, and explained Micah's predicament with her son. "I'm sorry, but you've got to take her off the table."

He was surprised that Lawrence didn't react.

"I'll move her to last. We probably won't get to her. Not sure how much she can help anyway."

He wondered what *move her to last* meant. He asked.

"She's been deposed. We can withdraw it, but I'd rather not. We can control the scheduling. By moving her to last, we keep her on the list if we need her for some reason. Chances are we'll never get that far."

He started to push the issue, but figured it was wise to take what was offered at this point. If he ever got the chance to have a real conversation with Micah, he'd explain. If she insisted, then he'd have Lawrence withdraw it.

At the gym, Warren walked into the locker room. Tim was already there, changing clothes.

"You sounded pissed," Tim said. "What's going on?"

Warren dropped his bag on the bench and opened his locker. "Fucking attorneys," he said, as he stripped off his suit and put on shorts and a T-shirt with Bitter End emblazoned on it.

"That's profound. What happened?"

"Your damn Doberman is out of control."

"*My* Doberman? He's *yours,* my friend. I warned you."

They finished getting dressed, then walked out to the court. He was picturing the face of Lawrence Dalton on the blue rubber ball he squeezed in his hand. As they warmed up, he told Tim about the phone call from Dalton.

Warren won the first game, 15-10. They set their racquets down inside the court, and went for a drink of water.

"It's been a while since you've beat me that bad," Tim said, as he wiped the sweat off his face. "I was taking it easy on you because of your arm, but no more mercy."

"Sure. One thing you attorneys know is how to make excuses."

"Remind me never again to play you after you've had a run-in with an attorney."

Warren had spent some of his frustration in the first game and was a little calmer. "Tell me, what do you think?"

Tim filled up his water bottle and took a long drink. "Hard to say. These kind of cases can be huge rat holes, into which you'll pour a lot of time and money. While you're certainly loaded, you don't have anywhere near the kind of pockets that the top three health insurance companies have. But if Lawrence Dalton smells blood, then I'd tend to trust him. He didn't get to where he is by losing."

Warren drained his water bottle and refilled it before they stopped by the restroom on the way back to the court. Standing next to his friend at the urinals, he said, "I told him from the start that I was interested in answers, not dollars."

Finishing his business, Tim walked over to the sink and washed his hands. "Then get Lawrence to give you the specifics on their offer. But listen to him, Warren. That's why you're paying him the big bucks."

They finished the second game, and Warren won 15-13. He didn't have the intensity he had in the first game, and he was lucky to win. Afterwards, they went over to Barney's for a beer, taking a seat at the bar since the place was empty.

"Is that all that's bothering you?" Tim asked.

"Just a lot on my mind," he said to Tim, at last. "This thing has mushroomed out of control. You know me—I don't do well with things I can't fix."

After the second beer, Tim said he had to run. Barney brought the check over and laid it down in front of Warren.

"Why are you giving it to me?" Warren said, passing it over to Tim. "Loser always pays."

Barney moved the check back to Warren. "Yeah, but I figure he's doing you a favor by being seen in public with you. He's the only one I've seen you out with, since you decided to take on the entire town."

Tim laughed. "Got a point, Barney."

Warren just shook his head. "What else have you heard, Barney?"

A thin smile crossed the stocky bartender's face. "Costing you some business, I hear." He took the towel off his shoulder and wiped the bar in front of the two men. "Probably going to lose some more before you're done."

Tim stopped smiling and looked at Warren, as Barney walked off. He had a questioning look.

Warren shrugged. "A couple of clients bailed. Nothing I can't manage." He finished what was left of his beer.

"How bad is it?" Tim asked.

He told Tim about the three clients who'd cashed out, but left out the part about Clay Fortson and Garrett Thomas.

"I started with nothing. If I lose the whole damn business, I've still got enough stashed away to get by. I won't starve."

"That serious, huh?"

Warren shrugged. "I don't know. Forte's got a lot of clout. Not sure how this is going to end."

"Have you heard from Micah?"

Warren snorted. "Finally—after I almost got arrested at her condo."

The worried look on Tim's face made him laugh. "I didn't do anything stupid. Well, not that stupid. She dressed me down in the hospital cafeteria, so I met her at her condo."

"And?"

"I forgot to stop and get a visitor pass at the gate."

"Nice. Just what you need—to get arrested for trespassing and have your picture on the front page of the *News-Press*. You have got to tread softly, my friend. There are a lot of people in this town who would love to burn you for even the slightest infraction."

He nodded and said, "Tell me about it."

"What'd she say?"

"I think she accepted my apology. I told her I'd call Dalton and tell him to take her off of his list."

Tim shook his head. "Talk to him yet?"

"Before I came over here. He told me he could withdraw it, but would rather move her to last. He said they'd probably never get to her."

"Makes sense. Will she agree?"

"Don't know. Haven't talked to her about it yet."

"You sure you got the stomach for this?"

Warren shrugged. "Nothing about my life has been easy. You know that. I've told you—I want answers, and I'm determined to get them. He's just going to have to figure out how to do it without involving her."

Tim stood and put his hand on Warren's shoulder. "I know, but don't let this consume you. The price may not be worth it."

Chapter 21

Trip Carter's on line two," Becky said, on the intercom. "Want me to take a message?"

Warren smiled. "No, I'll take it." Trip Carter was an old friend of his from New York, a financial journalist with the *New York Times*. They'd been drinking buddies when Warren had worked on Wall Street.

He picked up the handset and punched the blinking button for line two.

"Got any hot tips for me?" Warren asked, laughing.

"Yeah, don't go into the newspaper business. You make more in an hour than I make all year," the nasal voice of his friend replied. "How's life in southwest Florida?"

"Okay," Warren replied, a note of sadness in his voice.

"Sorry I couldn't hang around after the funeral. I had to get to Washington. How're you doing?"

"It's hard. Good days, and bad ones. I just hope there will be more of the former and less of the latter."

"I know. I still find it hard to believe."

I don't know what to believe anymore, Warren thought. Trip had met Alex in December when Warren had taken her up for the holidays. It was her first trip to the city, and she was enchanted. Warren, who'd lived there and visited countless times, took it for granted, but on that trip, it was like seeing it for the first time.

They'd had dinner a couple of nights with Trip, and he'd taken a liking to her. Now Warren was starting to wonder how much of what he had with Alex was real.

"I hear you've stirred up a hornet's nest," Trip said.

Warren chuckled. "I didn't know news from Fort Myers made it to New York."

"Oh, trust me, this news did."

Warren was curious. "What have you heard?"

"Just what I read in the *Times*. You know, 'all the news that's fit to print.'"

He knew better. Trip Carter had spent the last fifteen years working Wall Street, and had more sources than the Chairman of the Federal Reserve. Trip was fishing for something.

"You working this?" Warren asked.

Trip laughed. "I'm always working. Like I said, I'm just a starving reporter, trying to make ends meet in one of the most expensive cities in the world. You planning on coming up anytime soon? We need to get together."

This was Trip's way of saying he wanted to talk to him. He was too smart to say anything on the phone. Warren looked at his calendar. He needed to go to New York for business anyway, and it'd be good to see Trip.

"Matter of fact, I need to be up there next Wednesday. You available?"

"For you, Mister hedge fund whiz, always. Same spot?"

Their favorite hangout had been Dina's, a small, dingy Italian restaurant two blocks up from the *Times* building. Warren was surprised it was still there. Not big on ambience, it served some of the best Italian food in New

York. Dina's was a local place, not on anyone's guide to New York City, and everyone liked it that way—especially Dina.

"Why don't I come in early and meet you for dinner Tuesday night. Say around eight?"

"See you then, bro. Safe travels."

Warren hung up the phone. He had too much work to catch up on, so he told Becky to schedule the jet for Tuesday to get him to the City in time for an eight o'clock dinner. Last year, he'd leased a Lear 70, a small, six-passenger business jet. He didn't require it often, but when he did, it was convenient.

"Can I ask you something personal?" he said before she walked out of his office

She gave him a puzzled look, and answered, "What?"

"Do you think Alex was happy with me . . . with *us*?"

She shook her head. "Of course. I know she was. Where in the world is this coming from?"

He hesitated, sorry he'd mentioned it. "A friend of hers made the comment that Alex should've . . . found someone else." He studied her face for clues.

Becky frowned and shook her head. "I don't know who would say that, but they are crazy, and you're crazy for listening."

"Sorry. I shouldn't have said anything."

Her face softened. "It's okay. Obviously, it's been bothering you, but you need to cross that one off your worry list, you hear? And if I find out who said it, I'll personally kick their ass."

He couldn't help but laugh as she turned and walked out the door.

* * *

At a little after seven, Tuesday evening, the Lear touched down in Teterboro Airport in New Jersey, just across the Hudson from Manhattan. Only twelve miles from the city, it was one of the busiest general aviation airports in the world.

Warren hopped in his waiting limo for the brief ride into Manhattan. Although a helicopter would've been only ten minutes, he had plenty of time and was content with using a limo.

Forty-five minutes later, he walked through the door of Dina's. Trip was waiting at the bar.

"Good to see you, my friend," Trip said, greeting Warren with a hug instead of a handshake.

"Likewise," he said, glad to see his old friend.

A short, older lady walked up, hands on her hips. "What am I? Chopped liver?" she said, a smile crossing her face.

"Dina, you know I came up here just to see you." He opened his arms, and she stepped over to him, giving him a big hug and a kiss on each cheek.

"That was the right answer, you silver-tongued devil." A frown replaced her smile. "I'm so sorry, Warren. Trip told me."

Warren nodded, his eyes misting in spite of his resistance. He squeaked out a weak, "Thanks."

She grabbed his hand and led them to the back. "Come on, you two. I saved the best table for you."

Warren couldn't help but smile. She told every one of her regulars the same line. She led them to a table in the back corner, which was as private as possible in an open place like Dina's. But, with their backs to the wall, they could see everyone else with ease. Besides, anyone other than a regular would stick out like a sore thumb. With the place half empty, he'd known Dina to tell people she was booked if she·didn't like the looks of a stranger who showed up for dinner.

Dina brought them a bottle of her best Chianti, opened it, and poured them each a glass. Promising to join them for an after-dinner drink, she left them alone.

Trip picked up his glass, proposing a toast. "To good friends and good memories," he said.

After they had a sip of wine, Trip sat back and sighed. "This is the only time I can get wine like this—I can't afford it."

"What makes you think I'm picking up the tab?" Warren said, grinning. "You're the one who invited me."

"If you're expecting me to pay, then you better roll up your sleeves, 'cause there's a lot of dishes in the kitchen."

"What's up, Trip. You didn't just happen to call and see if I was going to be up here. You're chasing something."

Trip nodded. "I hear you've got some VIPs worried."

Warren shrugged. "I'm just a little ole hedge fund manager down in the swamps of Florida."

"Right, and I just work for a little old daily newspaper." Trip took another sip of wine, then leaned closer. "I'm serious. You've got some biggies scurrying for cover. I smell a story. I think I can get the green light on a story about your lawsuit."

"Tell me what you've heard, and maybe I can fill in some blanks," Warren said.

Trip shared what he'd heard, although Warren knew that Trip never disclosed everything. Always the sly reporter, he told only enough to get people talking. Warren took it easy with the wine, careful with what he said. Trip hadn't prospered at the *Times* by being tentative.

He knew a surprising amount of detail, and threw out a few tidbits for Warren. Lawrence Dalton had the Big Three worried, and Trip's sources felt that Tully Boone would be presenting an offer soon—all of which was old news.

What he did find out from Trip was that the timing was critical. Forte was going to market with a bond offering within a month. Bad publicity now could be disastrous as well as expensive.

"Sounds like Lawrence was right—he told me last week that he had them on the run," Warren said.

"Are you thinking settlement?" Trip asked, taking a sip of his wine.

He truthfully didn't know how to answer the question, for a variety of reasons. With no idea of what the offer might include, he had no way of knowing what his reaction would be. Whatever it was, he suspected that Lawrence smelled blood, and would want to keep pushing.

"I honestly can't say, Trip." When Trip lowered his head and raised his eyebrows, Warren continued. "And no, I'm not being evasive."

He settled back in his seat, holding his glass of wine. He told Trip why he sued, and what he hoped to get out of it.

"It's never been about the money. In the beginning, I just wanted to know what happened to Alex. Now, I'm determined to see that it doesn't happen to someone else."

He told Trip the story about Ciel and her daughter. "You want a story—there's your story. Someone needs to get that out in the open. Just leave me out of it."

"I'm just reporting on the lawsuit. You think Lawrence Dalton will talk to me?" Trip asked.

Warren knew Trip wanted to get him to open the door. "Sure. Like the rest of his kind, he loves the publicity. Give him a call."

He asked Trip if he'd ever heard of Dr. Samuel Abrams.

Trip shook his head.

"Look him up. He's someone you should talk to. He certainly opened my eyes." He noted that Trip wrote his name down in his notebook.

"This lawsuit could be hazardous to your health," Trip said. "I hear you've already lost some clients."

Warren nodded. "And, I'll probably lose some more before it's over. But, I don't care, not anymore."

Trip laughed. "Never thought I'd hear a hedge fund manager say he didn't care about money."

Dinner lasted until midnight. Dina had joined them for a grappa after the meal. Trip confided that he was considering a story on the lawsuit, with the angle being the small-town lawyer taking on corporate America. What he really wanted was an interview with Lawrence Dalton.

Warren told him he'd call the attorney tomorrow and do what he could to help his cause. When they left the restaurant, Trip promised he'd be in touch.

Blaine's phone buzzed in his pocket. It was not his company phone, since that one was setting on the desk in front of him. He pulled the vibrating phone out and answered without looking at the number.

"What?"

"Our friend was out to dinner in the Apple with a reporter."

Shit. Not what he wanted to hear.

"Legit?" That was his way of asking if the meeting was with a reputable reporter. There were a lot of reporters in New York City. Most were not associated with credible organizations.

"Completely."

More bad news. That meant it was a highly-regarded person with a well-known news outlet.

"Send me details and keep me posted." Blaine ended the call. He needed to know who and what organization. Mark would find out. He always did.

Mark was a known "fixer," the title accurately describing his line of work. Blaine had gotten his name from a contact he had with a murky corporate security firm that had done a lot of military contract work in Iraq.

Blaine knew that "Mark" was an alias. He didn't know his real name and didn't care to. Early on in their relationship, Mark had made it clear that the less Blaine knew, the better off they both were. Blaine was happy to oblige.

He'd never met Mark, at least he didn't think he had. All contact, except the initial call, was through a cut-out, or intermediary who knew nothing. He knew the initial call was simply a drop, and forwarded to Mark through means unknown to Blaine.

Within twenty-four hours, on a separate disposable phone he kept for such purposes, he would receive a call from an unknown number, which Blaine figured to be a throw-away phone. An electronically-modified voice would direct him on how to leave instructions.

After that step, the process was incredibly simple, and relied on non-technical means, presumably to avoid various technology traps. No computers, no Internet. Concise, handwritten instructions would be left at a pre-arranged drop point.

Once the job was completed, Blaine would arrange for funds to be transferred from one offshore account to another, the amount and receiving account number mailed to Blaine's house via snail-mail, disguised as a routine solicitation from an obscure charity.

The amount was not negotiable. Once, Blaine had asked their mutual friend what would happen if he didn't pay. His contact, a former Special Forces operative, simply shook his head and told Blaine he didn't want to find out.

Chapter 22

Warren's cell phone chirped at six thirty the next morning. Figuring it was Becky, he picked it up and answered without bothering to see who was calling.

"Hello?"

"Where are you?" It was Lawrence Dalton.

"I'm in New York, at the Intercontinental. Why?"

"When are you coming back?"

"This afternoon. I've got meetings this morning."

"Can you come back through Tallahassee?"

"Sure. I took the jet, so no problem."

"Good. I'll see you this afternoon. Give me a call when you're in the air, and let me know your ETA. I'll have someone pick you up at the general aviation terminal."

Before he could ask what was going on, Lawrence had hung up—again. Damn, that was getting to be annoying. Shaking his head, he called Becky and asked her to change the itinerary to bring him back home through Tallahassee.

"I have no idea," he said, when she asked for details. He was frustrated with Lawrence's lack of explanation. "Call Lawrence's office, find out the particulars, and adjust accordingly."

That afternoon, in the limo on his way back to Teterboro, he called Becky to find out his schedule. According to her, Lawrence said they'd be done by eight. He looked at his watch. Two o'clock. They were leaving at three. Flight time from Teterboro to Tallahassee was right at two hours, which meant they'd be landing in Tallahassee around five, depending on how long it took to get out of Teterboro—always a question.

With the flight time from Tallahassee to Fort Myers at less than an hour on the Lear, that would put him back in southwest Florida before ten. He wondered what was so important that Lawrence needed to see him today.

They touched down at Tallahassee Regional Airport at ten minutes after five. After turning off the runway, the Lear taxied over to the MillionAir terminal and stopped.

Once the door was open, Warren grabbed his briefcase. At the cockpit, he paused and told the crew he would be back by eight thirty. He walked down the steps of the jet and the short distance over to the general aviation terminal.

Inside, an attractive blonde standing at the registration desk greeted him when he entered.

A young man wearing jeans and a casual shirt sat in the lobby. He had a rumpled look, with his curly brown hair and at least one day's growth of beard. He rose when Warren walked in.

"Mr. Thompson?"

"Yes."

"Hi, I'm Jim. I'll be taking you to our office. Can I take your bag?"

Warren followed him out to a silver Jeep Wrangler parked out front of the terminal. He was surprised at

Dalton's driver and vehicle, but figured Tallahassee must be more casual with two universities.

They chatted a bit about sports and the weather as Jim drove to an office building off Monroe Street, near the capitol. It looked like a historic building that had been renovated. Jim turned down an alley alongside the building, and parked next to a shelter that looked big enough for two cars. It was occupied by a shiny green Bentley.

"Nice car," Warren said, admiring the Bentley.

Jim laughed. "That's Mr. Dalton's. As far as I know, no one else has ever driven it. You could count on one hand the number of people who have ridden in it."

Inside the office, Jim led him past the receptionist and up the stairs to Lawrence's office. It was a corner office, with a view of the capitol. Although it was nicely appointed, Warren was surprised at how modest it was, given Lawrence's reputation.

Lawrence was on the phone, and motioned them in. He finished his call, hung up the phone, and came around the desk to greet Warren.

"Thanks for coming. Hope your flight was fine. Have a seat," he said, motioning to the small conference table opposite his desk. When Jim sat at the table, Warren looked at Lawrence, then back at the young man who had driven him from the airport. Lawrence was in a starched white shirt and tie, complete with gold cufflinks.

Lawrence picked up on the confusion and chuckled. "I'm sorry. Warren, this is James Woodward, my associate. I've asked him to sit in on the meeting, since he's my second on the case."

Warren flushed, and looked at the scruffy man who was grinning. "We've talked on the phone, but never met."

"Don't worry, he dresses up nicely when he has to. And, he's a pretty decent lawyer. Grady, our driver, was out, so Jim offered to go out to the airport and bring you to the office.

"How was New York?" Lawrence asked as they settled in their seats.

"Good. I had a chance to see an old friend—Trip Carter. He's a journalist friend of mine."

Lawrence wrinkled his forehead. "I trust you kept your comments to a bare minimum."

Warren laughed, and nodded. "He's a financial reporter for the *New York Times*. He actually told *me* a few things."

Intrigued, the attorney held his hands out, waiting for more.

"He told me that you've got the Big Three worried, and the rumor is that Tully Boone is going to present you with a settlement offer," Warren said.

"That's old news. In fact, that's what I wanted to discuss with you. T-Bone flew down last night to meet with me. No entourage—just him. I tried to call you." Lawrence passed a document across the table toward him.

It was two pages, marked draft, and with other disclaimers on both pages. After Warren scanned it, he looked up at Lawrence.

"We talked until midnight, then he gave me that first thing this morning. As soon as he left, I called you. He wants an answer by tomorrow," Lawrence said.

Warren reread the document. It outlined a simple structure for a settlement. The defendants would pay Alex's estate a lump sum payment of five million dollars. The defendants would acknowledge no liability, and Warren would agree to drop any claims, present and future, related to her case. The terms of the agreement would be sealed, and all parties would be forbidden to discuss it. Violation of that clause would trigger a penalty equal to twice the amount of the settlement.

He threw the document on the table, and stared at Lawrence. "You're kidding me, right?" The offer contained nothing in the way of disclosure, which was all that he wanted. Yet, half of the money, which was what would be left after Lawrence's share and expenses, would be huge for Alex's mother and her aunt. He was curious as to what Lawrence was thinking.

Lawrence snorted, and gave him an incredulous look. "You have to ask? Surely you're not serious? It's a joke, and that's what I intend to tell T-Bone. But, I'm required to discuss it with you first, as my client," Lawrence said.

Warren eased back in his chair. "They say nothing about the fact that they didn't authorize another antibiotic—or failed to do necessary tests."

Lawrence shook his head. "I didn't expect it, and doubt they'll ever offer that. What they will offer is a lot more money for our silence."

"I keep telling you, it's not about—"

"And I keep telling you, it is. Money is the only thing that corporations understand, right, Jim?"

Jim, who had been quiet so far, nodded in agreement and said, "They want to settle soon, before their bond issue and the Congressional hearing. If it's not, it will cost them much more than five million dollars."

Unable to keep his seat, Lawrence stood and paced as if he were in a courtroom. "You want answers. I want money. T-Bone didn't fly all the way to Tallahassee—

alone—for five million dollars. If we play this right, we'll both get what we want."

He explained his strategy was twofold. First, he was pursuing the discrimination angle, a new wrinkle in a suit like this. Forte, and the other defendants, were well insulated from a malpractice or wrongful death claim, thanks to the favorable laws in Florida enacted as part of USCare. But, no one had ever pursued it from a discrimination perspective. That was the angle that had everyone scrambling.

"Sounds like legal mumbo-jumbo to me. I don't care, as long as it puts heat on Forte," Warren said.

"It'll keep Tully and his minions busy," Lawrence said.

"This is more than a wrestling match between you and Tully," Warren said.

"It puts heat on them from the perspective that it was something they weren't expecting," Jim interjected.

Lawrence appeared to ignore Warren's comment. "The second part of our strategy is to maximize the media exposure. That puts enormous pressure on them."

He explained that media attention was precisely what Forte wanted to limit. With a debt issue coming out soon, they couldn't afford a lot of negative publicity. Not only would it cost Forte in reputation, it would cost them hundreds of millions in interest expense. The timing was critical.

"Why aren't you getting a deposition from Sam Abrams?" Warren asked.

Lawrence shook his head. "That plays into Forte's hands. In the public view, Abrams is a joke, an unethical and discredited physician. Putting him out front helps them more than us."

"But his credentials—"

"His credentials are trumped by appearances—literal and perceived. How do you think an Ivy-League doctor subject to sanctions who looks like a holdover from the sixties is going to play in a Florida courtroom? How he *could* help us, is to give us some proof that the insurance companies are discriminating based on economic factors."

Jim nodded, agreeing with his boss.

"Okay, I'll talk to him again. By the way, Trip Carter wants to interview you," Warren said.

Lawrence grinned. "Tell him to call me. Now that's the kind of help we need—an article in the *New York Times*."

On the flight back to Fort Myers, Warren thought about his discussion with Lawrence. The attorney was right. Forte wasn't afraid of having to write a check to Lawrence Dalton. What they were afraid of was jeopardizing their upcoming bond issue.

Warren had to speak with Sam. Soon.

Chapter 23

Late the next morning, Warren went over to the hospital. Since he was no longer on the Foundation board, he had no reason to be there. But he wanted to see Micah Rollins and he figured this was the easiest way.

He wasn't sure when Micah might take a break, so he decided to hang out in the cafeteria around lunch in hopes of catching her. He got a cup of coffee from Ciel, asking about her daughter.

"She's doing fine. Already back in school," she said, beaming. "It was a miracle."

Warren smiled and nodded. "That's great," he said. He took his coffee and found a seat at a table where he could watch the entrance.

The lunch traffic was picking up, but no sign of Micah. Every time a female in scrubs came in, he strained to see if it was her. He kept looking at his watch as he finished his coffee, wondering if she was even working. He tapped the empty cup on the table, debating on whether or not to get another coffee.

Before he could decide, Micah walked in with another person. He waved, trying to get her attention. When she saw him, she shook her head, whispered something to her colleague, and walked over to his table.

"Are you stalking me?" she asked.

He laughed and held his hand up. "Guilty. I was afraid you wouldn't take my call. Can I buy you a cup of coffee?"

After she got her own coffee and yogurt, she sat at his table, putting a cream and sugar in her coffee. "Well, based on what I heard, you're not on the Foundation board anymore, so what's your excuse for being here?"

"I told you. I wanted to talk to you, and I was afraid you wouldn't take my call. And, I didn't want to get arrested trying to crash the gate at your condo. I don't think Frank cares for me."

"Did you call your attorney?"

"I did." He took a deep breath, not wanting to discuss this here. But, he was determined to be forthright with her. "He has moved you to the bottom of the list—"

She shook her head. "I want to be *off* his list. I thought I made that clear."

He held up his hand. "Let me finish—please. He's moved you to the bottom of the list, and he says that he doubts they will get to you. *But*, he would *prefer* to keep you on the list, just in case."

He pulled out his phone and held it up. "If that's not acceptable, I'll call him right now and demand that he take you off the list completely."

Her blue eyes studied him with incredible intensity. "If I get called, or receive another—"

"I promise you won't."

Her face relaxed a tiny bit. "You know, I was tempted to let them take you the other day at the condo."

"I know. That's why I wanted to see you in person. I wanted to ask you something and didn't want it to be misinterpreted in any way. I was wondering if you would have dinner with me—and Sam Abrams—this week."

She looked at him, puzzled. "Sam could've asked me."

"I know, but I wanted to ask you. I'm a big boy, and I didn't want you to think I was using Sam. I want you to join us, and I wanted you to hear it directly from me."

She gave him a slight nod. "Only night I have open is tomorrow, and that's if I can get a babysitter. Gabe's ten, old enough to stay by himself during the day, but I still don't like leaving him in the evenings."

"I understand. I'll be happy to pick you up, now that I know where you live," he said, smiling.

"I'll meet you at Jimmy's. Seven o'clock. If I can't get a babysitter, I'll let you know."

"Great. I'll call Sam and let him know. Thank you."

The next evening, at ten minutes before seven, he walked into Jimmy's. The hostess recognized him, and he looked around the small waiting room, not seeing Micah or Sam.

"Mr. Thompson, may I help you?" the tall brunette asked.

"Yes, I'm meeting Dr. Abrams and Ms. Rollins for dinner. Is she—"

"She hasn't arrived yet," the young girl said. "Neither has Dr. Abrams."

Warren stepped to the side, electing to wait. As he stood there, several arriving guests recognized him and stopped to briefly chat. Five minutes later, Micah Rollins walked in.

She wore a simple, blue dress that ended just above the knee, and low heels. The presentation was classic, dressy enough, but not too conspicuous. She walked with an air of confidence, not intimidated or hurried.

"Ms. Rollins," the hostess said, recognizing Micah. She turned to Warren and said, "Would you like to be seated? I'll bring Dr. Abrams as soon as he arrives."

She led them to a secluded alcove located just off the main dining room. Warren had used it many times, as it was private and the occupants had a clear view of the main dining area. He didn't remember requesting it when he made the reservations for this evening, but figured they'd booked it for him out of habit.

After they were seated, Micah asked him how he was doing, grilling him on his recent eating and sleeping routine.

He told her he was trying to eat better and exercise more regularly. Sleep was better, though not where it probably should be. "So, do I pass inspection?" he asked.

She laughed, her face lighting up and her eyes twinkling. "Sorry, once a nurse, always a nurse. Just habit."

Warren's phone buzzed. He started not to look at it, but Micah insisted.

It was Sam. He was calling to say he wouldn't be able to make it. He was stuck in a traffic jam on I-75 and had no idea when he'd make it through.

"That was Sam," he said, putting his phone back in his pocket. "He's stuck on 75 on the other side of the river and sends his regrets. He'll make it if he can, but said not to wait on him."

Their server came and took their orders for dinner. Warren asked Micah if she'd like a glass of wine with dinner, and she nodded, so he ordered a bottle of Sancerre, since they both ordered seafood for dinner.

Catching her quizzical look, he smiled. "I don't like ordering wines by the glass. No way of knowing how long they've been open. Don't worry, we don't have to finish it."

"And your health?"

"Oh yes, back to your question—I appreciate your concern. I really am doing fine." He held up three fingers for her to see. "Scout's honor."

He studied her face for a moment, trying to figure out how to turn the conversation back to what he wanted to discuss. It would have been easier with Sam present, but that didn't look promising. A fleeting thought crossed his mind.

"Have you ever heard of a doctor with the nickname of 'Benefactor?'"

Her eyes narrowed. "Where did that come from?"

"My attorney. He's heard some rumor, and he's trying to run it down." He shrugged. "Not important. But, why don't you tell me what I don't know about health care?"

Her smile disappeared, and her expression turned serious. "Look," she said. "I'm afraid I came on a little strong the other day, and I apologize. I appreciate your asking me out for dinner, but I think I've said enough about that subject. I thought I made that clear."

He realized he'd pushed too hard, and held his hands up. "Sorry, not trying to ruin the evening. I just have a lot of unanswered questions, okay?"

She regarded him with a look of suspicion. "Let's talk about something else."

He thought about protesting, then said, "Okay, what would you like to talk about?"

"Tell me about yourself—not what appears in the magazines, but the real you."

He looked at Micah, trying to gauge what she wanted to know. Reading people was something he was usually good at doing. When he looked into her eyes, all he saw was genuine compassion, a rarity in his world. She had a disarming way about her that made him want to drop the pretense and get to know her.

He told her about growing up in east Fort Myers, and found himself describing things he'd long since forgotten. They'd finished the main course, when he realized he'd been talking about himself the entire time.

After ordering coffee, but no dessert, he folded his arms and sat back in his chair. "Enough," he said. "I've negotiated with the best, and now I suddenly realize I've been selfishly doing all the talking and heard nothing about you. You're good," he said, shaking his head. "If you ever decide to get out of nursing and want a job, let me know. Now, at least over coffee, tell me about yourself. I refuse to say another word about me."

She laughed again, and he loved to hear that sound. It was a cross between a girlish giggle and a laugh from the heart. Again, the word *sincere* crossed his mind. Never had he met someone so genuine.

"Not a lot to tell," she said. "I was an only child. My mother died when I was a teen. I got my degree in nursing, been working in the field ever since."

"Sorry to hear you lost your mom so early. What about your father?"

"What about him?" she bristled.

He remembered Sam's comment about her and her dad not speaking. Obviously, that was a sore subject.

"Just curious."

Micah eyed him for a moment before replying. "My father and I didn't speak for years. When he realized he was dying two years ago, he reached out and we reconnected for a brief time before he died."

"What happened between you and your father?"

She paused, studying him. Not answering, she took a sip of wine.

"I'm sorry," he said, "I didn't mean to pry."

She shook her head. "It's a long story." She looked away, then back at him. "The short version is that I was unmarried and pregnant with Gabe. My father refused to accept it."

Micah watched him for a reaction, and waited for him to speak.

"I can relate," Warren said. "My father and I didn't speak for a long period of time. Unfortunately, he died before we could reconcile."

She cocked her head in surprise. "That's sad. What happened?"

"My father left my mother and me when I was eight. Just disappeared. My mother worked two jobs to support us." He paused to clear his throat. "He got in touch with her right before I started college. He wanted to see me. She left it up to me, but encouraged me to see him. I agreed to see him, but he never made it back to Fort Myers."

"Now I feel like I owe you an apology." Her voice was gentle and compassionate.

He shrugged. "None necessary. I started it."

Changing the subject, he said, "Tell me about Gabe."

Her face lit up at the mention of her son. She pulled her phone out and showed him a picture of a handsome ten-year-old boy with a snaggletooth grin.

"He's all boy. Loves sports, especially baseball. I used to be afraid to let him play, with his epilepsy. But after we got him on the Metaprozine, I started relaxing a little. He loves fishing. Every weekend, he wants to go out on the dock at the condo and fish."

"Does he know how to swim?"

She smiled. "Like a fish. I had him in lessons when he was four. If you live in Florida that should be a requirement."

"I agree."

Warren realized he couldn't remember the last time he'd been out on his boat. He used to love to go fishing and found it therapeutic. It had been too long.

"Look, I've got a boat. Some weekend, the three of us should go out fishing." He sensed her reluctance and shook his head. "I'd like to do it, okay? I love getting out on the water, and it'd do me good to get out. I don't use the boat enough as is. Think about it, okay?"

A smile crossed her face. Encouraged, he continued.

"We could pack a lunch and go out behind Sanibel. Do a little fishing, go swimming. Gabe would enjoy it. It'd do us all good."

"We'll see," she said, but she was still smiling.

He chuckled. "After all I've put you through, it's the least I can do. Check your calendar for the next few weekends. Promise?"

She nodded. Changing the subject, he said, "You were right about health care. I've been trying to bone up on the subject, but it's like trying to eat an elephant. What am I missing?"

She exhaled, took a sip of her coffee, and with her hands wrapped around the cup, pondered the wall behind him.

"Things aren't always as they seem," she said.

"I realize that," he said. "What am I missing?"

She looked around the room. "You talked to Sam. He told you about the rating system?"

"Yes, a lot of people don't believe it. But he convinced me. It's true, isn't it?"

She nodded. "It is. You understand why I can't say anything?"

"I think so. I'm curious about something else, something you said to me that day at lunch. You hinted that I might want to investigate the difference in insurance plans. You said there was more to it than I realized. Remember?"

She looked down, but nodded in agreement. She looked back up at him.

"I could see how pained you were, losing your fiancée. Your pain was deep, and it was real. I've seen enough to know the difference. And I felt sorry for you and said something I shouldn't have. That's why I wanted you to meet Sam. Believe me when I tell you I can't say any more. You understand there's too much at stake—for me and for Gabe."

His heart sunk at the mention of Alex, and he lowered his head.

She reached out and put her hand on top of his, the first time she'd touched him outside of the hospital.

"You're a good person. And I know you truly cared for her. I just hated to see you hurting like that."

"It was my fault."

Micah sat back, shocked at his comment. "What are you talking about?"

"I was in a hurry, as usual. I was driving too fast. She told me to slow down."

Micah looked at him, slowly shaking her head. "It was an accident."

"Yes, but it happened because of me. If I'd been paying more attention—"

"If? If? Do you think you're in control of everything that happens around you?" Her voice was getting louder. "You didn't decide what kind of care she received, did you?"

His eyes met hers, his face wearing the burden of his guilt. "She wouldn't have been in the hospital if—"

"You say 'if' one more time, and I'm leaving, I swear," she said. Realizing her voice had gotten louder, she lowered it and continued. "You can't live the rest of your life blaming yourself for things over which you have no control."

They fell silent as the waitress approached with the check. He pulled out his credit card and handed it to her without looking at the bill.

After she walked away, Micah said, "Please look at me, Warren." He did, and she continued, "As a nurse, and as a person, I've learned that so much of what happens in this world is beyond our control. Don't destroy yourself with guilt. You are *not* the one responsible for her death."

The waitress returned, and set the check on the table next to Warren, not waiting for him to sign it. After he paid, he walked Micah out to her car.

When they got there, he said, "Thank you."

She unlocked her car, and before getting in, she turned to face him. "Thank you for dinner."

"Thank you . . . for listening."

After settling in the driver's seat, she looked up at him and smiled. "I'll let you know about a weekend for boating. I'm holding you to your offer."

A tiny smile creased his face. "Good. I'd like that. If you don't, I'll come back over to your condo and Frank will have to deal with me."

She laughed as she started her car. "Please don't do that. I'll call—I promise."

"You better," he said as he closed her door.

Chapter 24

Mr. Thompson?"

"Yes?" The call came from an 850 area code, but Warren didn't recognize the number or the voice. He knew 850 was Tallahassee.

There was a hesitation on the phone, then an unsteady voice said, "This is Jim Woodward. Mr. . . . Mr. Dalton's . . . associate."

Warren thought back to the confident, scruffy looking attorney he met a few days ago in Tallahassee. This didn't sound like the same person.

"Are you okay, Jim? What's the matter?"

Jim cleared his throat, and didn't speak for several beats. Finally, he said in a trembling voice, "I'm afraid I have bad news."

"What kind of bad news? For Christ's sake, Jim, what's going on?"

Warren heard Jim exhale, then stammer, "Mr. Dalton . . . Mr. Dalton was in a car accident early this morning."

"Oh my God, is he okay?"

Jim sniffled, then said, "He didn't make it."

Warren slumped in his chair, shaking his head in disbelief.

"What . . . how . . . what happened?"

"Last night. He had a late dinner meeting in town." Jim took a deep breath. "He was on his way home, driving out to his farm. They said he ran off the road and hit a tree. That's all I know."

Warren was stunned and speechless.

"I thought you'd want to know," Jim said. His voice sounded like that of a little boy.

"I'm so sorry, Jim. I'm just . . . in shock, as I'm sure you are. I don't know what to say." He took a couple of deep breaths, shaking his head. "Thanks for calling, Jim. Please let me know when the . . . arrangements have been made."

"I will," Jim said, his voice sounding far away.

The call was disconnected, and Warren sat there for a few minutes, stunned. He'd just talked to Lawrence two days ago. The attorney was relishing the battle ahead. What was that Micah had told him last night? *So much of what happens in this world is beyond our control.*

He couldn't believe the news. He Googled Tallahassee newspapers, and got the website for the *Tallahassee Democrat.* Sure enough, the lead article was about Dalton. Warren read the article, which didn't add much to what James had told him.

Local Attorney Killed In Car Crash

Lawrence Dalton, III, was killed late Wednesday night when his car left the road and hit a tree in northeast Leon County.

A local resident, driving east on Miccosukee Road at 11:44 p.m., noticed the car, and stopped to offer assistance. Finding the driver unresponsive, he called 911.

Investigators don't think alcohol was a factor, but say speeding may have been involved. There were no witnesses.

Miccosukee Road is a narrow, tree-lined canopy road. This relatively uninhabited section has been the site of previous fatal crashes.

Becky buzzed him on the intercom, but he ignored it. *Lawrence Dalton was dead. Now what?*

She knocked, and walked into his office. Standing in front of his desk, she asked, "Are you alright?"

"Lawrence Dalton was killed in a car accident early this morning."

She put her hand over her mouth, then crossed herself, shaking her head. Remembering why she'd come in, she pointed to the phone, a button blinking.

"Trip Carter's on the line. I'll take a message." She turned and started walking out of his office.

"No, Becky. I'll take it," he said, picking up the handset.

"Hello, Trip." His voice was flat and unenthusiastic.

"Warren. Are you okay? I just heard the news."

Even though Trip couldn't see him, he nodded. "I just heard about it. His associate called a few minutes ago."

"All I read was that his car hit a tree. Did his associate have anything to add?"

Warren shook his head, again, as if Trip were in the same room.

"Warren?" Trip asked.

"Sorry, uh, no, he just said that Lawrence hit a tree and didn't survive."

"I'm really sorry, my friend. Give me a call later, once you get your bearings."

"Sure." Warren hung up the phone in slow motion, realizing he had already forgotten what Trip asked. He sat there for a full thirty minutes, staring out the window. Another beautiful day in Fort Myers, the sunlight reflecting off the river. Cars still moved along the streets, boats motored up and down the river. Life carried on. For some.

Warren felt like he'd been punched in the gut. Lawrence Dalton had won his confidence and trust. As Warren shared with Sam, he felt the attorney had a chance against the system. Now, thanks to fate, that chance was gone.

He called Tim to tell him the news.

"I just heard about it a few minutes ago. Damn, I hate that. He was one of those people who are larger than life," Tim said.

"I'm having trouble believing it." He thought back to the cocky, brash persona that was Lawrence Dalton, and how they had initially butted heads. In many aspects, they were alike. He was going to miss the arrogant lawyer, in more ways than one.

"Where does that leave me with the lawsuit?" Warren asked.

"Good question. Since he was basically a one-man show, it would be tough for anyone else to pick up the pieces. What about Woodward? Did Lawrence have any other associates who worked for him?"

"Jim was really the only one. He had several other attorneys and paralegals, but they were mainly gophers. Lawrence was the heart and soul of that firm."

"Well, there are other law firms. It would just take time."

But none like Lawrence, Warren thought. He couldn't imagine anyone else posing a threat to the Big Three. And they'd lost the advantage of timing. By the time another attorney picked up the pieces, time would no longer be an ally but an enemy.

"Maybe I should reconsider the whole thing," Warren said.

"Why don't we get some lunch? Meet me over at Centennial Park? We can grab a bite from one of the food trucks."

Centennial Park was on the Caloosahatchee River, only a few minutes' walk from his office. He wasn't hungry, but figured the fresh air would do him good.

"I'll see you there at noon," he said, hanging up the phone.

He called Sam and told him the news.

"What happened?"

He told him what he'd read in the Tallahassee paper.

"I'm sorry to hear that. I was beginning to believe you had a chance."

"Me, too."

"Give me a call later. Maybe we can get together for coffee."

A few minutes before noon, Warren met Tim at the park. Most weekdays, there were a half dozen street vendors peddling lunch. This was not your basic fair food, but gourmet food on the go. Tim settled on a pulled pork sandwich from the Hog Wild trailer, while Warren went to King Neptune's for a shrimp po'boy.

They took their food over to a picnic table overlooking the river, underneath a pavilion providing some relief from the hot sun. A nice breeze stirred off the water.

"You're not serious, are you?" Tim asked, as he took a mouthful of the pork sandwich in his hand.

Warren gave him a puzzled look, then asked, "About reconsidering?"

His friend nodded.

He finished chewing his potato chip. "Good time to think about the possibility, don't you agree? I mean, with Lawrence gone, it'll take someone else a while to get up to speed. Timing was a big part of Lawrence's strategy. I think we're screwed. I don't like it, and I wish I could change things, but . . ."

"Maybe you should at least talk to someone else— another attorney—before you decide," Tim said.

"I'll think about it."

Blaine watched and listened as Tully Boone talked on the Iridium handset, one of the extras on Forte's well-equipped Gulfstream G450 business jet. The satellite phone could connect in flight anywhere in the world. At the moment, they were forty thousand feet over Maryland, headed home to Atlanta.

"When?" Tully said, into the phone. He looked over at Blaine.

"Arrangements?" Tully asked, still talking into the phone. He listened, nodded, and then said, "Thanks." He hung up the handset, his eyes never leaving Blaine.

"Bad news?" Blaine asked.

"Lawrence Dalton was killed early this morning. Single car accident in Tallahassee." His expression was blank.

"Oh my goodness," Blaine said. "Sorry to hear that. He was a friend of yours, wasn't he?"

Tully nodded, his penetrating glare still focused on him. "My nemesis in the courtroom, for sure, but a friend nonetheless." He turned and looked out the oval window of the jet. "I shall miss him terribly."

Blaine waited a few minutes, then said, "Not to be so callous, but what does this do to our case?"

The attorney returned his eyes to him. "My initial reaction is to file for a continuance. I'll have to consult with my team."

He frowned. "Wouldn't that give the other side more time?"

"Exactly," Tully replied. "It'll push things out past the bond issue."

"Doesn't Dalton have a second?"

Tully shook his head. "Not really. Lawrence had several slaves working for him, but he was the heavy lifter. On a case like this, without him, it's in complete disarray."

Blaine smiled and nodded.

Two days later, Jim Woodward called Warren.

"Mr. Thompson?"

"Yes?"

"Jim Woodward. Got a minute?"

Jim explained that the defense had petitioned the court for a continuance, in order to give the plaintiffs time to regroup, considering Lawrence Dalton's untimely demise. The judge had been inclined to agree, but at the last minute, decided to check with Jim.

"We would want that, wouldn't we?" Warren asked.

"I don't think so. I strongly recommend that we stick to Lawrence's original timetable."

When Warren started to resist, Jim reminded him that their biggest advantage was timing. A ninety-day delay would not only negate that advantage, but give the edge to the defense. They could then settle into their siege mentality.

"I need to think about this, Jim."

"I figured as much, and asked the judge for forty-eight hours to confer with you. We've got until this time Thursday to give her an answer."

"While I've got you, what can you tell me about Benefactor? Do you think he's real?" Warren asked.

"Oh, yes. He—and we're pretty sure it's a he—he is a real person. I'm convinced of it. He's a physician and in Fort Myers, of all places. There seems to be a small underground network of like-minded people across the country. I've made a few contacts, but no names so far. Their identities are a closely-guarded secret."

"How many doctors are there in Fort Myers?"

"Roughly two thousand."

"And, what, sixty percent are males? So you've narrowed it down to twelve hundred or so doctors? Progress, maybe, but still a long ways away."

Warren hung up. How could Sam Abrams not know Benefactor, he wondered. That made no sense at all. Sam had to know about this doctor. In the beginning, when he'd first heard of this person, he thought it may have been Sam, but that didn't fit. But Sam had to know something about this mysterious doctor. Despite his protestations to Woodward, Fort Myers wasn't that big.

He called Tim. "Can you meet me at Barney's this afternoon?" He heard the keys on a keyboard clicking.

"How about tomorrow? I've got—"

"I need to talk with you today. It's important."

"Okay, but you're going to owe Karen dinner and an explanation to keep me out of the doghouse."

Later that afternoon, Warren found Tabby sitting at the bar in Barney's, sipping on his customary after-work beer.

"Do the employees at the Sheriff's office have a payroll deduction plan with Barney?" Warren said, slipping onto the stool next to his friend and patting his broad shoulder.

Tabby chuckled. "We should."

Tim walked in, spotted them at the bar and walked over. He put his arms around the two men, and looked at Warren, shaking his head.

"I'm not real popular at my house right now, and neither are you, pal," he said. "Karen had already lined up a babysitter and everything. It was going to be my lucky night. Now, I'll be lucky if I get any this week."

"I'm not real popular with anyone in all of Fort Myers. Tell her to take a number," Warren said. "On second thought, maybe you shouldn't tell her that."

"I think that would be very wise, my friend. This better be good."

Tabby finished his beer and rose, saying he had to go.

Tim took his seat, where Warren told him about Jim Woodward's call.

"Our biggest advantage is timing. Lawrence himself said that last week when I stopped in Tallahassee. We let those bastards have a ninety-day delay, then we're screwed."

"How comfortable are you with Woodward?" Tim asked.

Warren shook his head. He was on the fence. Certainly, Jim had the advantage in that he was familiar with the case, and had worked with Lawrence for six years. But, he wasn't convinced that the young attorney was up to the task. What he really wanted was more time to evaluate everything, but that was a luxury he didn't have.

"That's what it comes down to, doesn't it? I either roll the dice on young Mr. Woodward, or fold up my tent."

"You could go with another firm," Tim said.

"No, not an option. I've thought about it. It'll take too long for someone else to get up to speed, so we lose the timing leverage. And I'm convinced we can't win playing Forte's game."

His instinct was telling him to give the young attorney a chance. At this point in the game, what did he have to lose?

"If you stick with Woodward, decline the continuance. That keeps the pressure on the other side. Plus, at least there's some continuity there. Sounds like your only choice, unless you're willing to give up the fight."

He narrowed his eyes and looked at his friend. "Have you ever known me to walk away from a fight?"

Chapter 25

Lawrence Dalton's funeral was set for Saturday. Warren invited Tim to fly to Tallahassee with him. He was always good company, and he wanted to get Tim's opinion of Jim Woodward.

He was still undecided about the young attorney. On the flight up, Tim gave Warren a little background on Lawrence Dalton. According to Tim, Lawrence was old Tallahassee money. His grandfather on his mother's side had been governor. Warren was surprised. Lawrence never mentioned it.

Tim also said he was a genius, with an uncanny gift for memorizing an extraordinary amount of details during a trial, yet couldn't remember where he'd last left his car keys. It was if his brain had the ability to hyper-focus for short periods of time.

They landed at Tallahassee Regional Airport, and taxied over to the general aviation terminal. Today, the ramp looked like a parking lot. At least eight jets were already parked on the ramp, including a Gulfstream G450 parked next to the Florida governor's Citation.

Warren and Tim piled into the waiting car for the ride into town. The funeral was at St. John's Episcopal Church, on Monroe Street only a few blocks from Dalton's office. The beautiful old church was packed, standing room only, by the time the service started. Tim was well-known by the legal community in Tallahassee, and greeted by a number of the people in attendance.

The burial was at St. John's Episcopal Cemetery, only a few blocks away. It was one of the oldest cemeteries in Tallahassee. As they headed toward the tent where a crowd was gathered for Dalton's graveside service, Tim pointed out the markers of Prince and Princess Murat. Achille Murat, the second mayor of Tallahassee, was the nephew of Napoleon Bonaparte. Murat's wife was the grandniece of George Washington.

After the graveside service, Warren and Tim walked over to Jim Woodward, who was talking with a small group. Jim greeted them and introduced the group.

An older, distinguished looking gentleman was Tully Boone. Warren tried to wipe the smirk off of his face as he shook Tully's hand. All Warren could think of was when Lawrence called the man T-Bone. That image would be forever etched in his memory. The two men with Tully were Pete Manning and Blaine Harris.

Two other suits stood a couple of feet behind them completing the entourage.

After shaking Tully's hand, Warren moved to the next suit, a tall, thin man with glasses.

"Warren Thompson," he said, shaking the man's hand.

"Warren. Pete Manning. Pleased to finally meet you."

Pete Manning. The CEO of Forte. Warren recognized the name, but not the face. The first three letters of the tail number on the Gulfstream at the Tallahassee airport were FHI. Forte Health Insurance. Now he knew who the Gulfstream belonged to.

"Blaine Harris," the last suit on the front line said. Warren had never heard his name, but based on his body language and position in the group, he was clearly a player. The other two minions behind them kept silent and didn't step forward or offer their names.

Manning said, with the polished smile of a politician, "I believe you worked for a friend of mine in New York. Mason? Mason Gilmore? I've heard a lot of good things about you from him."

Warren smiled. "Really? I'm surprised. How is Mason? I haven't spoken to him since he fired me ten years ago."

Manning glanced at his sidekick, uneasy with the sudden turn in the conversation.

"I didn't . . ." Manning hesitated, and Warren could tell he decided at the last minute not to complete the lie on his lips as Warren stared at him. "An occupational hazard, I guess, in our business," Manning finally said.

Our? Warren thought. Big difference. Someone like the man standing in front of him gets fired, he gets a big chunk of hush money, called a severance package, worth hundreds of millions of dollars. Warren barely escaped with the trinkets on his desk.

Tully stepped up to rescue his client. "Sorry to hear about Lawrence. Though we had our differences in the courtroom, I considered him a friend. I had nothing but the most sincere respect for him. His shoes will be difficult to fill." He eyed Woodward as he finished the last sentence, then looked back at Warren.

The Forte entourage bid their farewells, and moved along to another clump of suits, which included the governor. They received a much warmer reception there, Warren noted. Tim excused himself to go talk to a familiar face, leaving Warren and Jim alone.

"I appreciate you coming, Warren," Jim said. "We've got a lot to talk about, but now is not the time or place. I'll give you a call within the next couple of days." He looked around, and leaned in closer to Warren. "I have my doubts about Lawrence's accident," he whispered.

"What?"

"You remember how meticulous Lawrence was with that car. My contact in the sheriff's department told me they estimated his speed at over seventy when he hit the tree. There's no way he was driving that fast on that road."

Before Warren could ask anything else, Tim rejoined them with another man in tow. He introduced him as Davis Lamont, an attorney from West Palm. Lamont was a malpractice attorney who Tim had mentioned as a possible replacement for Lawrence.

Warren shook Davis's hand, but his thoughts were elsewhere. *What was Jim talking about? Lawrence's wreck wasn't an accident? Who would—* He caught another glimpse of the Forte entourage, still talking with the Florida governor.

After a few minutes of small talk, Tim shot Warren a glance and nodded toward his right at Lamont. Tim grabbed Woodward's arm and excused them, saying there was someone he wanted Jim to meet.

That conveniently left Warren and Lamont standing there alone. Seizing the opportunity, Lamont launched into his sales pitch. Warren tried to be polite and feigned interest, but all he could think about was Jim's comment.

Tim returned, sans Jim, and Lamont excused himself. "I hope you and Davis had a few minutes to chat," Tim said. "I tried to give you some time."

"What did you do with Jim?" Warren asked, as he looked around trying to find him.

Pointing to the other side of the large crowd, Tim said, "He's over there somewhere. Did you not like Davis?"

"He's okay. I wanted to speak with Jim again."

Tim looked at his watch. "It's about time to head back to the airport. I don't want to keep Karen waiting, and neither do you. I'm on thin ice as it is."

"I was hoping to get a few minutes to talk with Jim before we left," Warren said.

Tim turned and looked over to the large group where Woodward was holding court. "Doesn't look promising."

Frustrated, but not wanting to be responsible for Tim being late, Warren relented. "Fine. Let's go, then." They headed back to their limo.

"Tallahassee changed much?" Warren asked, on their way back to the airport.

Tim smiled. "In some ways, yes. Others, no."

"You certainly seemed to know a lot of people here."

"Lots of attorneys in this town." Changing the subject, he said, "That was an interesting exchange with the crowd from Forte. I thought Manning was going to choke."

Warren laughed. "That's the reason I moved back to Florida. I can't stand people like that. I wasn't going to let him get away with his pretentious act. 'I've heard a lot of good things from him about you'—yeah, right. The only thing he's heard from Mason Gilmore about me is that I'm a total asshole."

"I think he was relieved to get away from you," Tim said.

"And did you see where he went? Our governor. Birds of a feather."

Rick Scott, the governor, had made his fortune in health care, as the CEO of Columbia/HCA. He and Pete Manning appeared to be old friends, which didn't surprise Warren.

"What's the deal on Harris? He didn't say much, but he seemed to be in Manning's hip pocket."

"Didn't recognize him," Tim said. "If he was with Manning and Boone, then you're right—he must be pretty high up the food chain."

He was clearly pals with the CEO, and he looked very comfortable in the presence of the governor. Blaine Harris didn't seem like someone who was easily intimidated.

At the airport, they boarded Warren's jet, and took their seats as the co-pilot closed the door. As they were getting buckled in, the soft whine of the engines starting broke the quiet as the crew wasted no time in getting ready to depart.

"So, what did you think of young Jim?" Warren asked.

Tim shrugged. "Hard to say. He seems nice enough, and from what I gathered from talking to acquaintances, he's very bright. But, Lawrence Dalton was such a larger-than-life figure. Not fair to compare, I know, but . . ."

"Kinda like comparing me to the other Warren—Warren Buffett."

Tim laughed and looked around the cabin of the Lear. "Looks like you're doing pretty good to me. I can't afford one of these."

"Bullshit. You're just too cheap." Warren gazed out the window at the towering clouds building in the distance.

"Do you think Woodward can hold his own against T-Bone?" he said, chuckling at the invoking of Dalton's nickname for Tully. "That's all I could think about when we met him—T-Bone."

Tim shook his head. "Tully's like Lawrence, not many like him. Jim doesn't have the experience or the kind of resources that Tully has. But he reminds me of a young Lawrence Dalton. I wouldn't underestimate him."

"You think I should dump him? Is that why you brought Lamont over to meet me?"

Again, Tim shook his head. "Didn't say that. I just tried to answer your question. Head-to-head, no, at this point in his career, he's outmanned against Tully. But, you dump him, you lose valuable time and a decided advantage. Tough call. I just wanted you to meet Davis, since he happened to be there. I'm not pushing him, just saying he's a potential replacement. He's a seasoned trial attorney."

"He's a dick."

"You arrived at that conclusion after spending a total of five minutes with him? So much for trying to help you," Tim said.

"Sorry. I appreciate your trying to help. I'm just bummed about Dalton. Did Jim mention anything to you about Dalton's accident?"

"No, why?"

"He said . . . never mind, it was nothing."

Tim had a puzzled look on his face. "What did he say?"

"He was just shocked, is all. Doesn't understand. None of us do."

Warren looked out the window, seeing Fort Myers in the distance. His gut was telling him to keep Jim. He thought back to what Micah had told him. *Listen to the voice.*

The next day, Warren called Tabby.

"Wilkins," he said, answering his cell phone. Tabby was not much on chit-chat.

"Hey, old man. How's it hanging?" Warren said.

A deep-throated laugh emerged from Warren's phone. "How's the arm doing? Ready to ride?"

"Close. I miss it."

"You calling to buy me lunch?"

Warren laughed. "Matter of fact, I was. Got time today?"

"I always have time for rich friends. Nick's at noon?"

"See you there." Warren hung up his phone. Nick's was an old haunt in downtown Fort Myers that had so far evaded the wrecking ball, and served as a hangout for the people in the sheriff's office. Warren didn't know what they'd do if it ever sold. He suspected Tabby and his friends would make life miserable for the new owners if they tried to yuppify it.

At a few minutes before noon, Warren walked into the deli and let his eyes adjust to the low lighting inside. He spied Tabby occupying the majority of one side of a booth near the back. He slid in opposite his friend.

"I ordered you a Philly cheese steak," Tabby said.

"Thanks."

"What are you wanting?"

As usual, Tabby got right down to business. Sometimes Warren would string him out a bit to toy with him, but today he wasn't in the mood.

He relayed the information about Dalton's accident as impartially as he could. When he finished, he asked Tabby if he thought it was an accident.

"Hard to say, sitting here. It happens. People get distracted, an animal darts out across the road or the phone rings. Sometimes you don't ever know."

Warren shook his head. "I thought about those possibilities, but that doesn't explain the speeding. That's the part that doesn't fit. Something keeps nagging me about it. You know me, I'm not big on conspiracies, but something about this one doesn't feel right. According to people who knew him, he never drove over the speed limit, and I know for a fact, he was a fanatic about that car. That's why I wanted to bounce it off of you, get your take."

He didn't mention his conversation with Jim, wanting to get a fresh and impartial opinion.

The waitress brought the two sandwiches to the table. Warren noticed that Tabby had gotten the large, which was at least twice the size of his. He shook his head. Tabby was a big man with a big appetite. Some things never changed.

As they ate, Tabby asked a few questions. Warren knew he was breaking it down and analyzing it based on his past experience. As always, it was hard to tell what was going on in Tabby's head.

"I'll make a few calls. See what I can find out. I'll get back to you."

Warren knew better than to ask for a preliminary report. His friend was still mulling it over, and wanted to make sure he had the facts. Tabby was analytical, if anything, and not one to be swayed by speculation.

Two days later, Warren's cell phone buzzed. It was Tabby.

"I'm hungry. Meet me at Nick's. Noon?" Tabby's deep voice said, when Warren answered.

Warren looked at his watch. It was 11:30, and he had a call scheduled for 12:30. "I've got a call in an hour. Anything you can tell me over the phone?"

"How about tomorrow?"

Tabby wasn't going to discuss it over the phone. And Warren didn't want to wait. If Tabby was calling, he had some information, and Warren wanted to know what it was.

Twenty-five minutes later at Nick's, Warren slid into the booth opposite Tabby. The big detective looked at his watch and then at Warren.

"You? Early? What gives?" Tabby took a drink from the tall glass of iced tea in front of him.

Warren shrugged. "Trying to change my bad habits."

"Humph."

The waitress came over with a glass of water for Warren, took his order, and left.

"What did you find out?" he asked.

Tabby smiled, his grin bigger than normal. "You familiar with the road where Dalton had his accident?"

Warren shook his head.

"It's what they call a 'canopy road' in Tallahassee. Narrow, two-lane country road, lined with massive oak trees on both sides. Not much shoulder."

He had a puzzled look on his face, and Tabby continued.

"Not a lot of traffic. Speed limit is forty-five. My sources estimate he was going close to eighty. Hit an oak tree this big." Tabby extended his massive arms to show him. "No skid marks. Road was dry. Oaks that size don't give a lot."

"Okay, so he hit an oak tree going too fast."

"Seems there were a couple of unexplained indentations on the back bumper of Mr. Dalton's Bentley."

Warren waited for a further explanation. When none was forthcoming, he gave in and said, "So? Even Bentleys get bumped."

Enjoying the game, Tabby shook his head. "Not this one. You were right. This car was spotless. Not a scratch. He had two parking spots bought and paid for at the Governor's Club in downtown Tallahassee so he could park it himself. He paid a guy two hundred dollars a week to hand wash it, and another five to wax it once a month. The car wash guy had washed it that afternoon. No indentations."

"Maybe the tow truck did it?"

Sometimes it was hard to tell when Tabby was grinning, but Warren knew he was definitely grinning now.

"Tow truck driver knew the car. There's apparently only one green Bentley in Tallahassee. Before he even touched it, he walked around and took pictures with his cell phone so nobody could come back and lay anything on him. The indentations were there, just like they were on the accident investigator's photos."

Warren started to ask a question, but the waitress arrived with their sandwiches. Once she walked away, he asked, "Okay, you've got me. What are you thinking?"

Tabby bit off what looked like half of the sandwich in one bite, and waited until he finished chewing it before answering.

"Maybe he got bumped. A truck or SUV with bolt-on brush guard. Someone came up behind him, tapped his bumper and that's why he was speeding. No paint marks, no way to trace it."

Warren studied his friend's face for clues. Having played poker with Tabby, he should have known better. "Is that your thinking or someone else's?"

Tabby ignored the question. "By the book, have to rule it an accident. No way to prove otherwise. But if I was putting money on it, I'd say somebody got away with one."

Chapter 26

Warren had the boat loaded and ready to go. This was the first time he'd taken it off the lift in more months than he could remember. He'd originally bought the boat for fishing, but like many boat owners, discovered he didn't have the time he'd thought.

Paulo, his housekeeper Carmela's husband, took it out and ran it up the river every few weeks, just to make sure everything worked. Yesterday, after Micah called and said they'd be coming, Warren told him to top off the fuel, clean it, and make sure the rods and reels were onboard, along with some live shrimp. He'd told Carmela to make sure it was stocked with sodas, water, sandwiches, and snacks. He'd not discussed with Micah how long they'd be out, but he wanted to be prepared.

He looked at his watch. 10:12. Micah had said they'd be there by ten, and he wondered if she'd changed her mind. He pulled out his phone and checked, but there were no calls or messages.

As he walked up to the house, he heard a car out front. He went inside, and opened the front door just as Micah walked up.

With her was a skinny boy, with shaggy brown hair. He looked up at Warren with big brown eyes, then shifted his gaze down toward his well-worn boat shoes.

Micah was wearing white shorts, and a plain, light blue, stylish-looking tee top. She was carrying a small tote.

"Sorry," she said. "I missed the turn, then had to go down a ways before I could turn around."

Recalling her admonishment the first time they had lunch, Warren almost made a crack about not waiting, but didn't want to take a chance on starting off the outing on a bad note. "No problem. Come in." He stepped back as they entered the house.

"Warren, this is my son, Gabe." She squeezed the boy's shoulder, and he held out his hand. "Gabe, this is Mr. Thompson."

Warren took the boy's hand and shook it. It was surprisingly firm for a ten-year old. "Gabe. Pleased to meet you. Call me Warren, please. Mr. Thompson makes me feel old."

Gabe smiled at that, nodded, and looked up at his mom. She returned the smile, indicating it was okay.

"It should be a nice day out on the water," Warren said. You like boats?" he asked, directing his remark to the young boy.

Gabe nodded.

"You need anything before we leave?" he said to Micah. "There's a small head on the boat, but if you'd like to make a stop before we leave . . ." He nodded toward a door on the left, which led to a bathroom.

Micah looked at Gabe, who shook his head, then said, "I think we're fine, thank you."

He gave them a quick tour of the house before they walked out to the dock.

"Quite an impressive place," she said.

"Thank you. I enjoy being on the water, but don't get to use the boat as much as I'd like. I'm glad you came. Gives me an excuse to exercise the boat."

Gabe was a quiet boy, slight, with curly brown hair and matching eyes. His eyes darted around, seeming to absorb everything.

Warren had not spent much time around children, so didn't have much of an opinion one way or the other about them. Tim and Karen had a daughter, and Gordo had an older son, well-entrenched in his rebellious teens. At functions where kids were present, they always gravitated toward Alex, who was a natural.

Micah hadn't said anything about Gabe's father, and Warren wondered what kind of role he played in his son's life. He didn't want to pry, and decided if Micah wanted him to know, she'd tell him.

As they walked out to the dock, Micah noticed the boat. "A Grady-White. My dad had one when I was young."

Warren jumped on the boat, took the bag from Micah, and helped them board. He took them down into the small cabin and showed them where everything was located there.

"Life jackets are in this locker," Warren said, lifting the cover so they could see. He held it open for Micah to decide.

"Gabe's a good swimmer, but thank you. I think on a boat this size, he'll be okay, won't you, Gabe?" Again, the boy nodded, his eyes taking in everything around him.

"And how about you, Mom?" Warren asked.

Micah laughed. "I've been swimming since I was old enough to walk. But, thanks for checking."

He stepped up into the helm area and started the engines. Micah sat on the port seat while Gabe stood next to him. He pointed out where things were located on deck.

"Want to help me out?" he asked Gabe. The boy grinned, and nodded. Warren stepped down from the cockpit and led him behind the starboard seat. He lifted the lid of the livewell to check on the bait that he knew Pablo had loaded last evening. Gabe leaned over and looked inside at the shrimp swimming around, then looked up at Warren.

"I heard you liked to fish, so we have bait. Maybe we can catch dinner."

Gabe grinned, and looked up at his mom, her arm over the back of her seat, watching. She started to get up, but Warren waved her off.

Warren took him to the stern, took the dock line off the cleat on the boat, and handed it to him. What little breeze was stirring was pushing the boat against the dock, so no line handling was necessary. Micah smiled and nodded, as she realized what Warren was doing.

He walked up to the bow, took the line off, and threw it over the hook on the piling.

He came back to the helm and engaged the motors in reverse, telling Gabe to toss the line over on the dock as the boat slid past the piling.

"Thanks, Gabe. You're a big help. You want to come up here next to me, and I'll show you how the boat works?"

The boy was grinning from ear to ear as he made his way next to Warren, standing at the wheel. Micah sat on the chair on their left, watching her son and listening.

As they slowly motored out the narrow channel, Warren explained how the controls worked. Gabe soon overcame his shyness and peppered Warren with questions.

When they got to the main channel of the Caloosahatchee River, Warren turned left and told Gabe to sit in the chair on the right side of the helm.

"Well, madam. Where are we headed today?" he asked Micah, as he pushed the throttles forward. The twin Yamaha outboards brought the heavy boat up on a plane in a matter of seconds. He pulled the throttles back to a comfortable cruising speed and sat back in the captain's chair, scanning the water for traffic.

"What would you think about going out to the Sanibel lighthouse? Maybe anchoring on the back side and do a little swimming?" she said.

He smiled. That was one of his favorite places to go on a day like today. "You've got it," he said.

He looked down at Gabe. "Of course, I'd like to do a little fishing first. What do you think?"

The boy nodded without even looking at Mom.

Warren looked over at her. "There's some pretty good fishing over on the back side of Tarpon Bay. The tide's right, so why don't we try our luck there first?"

She nodded, and her grin seemed to be as wide as Gabe's.

When they came to the slow-speed zone on the other side of the Cape Coral Bridge, he slowed the boat, bringing it down off plane. He motioned for Gabe to step up to the wheel.

"Why don't you drive for a little bit?"

"For real?" Gabe asked.

"Absolutely." He told the boy to sit up on the captain's chair so he could see, while he stood next to him. He explained to Gabe how to hold the wheel, and told him about keeping an eye on the other boats as well as the markers.

After they passed through the slow-speed zone, Warren put his hand on the wheel and asked Gabe if he wanted to go faster.

"Can I?" he asked, looking at his mother for approval.

With some hesitation, she nodded, and he looked at Warren for further instructions.

Warren glanced around to make sure they were well within the wide channel and no other boats were nearby. He told Gabe to push the throttles about halfway forward while he helped him hold the wheel steady.

Gabe did as instructed, and the twin 300 horsepower engines sprang to life, pushing the boat up on top of the water, or planing, as Warren explained. Warren nudged the throttles back a bit, letting the boy get comfortable with the feel of the boat.

Satisfied Gabe was doing well, and after scanning the area once more, Warren took his hand off the wheel. "All yours, now."

The grin on Gabe's face was priceless. Warren thought back to when he was that age and how much fun it was to drive a boat. To see it through the eyes of a ten-year old again was exhilarating.

After five or six minutes, they came to a narrow part of the river, and Warren took over. The grin never left Gabe's face, and he was still grinning and talking nonstop about how much fun it was to be on the boat.

They left the channel opposite St. James City and turned south toward Sanibel Island. When the depth finder showed four foot of water underneath the boat, Warren slowed to an idle and peered over the edge. Once he spied the grass flats he was trying to find, he reversed the engines to stop the boat's forward motion. He flipped a switch on the dash to release the anchor.

Satisfied the anchor was set, he switched the engines off. Then, he removed the first rod and reel from its holder. Paulo had already rigged the tackle, so Warren put a shrimp on the hook and handed it to Micah.

"No, you guys go—"

"No way. Everyone has to fish until we catch dinner, right, Gabe?" With a huge grin, the young boy nodded until she took the rod.

Warren put a shrimp on the second rod and reel, Gabe watching intently as Warren explained how to hook the shrimp. "You can do the next one," he said.

Gabe took his and went to the back of the boat opposite his mom.

Warren baited his hook and as soon as he threw it out, Gabe hollered. "I got one, I got one." He put his rod in the holder, and walked back to the stern. Sure enough, Gabe had a fish on.

He coached him on properly handling the fish, and when he got it close to the boat, Warren reached down with the landing net and scooped up a nice spotted seatrout.

He took the hook out and measured the fish for Gabe's benefit, although he knew the fish was well over the fifteen-inch minimum.

"It's a keeper," he announced. "Twenty-two inches. Each person gets to keep one over twenty inches, so you've got yours. Nice trout. Looks like Gabe will be eating fish tonight."

Gabe couldn't contain himself. He jabbered ten minutes solid about fighting the fish. He insisted on baiting his hook by himself.

In all of the excitement, Micah's shrimp had been stolen by a sneaky fish, so Warren baited hers again and she threw it out. He reeled in an empty hook on his rod, but before he could replace the bait, Micah screamed out this time.

She, too, had a trout, though legal, not as large as Gabe's. This went on until they had five fish in the box, Warren content to act as a deckhand for his two guests.

"Well, we've got more than enough for dinner. I think we should leave some for the other fishermen and go for a swim," he said.

Micah looked at him, smiling. "I don't recall you catching anything? What are you having for dinner?"

Warren put his arm on Gabe's shoulder. "I'm appealing to the fisherman on board—the one who caught the most fish. I'm betting he's willing to share with the captain."

"You can have one of mine, captain," Gabe said, grinning.

"Very nice of you, Gabe," Micah said, winking at him.

They motored over to Sanibel, just north of the lighthouse, and when they got as close as Warren dared, they anchored, only thirty yards or so from the beach. Satisfied the anchor was set, he switched the engines off.

"Ready for a dip?" he asked. Before he could get the transom door open and the swim ladder down, Gabe had stripped off his T-shirt and was ready to go.

"Hold on, Gabe," Micah said, laughing. "Wait for me." She unzipped her shorts and pulled them off. She pulled the tee she was wearing over her head and put them both on her seat.

Warren couldn't help but notice how good she looked in the orange and white bikini she was wearing underneath. She was trim, and in good shape, a fact well disguised by the ubiquitous scrubs he'd seen her wearing at work.

Mother and son were soon in the water, splashing around and swimming like fish. Warren removed his T-shirt, and joined them. The water was refreshing.

They swam the short distance to the beach, and walked around toward the lighthouse. Gabe ran ahead, looking for shells.

"That was sweet of you to let him drive the boat. You made a friend for life," she said, as they strolled down the beach. "And, you were very sweet to let us fish while you tirelessly performed mate duties. Did you ever get to put your line back in the water?"

"I enjoyed it. Brought back fond memories," he said. He held his hands up and looked around. "I'd forgotten how much I enjoyed being out on the water."

"His dad never had the patience to do those kinds of things."

"That's a shame," Warren said, "but, easy for me to say. I'm not a parent."

"No children in your past? No ex-wives?"

Warren chuckled. "No, on both counts. Never found the right one until Alex came along."

A cloud seem to pass over them, and Warren apologized.

Micah stopped walking, turned, and looked him in the eyes. "Don't do that. There's no need to apologize. It's okay to talk about her, but only if you're comfortable. I don't want to intrude."

He nodded, and they started walking again. "As you can figure, I have a hard time letting my feelings show. The way I'm wired, I guess, plus the business I'm in."

Gabe ran up to them, handing his mother a few shells that he'd picked up. "You get the next ones," he said, pointing to Warren. He turned and ran back down the beach a few yards ahead of them.

"He likes you," she said. "He's usually pretty shy around strangers."

Warren smiled. "Good to know. I've not spent much time around kids. My friend Tim, he has a daughter, but she's about the only kid I am ever around, so not much experience."

"You're a natural. He doesn't have many male role models in his life."

"How about you? One ex-husband, it sounds like," he said, nodding toward Gabe.

She shook her head. "No, we were never married. He offered, but I knew it would be a mistake. He wasn't husband or father material. But Gabe means the world to me, so something good came out of that relationship."

"He's a good kid. And, a good fisherman, too. He has a great mom. I'm really sorry about getting you involved in all of my problems. I hope you'll forgive me. It wasn't intentional."

She stopped walking and turned to face him. "I realize that, now. And, you understand why I can't be involved."

He nodded. "I'm considering dropping the lawsuit."

She cocked her head. "Why?"

He shook his head. "Why? After all the trouble I've caused you?" He took a deep breath. "It won't bring Alex back. My lawyer's gone. I've got my answers. I don't like them, but all I ever wanted was an answer."

"I don't believe you. I heard about what you did for Ciel at the hospital."

He frowned. "How did you—"

"Calm down. Hospitals are notorious for their grapevines. Word gets out."

"I didn't want anyone to—"

"I know. But, what you did was incredible. You saved her daughter's life. That was the only reason I didn't have you arrested that day at my condo."

"All I did was write a check, nothing particularly impressive about that."

She smiled and her eyes bore into him. She glanced down the beach to check on Gabe. He was digging in the sand and playing with two other children, a safe distance from the water. Micah turned back to face him.

"Maybe not, but you did it. And you didn't have to. Unless I'm mistaken, you're the type of person who wants to fix things."

He thought about Sam's challenge, and knew she was right.

As if reading his mind, she said, "Don't drop the suit because of me. I can't help you, and now you understand why. But don't use me as an excuse. If you decide to drop it, do it for your own reasons."

"But, Micah. If I—"

She nodded. "I know. If you continue, there's a chance I may get pulled into it. As long as I don't cooperate, I'll be okay. Do what you've got to do, Warren. For you. And for everyone else."

Chapter 27

Monday morning, Warren was having coffee with Sam at Café Nation. "I met with my friend at the sheriff's office," Warren said. "I asked him to see what he could find out about Dalton's 'accident.'"

Abrams's eyebrows arched as he waited for Warren to continue.

"He—and I suspect his friend in the Leon County Sheriff's Department as well—thinks someone bumped Lawrence's car. But, no proof, so it goes down as an accident."

"Who?"

Warren shrugged. "Who do you think? Someone working for Forte." He told Sam the details involving the accident. "Seems too convenient to be a coincidence, don't you think?"

Sam stared at him. "No. That's way over the line."

"But it makes sense, especially considering the timing. Taking Dalton out delays everything. They get their debt issue done."

Sam shook his head. "Sorry, I can't buy that. Corporations are capable of evil, don't get me wrong, but . . . murder? You've been reading too many conspiracy novels."

He wanted to believe Sam, but maybe he'd worked too long in the corporate world. He wanted to believe in the goodness of people, but he also knew whenever huge sums of money were involved, all bets were off. Any person was capable of doing anything.

"Nothing that can be proven, anyway. Any ideas on how to proceed? I gave it some thought, and decided not to drop the lawsuit. But, I'm convinced that Jim Woodward is no match for the likes of Tully Boone."

"That bad, huh?" Sam said.

"No, Jim's a bright guy. He'll get there. Right now, he just doesn't have the experience or the resources behind him. The lawsuit is a longshot. It'll take too long, and the insurance companies can outlast me and outspend me. But, I've already gone this far with it, so I might as well see it through. It keeps the heat on Forte."

After his conversation with Micah on Sanibel, he had re-examined his approach. The best way to prevent the insurance companies from manipulating coverage was to flush their scheme out in the open. The question was how.

"I'm thinking I should be looking at a backup plan. What about going to the feds?"

Sam choked on his coffee and laughed, shaking his head. "You still don't get it, do you?" Before Warren could respond, he continued. "Who do you think controls the politicians? As you told me, 'follow the money.' You don't think I've tried going to the government?"

Warren's cell phone sounded. The ring tone was the opening horn of the Otis Redding song "Fa-Fa-Fa-Fa-Fa (Sad Song)." Micah was calling.

"Hey, I was just about to—"

"Those bastards," she said, sniffling.

"What? Who?" He was surprised at the emotion. He'd not seen this side of her before.

"I just got a new insurance card," she said.

No, he thought, *they wouldn't have.*

"They changed me from a four to a fucking seven."

He didn't say anything.

"Did you hear what I said? They downgraded my coverage—mine and Gabe's—to a seven. Do you know what you get as a seven?"

He knew all too well what that meant.

"I do. Alex was a seven," he said, in a calm, low voice.

Now there was a silence on the other end as she processed the response.

"Sorry. Of course you do. I didn't mean—"

"It's okay, Micah. I know you're upset. I'm having coffee with Sam at Café Nation. Why don't you and Gabe come down? We can go next door and get Italian. Pizza for Gabe and something else for us."

"He's got a lot of homework. Why don't you two come over, and we'll get it delivered here?"

"Hold on."

He said to Sam, "Micah. They downgraded her coverage. Can you join us over at her place?"

Sam shook his head and said, "I've got a meeting in an hour. Maybe after. I'll call."

He spoke back into the phone. "Sam's got to be somewhere, but I'll come. Frank's not going to shoot me, is he?" he said, trying to lighten the conversation.

She hesitated, then laughed as she realized what he was saying. "No, I'll leave your name at the gate this time. Just try not to antagonize him, though. I have to live here."

"Six thirty okay?"

"Perfect. I'll have it here so we can eat as soon as you arrive."

On the way over to Micah's condo, Warren thought about what Forte had done. This was no mistake; it was a deliberate shot across the bow, threatening him.

Although he'd made a big fuss about his insurance, the fact of the matter was that it really didn't make any difference. He had the resources to get the highest level of care. He knew it, and they knew it.

Micah and Gabe were a different story, however. Although he didn't know her financial situation, he doubted she had the resources, given her reaction to the downgrade.

Frank wasn't on duty at the gate. True to her word, Micah had left Warren's name with the attendant this time. When he got to the condo, he rang the buzzer and Gabe opened the door.

"Hello, Gabe. How are you?"

"Good. Pizza's here," he said, running into the kitchen ahead of him.

Micah was barefoot, in red capris and a yellow crewneck. Warren handed her a bag containing a bottle of Chianti and a Coke he'd picked up on the way.

"I hope the Coke is okay for Gabe."

She frowned, and pulled it out. It was a small bottle. Her frown morphed into a smile as she nodded. "I try to keep these at a minimum. At least you got a small one. Thanks."

He noticed the table had already been set, with lasagna and salad for the two adults, and a small, cheese pizza for Gabe, who was glued to the television.

She opened the wine and poured two glasses, which Warren took over to the table.

"Dinner's on," she said to Gabe, who jumped up and came to the dining room.

They had a pleasant dinner, with Gabe telling about his day at school. When they were done, Warren got up to clear the table, and Micah took Gabe to his room to start on his homework.

By the time she returned, Warren had cleaned up everything and poured them another glass of wine. They walked out on the lanai, overlooking the river. It was a beautiful view from the fourteenth floor.

"I'm sorry about what I said on the phone," Micah said.

"You were upset."

She showed him her new USCare card. The key digit was now a seven.

"I checked with Human Resources before I left. Of course, they assured me that the plan hadn't changed, that I had the same deductible, blah, blah, blah. Then I called Gabe's doctor, and gave them the new member ID. Surprise—he doesn't accept that plan."

"What about another doctor?"

She shook her head. "That's not the biggest problem."

The only medication that worked with Gabe was a new drug called Metaprozine, she explained. They had tried everything, including Tegretol, Keppra, and Gabitril. None of them were anywhere near as effective as Metaprozine.

Metaprozine was given as an injection, and had to be administered monthly by a physician. Blood levels and kidney functions had to be monitored very closely to avoid adverse side effects, but with Gabe, the drug had eliminated his seizures.

"I called the pharmacy," she said, shaking her head. "Metaprozine is not covered under the new plan. What am I going to do? His next injection is scheduled in a week."

Warren looked over at Micah and saw the frightened look on her face.

"I'll cover it. Don't worry."

"I can't accept—"

"It's me," he said. "Don't you see? They're sending me a message. They downgraded my plan. Now they're going after you. It's my fault."

She shook her head. "I can't be dependent on you for our medical coverage."

"I'll figure something out. I'll cover it in the meantime. It's only fair, since I got you into this mess."

"What are you going to do? Drop the suit?"

"I don't know. But don't worry. I'll come up with something. I promise."

Warren didn't sleep much last night. After he got home from Micah's, he sat out on the deck, trying to figure some way out of this. Forte had him in a corner, and he hated being in that position.

The bastards had figured out a way to get to him. He knew he could cover Gabe's medical bills for a while, but he knew that wasn't a long-term solution. He saw no choice but to drop the lawsuit in return for Forte restoring Micah's coverage. He would win the battle, but lose the war. And that rankled him most of all.

The next morning at work, he was getting ready to call Jim Woodward when the intercom buzzed.

"A Blaine Harris is on line three," Becky said. "Claims to be with Forte."

He started to tell her to take a message, then reconsidered. "Thanks. I'll take it." He punched the blinking button and answered.

"Warren, this is Blaine Harris with Forte. We met at Lawrence Dalton's funeral in Tallahassee last week." The voice was calm and even, not much of an accent. Confident and arrogant. Warren pictured the man he saw standing in the Forte entourage at the funeral.

"Blaine. What can I do for you?"

"I'm going to be down in south Florida this Thursday. Was wondering if you might have time to see me if I stop by Fort Myers on my way back?"

Warren looked at his calendar. "What time did you have in mind?"

"I leave Boca at four. I could meet you somewhere at say, five?"

He assumed Blaine was flying on the corporate plane and would be coming in to Page Field. "Why don't I meet you at Ray's? Five o'clock. It's downtown on the river." He didn't bother to give him directions.

"That would be fine. I'll see you Thursday."

Warren hung up the phone, wondering what this was about. He decided to hold off on calling Woodward until after he met with Harris.

At ten minutes after five, Warren strode into Ray's. Through the window, he saw Blaine Harris sitting out on the deck under an umbrella, a glass of water on the table.

He stopped a waitress, handed her a twenty and told her bring him a glass of water and keep the change for her trouble. He walked out on the deck, smelling the salt air. Blaine saw him and rose.

"Sorry I'm late," Warren said, as he shook the man's extended hand.

"No problem. I was just enjoying the scenery. Nice place. I thought we'd sit outside where it's a little more private."

Warren pulled out a chair and sat opposite the older man. He studied him as they settled in their seats. Harris was shorter and heavier than Warren remembered, dressed in a conservative blue suit, red rep tie with a starched white shirt. The round face was framed with dark glasses and thinning gray hair that was retreating to the rear. Warren didn't speak, determined to wait him out.

Harris cleared his throat. "I appreciate you agreeing to meet with me. I wasn't sure you'd do so."

The waitress appeared, set the glass of water down in front of Warren, and asked if they needed anything else. Both men shook their heads. After she walked away, Harris shifted in his chair and leaned forward. "You strike me as a 'no-bullshit' kind of person, so I'll get right to the point.

"This lawsuit is not good for either of us. We certainly have the resources to go the distance, but we don't want the distraction. I understand this is costing you business, which maybe you can afford over the short-term, but will eventually hurt. Pete Manning knows a lot of very wealthy people—people looking for good investment managers— which you are. He's the kind of person who's in a position to help you stop the bleeding and furthermore send a lot of business your way.

"Anytime you have something ugly like this, a lot of people may get hurt. Relationships could be damaged beyond repair."

He paused for this to sink in and adopted a more congenial tone. "The outcome of your lawsuit won't make a dent in our bottom line. You know that and we know that. Just the same, we'd like it to go away. We are motivated, you could say, to do so *if* we can do it expeditiously. The question is, 'what's the number?' What would it take?"

Warren smiled. He'd expected this. Maybe not the sweetener of additional clients, but the naming of a price. Everything has a price, and Forte wanted to know Warren Thompson's price.

Forte was prepared to write a substantial check to make it go away. The not-so-implicit threat was clear—you don't settle, and we're going to make your life miserable in every way.

It was tempting, as much as he didn't want to admit it. His business could be made whole overnight, even better. He chuckled inside as he thought Forte could probably even see to it that his position as hospital foundation chair would be restored.

Alex's mother and aunt would have enough money to live very comfortably for the rest of their lives. More money than they could ever dream of.

Most important, he could eliminate the increasing pressure on Micah Rollins. There were a lot of plusses in that column, too many to dismiss in a casual way. He convinced himself he'd be foolish not to consider it.

"Ten million. Non-negotiable," Warren said.

He detected an almost imperceptible rise in Harris's eyebrows as the man started shaking his head. He held Warren's eyes for five or six seconds before speaking.

"I don't have the authority to go that high."

"Bullshit. You've already offered five." Warren pushed his chair away from the table. "Your new bond issue is three billion. Fifty basis points more on the interest rate—which is what you can expect with this lawsuit in your filing—will cost Forte fifteen million dollars. So, ten million is a bargain and you know it. Call your CFO and ask him." He started to rise.

"Wait," Blaine said.

Warren sat back down, but didn't move any closer to the table.

"I'll have Tully draw up the papers and send them to Woodward. He'll have them within twenty-four hours." Harris leaned back in his chair and steepled his hands underneath his chin. "You've got forty-eight hours."

He rose from his chair, and Warren said, "That's not all."

Harris eased back down into his chair. "That's not all? You hold me up for ten million dollars, and that's not all?"

Warren shrugged. "I wanted to start with the showstopper. If that wasn't a go, then we were done. Probably should've asked for more."

Harris snorted and stared at him. "What else?"

Warren looked around to confirm they were alone, then leaned forward, his eyes locked onto Harris's. "You leave Micah Rollins and her son the fuck out of this. Forever. Forte so much as sends her a piece of junk mail, and I'll spend every last cent I have to make sure you and your buds regret it. Plus, you restore her insurance coverage to a level two."

Harris held his stare, then shook his head. "I have nothing to do with—"

"Your initial assessment of me was correct. Don't bullshit me, Harris. Her coverage is changed *before* my attorney does squat. Level two, not level four. And, an official letter stating that there was a clerical mistake, and they are guaranteed level two status, not to be downgraded."

"That it?"

"The suit against me is dropped. Make sure all of this is covered. Ironclad. Soon as that happens, we'll move forward."

He got up and walked out.

Jim Woodward called the next afternoon. "You won't believe what I'm looking at," he said, the excitement in his voice undeniable.

"Let me guess—a settlement agreement from Forte."

There was a pause on the line. "Is there something you forgot to tell me, by chance?" Woodward's voice was angry.

"Sorry, Jim. I had a discussion with Blaine Harris late yesterday. I was going to call you, but I've been slammed this morning."

"I'll fax you a copy." Woodward sounded mollified. "I'm assuming you already know the terms."

"Why don't you tell me, in case they conveniently managed to forget something?"

Jim went over the salient points in the agreement. Everything that Warren had asked for was covered.

"How soon?" Warren asked.

"I have a few changes. Within a couple of days. Boone said time was of the essence, so I'm assuming they will fast track it. We should have a check by the end of the week."

Perfect, Warren thought.

Chapter 28

I'm settling the lawsuit," Warren said. He was having lunch with Micah in the hospital cafeteria the next day.

"You're settling?" she said, in a surprised voice.

He shrugged. "They made a good offer, and I don't see any other way out. From the beginning, I wanted to know what happened. Now I know, even though I don't like it."

"And that's it? That's all?"

"Look, it's a decent offer. The money's going to Alex's mother and her aunt. Your insurance is raised to a level two. I wish I could keep those SOBs from doing it again— to people like Ciel who don't know any better and people like you, who know better but can't fight a huge corporation. But I'm beat and I know it."

"No offense, but did you really think a $50 million dollar lawsuit would do that? Think about it—you're just a nuisance to Forte. They've got you playing their game. With armies of lawyers and incredibly deep pockets, they can outlast you."

Her words stung, but she was right. He remembered the words of his high school basketball coach. *Don't let them make you play their game.*

It was the final game of his senior year. They were on the verge of making it to the state regionals. They had a good team, but not great. Unlike their cross-town rival, who had a court full of thoroughbreds.

Warren's team went in at the half down by seventeen points. The mood in the locker room was somber and everyone was dejected. They were expecting the inevitable tongue lashing from Coach.

Instead, he stood up and in a calm, collected voice said, "We can't beat them at their game. They're better at it than we are. If you want to win, we have to make them play *our* game. Don't let them make you play *their* game."

He reminded them what their game was—defense and patience. They went out and won the game by one point. They did it by playing defense and being patient.

Micah was right. Forte had Warren playing their game, and he couldn't win. He had to make them play *his* game. Only problem was, he wasn't sure what his game was.

"Okay, then, what's plan B?" he asked.

"Think about it. How can you hurt Forte? You get them to stop rating customers based on ability to pay. And in order to do that, you've got to make people understand what's going on."

"And, how do you do that?"

She gave him an exasperated look. "I don't know. A giant billboard on every corner, stating what they're doing."

He thought about what she was saying. He couldn't put a billboard on every street corner, but maybe there was something almost as effective.

On the way back to his office, he called Sam. "What are you doing?"

"My usual, having coffee at Café Nation, working on a few things, trying to make rent money. Why?"

"Fly to New York with me Thursday. There's someone I want you to meet. We can take my plane. We can make it to the city in time for lunch and I'll have you back in Fort Myers by ten that evening."

"Your plane?"

"It's a small one." He gave Sam instructions to meet him at the Base Operations Terminal at Page Field by 8:00 a.m.

The next morning, Sam was waiting for him there, along with the pilot and co-pilot. The jet was parked outside, ready to go.

"Business must be good," Sam said, as he settled into the seat across the aisle from Warren. The co-pilot closed the door on the Lear as the pilot went through his checklist. Within minutes, they were rolling.

Warren filled Sam in on the happenings of the last few days.

"You sure about this?" Sam asked.

"No, but what choice do I have? Keeping my foot up their ass is my only option, it's the only advantage I have. We've got to keep the pressure on. We miss this timing opportunity, it's game over."

They made good use of the flying time, and touched down in Teterboro at a couple of minutes before ten.

"I could get used to traveling like this," Sam said, as the co-pilot opened the door to the Learjet.

"All it takes is money," Warren said.

A limo was waiting for them. Warren and Sam climbed in, and Warren told the driver to take them to Dina's on 44th, near 8th Avenue.

Just after eleven, they walked in, where a trim, well-dressed black man with a shaved head and glasses greeted them.

"Warren. How are you?" He walked over and hugged Warren.

Warren returned the hug, separated, and introduced Sam to Trip Carter. "Trip is an old friend. I knew him before he went over to the dark side at the *Times*."

Trip laughed and said, "What he means is before I saw the light."

The maître d' ushered them back to a quiet booth near the rear of the dimly lit restaurant.

"Where were you before the *Times?*" Sam asked.

"Over at the *Wall Street Journal*. My editor started pushing too hard to change the tone of a story I was working on. When he finally admitted he was getting pressure from above, I walked out and went to the *Times*. That was eight years ago, and I haven't regretted it."

"What he's not telling you is he came this close," Warren held up his thumb and forefinger and squeezed together, "to a Pulitzer two years ago. Trip is a financial reporter for them, and a damn good one."

They ordered lunch, as Sam told a little about himself. Then, Warren started to explain what he'd discovered. Trip pulled out his digital recorder and set it on the table. Warren stopped talking and shook his head. "Sorry, Trip. This conversation has to be off the record."

"You know how I feel about that, Warren. Unless it's a matter of personal safety—"

"It may be. Hear us out today, and we'll decide later. Fair enough?"

Warren told him everything that had happened, including the meeting with Blaine Harris and the subsequent settlement.

Their lunch lasted the better part of the afternoon, with Trip taking copious notes.

"All of this sounds great for a story, but do you have proof?" Trip asked.

Warren looked at Sam. This was the moment of truth. He was hoping that once Sam met Trip, he'd be willing to help.

"What kind of proof do you need?" Sam asked.

Trip told them he needed verifiable data on actual patients, information that would corroborate what they were saying. He spent the next thirty minutes telling them exactly what he needed.

"What about Benefactor?" Warren asked.

Sam shot him a look and gave him a slight shake of his head. Trip was looking at Warren and missed the communication.

"Who's that?" Trip asked.

"Just an urban legend," Sam answered, before Warren could comment. "I think I understand what you need, Trip. I'll get back to you."

Warren made a mental note to ask Sam about this later. Since they were done, and it was getting late, Warren moved his chair out to stand, the others following suit.

"Thanks for meeting with us, Trip," he said. "We'd better get a move on. I promised Sam I'd have him back in Fort Myers by ten. What else do you need?"

"Nothing, now. If you can get that info, send it to me. I know there's a story here, and I think I can convince my editor to run it. I'll make some calls and let you know what I find out."

Trip turned to Sam. "You're certain about this? No offense, but this sounds a little like one of those weirdo conspiracy theories that's always making the rounds."

Sam laughed. "Not the first time I've heard that. No, sad to say, it's true. But I'll warn you it's going to be extremely difficult to corroborate. We've explained why no one wants to talk."

Warren nodded. "Be careful. You see how long it took them to send me a message, and it wasn't very subtle."

Trip smiled. "I've been threatened before, and in less subtle ways." He touched a scar over his left eye. "Remember how I got this?"

Warren nodded, and turned to Sam. "That was the story that almost got him a Pulitzer. Almost cost him his life, too."

"You guys be careful," Trip said as they walked out. "Sounds like they're already on to you, so watch your step."

On the way back to the airport, Warren said, "Why didn't you want to talk about Benefactor?"

Sam shrugged. "Nothing to say. No sense in mentioning a rumor to a reporter. It hurts our credibility. Let's talk about how much detail we need for Trip."

They talked almost nonstop all the way back to Fort Myers. Warren knew Trip would do his research, but Sam was worried that the reporter wouldn't believe it.

"I've been here before, Warren," the doctor said. "You don't think I've talked to reporters? When everyone else they talk to dismisses it, they lose interest."

There was a weariness to his voice, Warren thought. He had the look of someone who had taken more than his share of blows, and was still standing. But the battle had taken its toll. Warren wondered how well he would hold up to the same kind of abuse that had been showered on Sam Abrams.

"I know, Sam. I'm not naïve—I know what we're up against. But Trip is a stand-up guy. I'm in it with you. All the way, no matter what."

Sam stared out the window of the jet into the dark sky.

"I'll see what I can do," he said.

Blaine's eyes were barely open and his breathing was rapid. The buxom brunette straddling his naked body slowed down, drawing it out. He was mesmerized by her body, and he knew he was close.

She was one of his favorites. Lesly was an art student at NYU, uninhibited, and remarkable in bed. He'd met her at a gallery opening, and she'd come to his place that evening after a celebratory dinner at Aureole.

The settlement agreement with Warren Thompson had been finalized. The check had been cut, and the announcement that the lawsuit was being dropped was circled on the page of the *Wall Street Journal* on the nightstand.

His phone buzzed—the other one. Lesly hesitated and looked at the nightstand. *Shit,* he thought, exhaling. So close. He'd silenced his regular phone, but never did that with the other one.

It buzzed again. The moment was gone. She knew it, and so did he. He patted her thigh, and she got up and walked to the bathroom. He watched her as he reached for the phone. Maybe they could start again after the call, he thought.

He picked up the phone and punched Answer. "Yes," he said, still breathing heavy.

"Did I interrupt something?" the voice said.

He ignored the question. "What is it?"

"Dollar boy and his doctor buddy just met with the reporter again."

Dollar boy was their code name for Warren Thompson.

"Both of them? You sure?"

"No doubt. A long meeting. All afternoon."

What was that about? Maybe Thompson and Abrams were celebrating the settlement. But why would they be meeting with the reporter? He thought for a moment, then said, "See what you can find out."

He disconnected the call. He knew from Thompson's last trip to New York that the reporter was Trip Carter, a seasoned financial reporter with the *New York Times*. Before, he had been working on an article about the lawsuit. But since that was settled, and Thompson was under a gag order, what could they be meeting about? In the morning, he'd have to work his contacts to find out what was going on.

He was still thinking about the call when Lesly walked back into the bedroom, wearing nothing but a smile. She stood at the edge of the bed, letting him admire the view.

"Done with business?" she asked, caressing her breasts.

"That business."

He reached out and ran his fingers down her body until his hand was between her legs. "But not this business."

Chapter 29

Friday morning, Sam called Warren and asked to meet at Café Nation.

He walked out on the patio and saw Sam sitting in the corner, under an umbrella. A student sat at the table next to Sam. He looked nervous and kept looking out toward the street.

Warren made his way over and sat across from Sam, eyeing the student, suspicious about his proximity to them. He was about to suggest to Sam that they move to another, more private table, when the young man broke into a grin, and waved.

Warren was confused, then out of the corner of his eye he caught a young girl on the sidewalk behind him, waving. She came in through the coffee shop and out on the patio, where the young man stood and gave her a kiss.

He smiled, scolding himself for being so paranoid.

"You okay?" Sam asked.

Warren nodded, ignoring the couple and turning his attention back to Sam.

"I think I can get the information that Trip asked us for," Sam said.

"How?"

Sam glanced around, then learned over the table. "Benefactor," he said, in a hushed voice.

"Benefactor?" Warren said, a little too loud, as Sam raised then lowered his outstretched hand over the table, imploring Warren to keep his voice down.

"But you said—"

"I'm sorry about lying to you, but I hadn't made my mind up yesterday. And, I wasn't about to confirm it in front of a reporter."

Warren was astonished at the revelation. "So it *is* true?"

Sam nodded. "I've already requested the information and should have it tomorrow. I don't want to say anymore in public. Can we plan on meeting at your house tomorrow evening?"

"Sure. When?"

"I'll give you a call and let you know."

"No problem. I'll be there," Warren said, full of questions about Benefactor and knowing they would have to wait.

Saturday afternoon, Mark watched as the silver Honda Accord turned right into the main entrance for Rivers Community Hospital. He was driving a non-descript white Chevrolet Cavalier rental two cars behind the Honda. He slowed and turned behind the Honda, which he knew was driven by Doctor Samuel Abrams.

He'd been following the doctor, and was impressed by his counter-surveillance savvy—not bad for an amateur. Although Abrams couldn't know who he was, he was taking no chances on being followed. He turned in to several strip shopping centers, and even made a U-turn on McGregor. Of course, the GPS device that Mark had put under the right rear bumper of Abrams's car a few days ago had made it easier to track Abrams's movements without being seen.

Abrams parked, and Mark found a parking spot in the next aisle. He followed him inside the building. When Abrams went to the doctor's lounge, he had to break off surveillance.

He went back out to his car, and waited for the doctor to come out. Thirty minutes later, the doctor emerged, carrying a manila folder.

He felt sure Abrams had met with Benefactor, but still had no clue as to who the elusive doctor was. Thanks to a college student he'd paid to sit at the table next to Abrams and Thompson at Café Nation, he knew that Abrams had agreed to help Thompson by getting information. And the student had overheard the word "Benefactor."

Abrams's phone was tapped, so he also knew that the doctor had called Thompson to set up an appointment this evening at eight. The only conclusion was that Abrams had just picked up something to give Thompson.

He pulled over into a Hess station to call his contact for further instructions.

Blaine Harris answered his throwaway cell phone, and listened as Mark explained the current situation.

"You're convinced that Benefactor works at the hospital?" Harris asked.

"Absolutely."

"Any way to find out what the doctor gave our friend?"

Mark had explained that Abrams had come out of the hospital with a folder in his hand.

"There are always ways. Depends on how fast you want to move."

Blaine knew that son of a bitch Thompson was double-crossing him. He'd found out through his contacts at the *Times* that Trip Carter was working on an exposé on the top three health insurance companies. Since nothing was officially known, Thompson wasn't violating the gag order imposed by the settlement. But, Thompson had put Abrams in touch with Carter and now Abrams was providing information to the reporter. Information he'd acquired from the mysterious Benefactor.

"All I know is we've got to derail this thing—and fast, before it spins totally out of control. Can you get the documents?"

"How soon do you want them?"

"I want them now, goddammit."

"Can do. It'll be extra. Extreme measures may be required."

Blaine thought a minute. He wanted to ask, then realized he didn't want to know. Extreme in Mark's lexicon usually meant someone was going to get hurt. He hated being in the dark, but knew Mark could be trusted to carry out whatever needed to be done and do it as discreetly as possible. The man had never failed before.

He took a deep breath, unsure as to what he was sanctioning. "Proceed," Blaine said, ending the call.

Mark liked to work alone whenever possible. There were few people he trusted, and the fewer moving parts any project had, the less chance for problems. Some projects required additional help, and he wished he could bring in an associate for this one. But that was out because of the time constraints.

He looked at his watch. He had six hours before Abrams was going over to Thompson's house, which was probably the best place to try and snatch the documents.

On his phone, Mark located a boat rental place in North Fort Myers, on the Caloosahatchee River across from downtown Fort Myers. Donning a simple disguise, he drove there. Like many Special Forces personnel, he didn't stand out in a crowd.

He stopped by the flea market on his way and purchased some used fishing tackle. He transferred his gear into the beat-up tackle box and scuffed cooler and put everything in the trunk of his rental car. At the marina, he rented a boat for the evening under an assumed name, claiming he wanted to go fishing. He made sure the man at the office saw him loading the gear onboard.

In the boat, he pulled away from the dock and waved at the office, figuring the clerk was watching. As soon as he got to the main channel, he turned southwest and went under the bridge where US 41 crossed. He wanted to locate Thompson's house from the water in the fading daylight so he'd have his bearings when night came.

When he got to a point opposite Thompson's house, he moved out of the main channel and throttled the boat back to an idle. He removed his binoculars from the tackle box and scoped out the house.

He had a good sight line from this vantage point, so he threw the small anchor out and made sure it was set. He turned off the motor, took out the spinning rod, and cast it out toward shore. To the casual observer, he was just another fisherman enjoying what was left of the daylight.

He picked up the binoculars again for a closer look at Thompson's house. An older, Hispanic-looking man puttered about the yard, tending the plants and shrubs. Occasionally, a heavy-set woman wearing an apron would appear on the deck, waving, and shouting at the man. He would stop and listen for a minute, then wave her off and continue about his business.

They wouldn't be a problem, but it would be easier if they weren't around. He set the binoculars down and plotted out a course of action. Now, all that remained was to wait for nightfall.

As darkness descended, Mark picked up the binoculars and scanned the house. Lights came on, which made it easier to see inside. He saw the caretaker and housekeeper in the kitchen. The woman had her apron off and was holding a large bag.

The old man was nodding, looked around, and then they walked out of the kitchen, turning out the lights as they left. In a few minutes, he saw lights going out the driveway. He shifted the binoculars and watched as an older model sedan left through the gated entrance. He put the binoculars down and nodded. The plan just got simpler.

He leaned back in the boat and waited. Before long, he saw a white BMW come through the gates and disappear behind where the garage was located. Earlier that afternoon, he'd researched the online property records for Lee County, so he knew how the house was situated on the lot.

In a few minutes, another light came on in the kitchen, and he made out a man he recognized as Warren

Thompson. No one else appeared to be in the house. Abrams would be there soon with the documents.

With the old couple out of the way, that left Thompson and Abrams to deal with. That wouldn't be a major problem. Although he would have preferred stealing the documents when no one was home, that didn't appear to be an option.

He started getting his gear ready.

About quarter after eight, Warren heard the buzzer at the gate. He opened the door, and Sam was standing there with a manila folder in his hand.

"Hey Sam, come in." Once inside, Warren offered him something to drink.

"A beer would be nice, thanks," Sam said.

Warren took a couple of beers out of the refrigerator, opened them, and led Sam out on the lanai to talk.

After they sat at the table, Sam opened the folder, pulled out a sheaf of paper and pushed it over to him.

"As you can see, you have confidential patient information. This could land me and others in prison, along with owing millions of dollars in fines. I'll deny ever giving it to you, but rest assured, it is totally accurate. Are you familiar with HIPAA?"

Warren had learned that The Health Insurance Portability and Accountability Act of 1996, known as HIPAA, established rules to protect the confidentiality and privacy of health information. Failure to comply could result in stiff civil and criminal penalties.

A willful violation, such as this, called for at least a $50,000 fine for each violation, in addition to a possible jail sentence of ten years. This was one of the primary reasons that no one was willing to breach confidentiality.

He nodded, and looked at the papers. Each page contained a simple consecutive number, followed by a single digit, diagnosis, and complete medical record.

"You have patients with the same diagnosis, and with roughly the same 'health status,' so you are looking at an apples-to-apples comparison of like pairs—eighteen patients, to be exact."

Warren looked at the first pair. For the first patient, there was an extensive list of diagnostic tests, drugs, and procedures. For the second patient, the list was much shorter, although the diagnosis was exactly the same.

"The consecutive number at the top of the page is what Benefactor substituted for patient number. He's the only one who can reference it back to a specific patient. The single digit that follows is the third digit from the right of their Insurance Member ID—an abbreviated insurance ID, if you will. The same digit that I showed you on your insurance card, remember?"

Warren nodded, and looked at the insurance ID for the first patient. It was a four. On the second, it was an eight. The difference in care provided to the comparable patients was striking.

Every pair of patients he looked at shared a similar story. For the same diagnosis, the work performed was radically different. The lower number always received considerably more effort.

He looked up at Sam. "This is un-fucking believable. Where did you get this?"

"What? You didn't believe me?"

He shook his head. "I did, but to see it in black-and-white. This is incredible. So there really is a Benefactor?"

"Let's just say I have contacts at the hospital."

Warren wanted to ask more, but had the feeling that Sam wasn't going to tell him anything else.

"Couldn't the discrepancy be attributed to other issues, like for example, the patient in one case is a diabetic or something?"

Sam nodded. "That's why . . . that's why the person assembling the information did the best they could on such short notice to only include pairs that were very similar."

"Alex never had a chance, did she?"

Sam looked him in the eye, and shook his head, not answering the obvious.

"I can't believe those sons of bitches at the hospital—"

Sam held up his hand, speaking in a calm voice. "It's not just Rivers, and not just Fort Myers, and not just her doctors. It's the entire system, Warren."

Sam also provided him with copies of screen pictures of the treatment protocols. The resolution wasn't the greatest, but clear enough to read. The lower the number of the insurance level, which is what they were now calling the third digit of the member ID, the more exhaustive the protocol, even for the same diagnosis.

The difference was striking. For a patient with a three, like Warren, the protocol ran several pages, listing numerous tests and patent drugs. For the unlucky patient with level nine, the treatment protocol didn't even come close to filling a page.

"And these are for patients close to the same age, in the same medical condition, with the same diagnosis?" Warren asked, still finding it impossible to believe.

Sam nodded. "And, if you look at the timeline, the discharge for the nine is the same day, while for the three, it's three days later."

"So, they're doing nothing for the nines? It's the moral equivalent of leaving them on the sidewalk. Talk about fucking death panels. And it's all driven by the money."

"Afraid so, my friend."

"Do you have more information like this?"

"Tons," Sam replied.

"And Benefactor can tie these to specific patients?"

"Absolutely."

Warren called Trip on his cell, putting him on speaker.

"We've got it," Warren said.

"Got what?" Trip asked.

Warren told him that Sam was with him. He described the documents he was holding in his hand.

Trip Carter let out a low whistle. "Can you scan those into your computer and send them to me?"

"Sure."

He hung up the phone.

"I've got to run," Sam said. "I'll just leave them with you. Go ahead and scan them and you can get them back to me tomorrow."

Warren walked Sam to the door, and came back to the kitchen. He was hungry, and figured he'd fix a sandwich before he scanned the documents in.

After he finished his sandwich, he rummaged around in the refrigerator and found a key lime pie that Carmela had baked for him. He cut a generous piece, then decided a cup of coffee would go great with it. When the coffee was done, he poured a cup and sat down to scan the pages Sam had left with him.

He had just finished scanning the pages into the laptop that Dalton had provided, and clipped the pages together, when his cell phone buzzed. It was a text from Sam.

Meet me at Café Nation at 9:30. Important

He looked at his watch. It was ten after nine, and would take him a good fifteen minutes to get there. He started to call Sam and ask what was so urgent, then decided that Sam wouldn't have texted him if it wasn't.

It would only take a couple of minutes to send the document to Trip. He composed a quick email, attached the document, and hit Send. The Send/Receive box popped up and he waited for the computer to show it was complete.

The message popped up on the screen:

Unable to send - server unavailable.

Shit. He tried it again with the same result. He looked at his watch. It'd have to wait. He'd send it when he got back.

Warren rounded up his shoes and keys, and went to the garage, leaving the document on the counter.

Chapter 30

Mark watched everything through the binoculars. Just as he was getting ready to come ashore and attack, he'd seen Abrams leave. That left Thompson alone in the house. The opportunity had given him an idea and he'd modified his plan.

He'd spoofed Abrams's number to send the message to Thompson, making it appear as though it had come from Abrams's phone. As intended, Thompson had left soon after receiving the text. He knew it would take Thompson at least fifteen minutes to drive to the café and the same amount of time back—not including fifteen or twenty minutes at the café to figure out what the hell was going on. That gave Mark forty-five minutes to break and enter the house, find what he needed, and leave. Plenty of time.

After Thompson drove away, Mark checked the house to confirm it was empty. He started the motor and carefully made his way to the dock at Thompson's house. As soon as it had gotten dark, he'd put black tape over the registration numbers on the boat. As he approached the dock, he pulled a thin, black mask over his face and super-thin black gloves. He hadn't spotted any surveillance cameras on the property, but since he'd not had a chance to do a thorough recon, he wasn't taking any chances.

He tied the boat up and stepped up on the dock, carrying a small black duffel bag. He checked his phone to see where Thompson's car was. Fortunately, he'd managed to stick a tracking device on it earlier today. The red dot appeared on the screen, several blocks away and moving toward the coffee house.

Putting his phone in his pocket, he made his way toward the house, where he saw a sign stuck in the ground.

Home Security of SW FL

He smiled. He was in luck. He was familiar with the security system they used; it was one of the more popular ones. And, one of the easiest to circumvent. He walked around the house until he found the utility entry point.

He disabled the phone line and turned his cell phone jammer on to block the cell phone option if it was installed. Of course, this also blocked his phone, but since he wasn't expecting any calls, he wasn't worried. He didn't bother to cut the power. This alarm system had a battery backup, so there was no need to waste the time.

On the deck, he picked the lock on the door leading to the kitchen, opened it, and stepped inside. He listened for the beeping of the alarm system, and made his way to the keypad inside the garage door. Although it couldn't send a signal to the monitoring company, the alarm could still sound an external siren which would attract unwanted attention.

He opened the hinged cover and clipped the leads from his electronic black box onto the black and yellow wires in the panel. In a few seconds, the code displayed on the box and sent the proper signal to the alarm.

Mark checked his watch, on which he had set a countdown timer. Thirty-six minutes left. Now to find the documents.

Thompson had made it easy for him. Both the laptop and the paper documents were still on the counter. He glanced through the papers, folded them, and put them inside a pocket on his vest. Thirty-one minutes.

Now to the computer. He powered up the computer, and was impressed when he saw the login screen. It was one he recognized. He had the same security software installed on his own computer. It was one of the best, and close to impossible to hack into in a short amount of time.

The problem with security is that any system, regardless of what type, was only as strong as its weakest link. With his background, he knew to assess the entire system and not waste time on the strengths. Find the weakest link as quick as possible and exploit it.

In this case, the software was top-drawer. It would require an experienced person with considerable computer power a significant length of time to break. However, the notebook was a garden-variety Apple, the kind you could buy at any Apple store. This was the weak link. He was hoping to find out whether or not Thompson had sent the documents anywhere, but that was now out.

He stripped all of his electronic gear he was wearing and set it on the corner of the bar, several feet away from him. He took a magnet out of his bag and plugged it in to the portable battery pack he had also removed from the bag. The result was a super-strong electromagnet, capable of deleting the memory of any but the hardened versions of electronic devices within six inches of the magnet. More than one person had wiped out their phone or watch being careless with such a device. It was a mistake that was only made once.

He switched the magnet on and ran it around the top and bottom of the computer. The screen went black. He pressed the power button down for several seconds, waiting for something to happen. Nothing. He pressed the power button again. Nothing. The computer's mind had been completely erased.

Satisfied, he packed everything up, went back to the alarm keypad, and entered the code. With the alarm beeping, he made his way out the door he'd entered and closed it behind him, checking to make sure it was locked. When he got back to the access point, he disconnected the device he'd left there and deactivated the jammer.

He took a few seconds to check the tracking app and see where Thompson was. *Shit.* The blinking red dot was on McGregor, headed this way, only a few blocks from the house. He'd either miscalculated or something had changed. No time to analyze it now.

He gathered his things, did a quick check to make sure nothing was left behind, and walked over to the dock. Before he got to the boat, he heard the car turning in the drive. He couldn't remember if the dock was in the sight line from the drive, but he wasn't slowing down to find out. That was the problem in planning a project on such short notice.

Warren punched in the alarm code after entering through the garage. In the quiet of the kitchen, he heard an outboard motor that sounded close to his dock. He shrugged. Someone fishing probably, nothing unusual on the river.

When he'd got to Café Nation, Sam wasn't there. He tried calling him, but it went straight to voice mail. After ten minutes and several unsuccessful attempts to reach Sam, he left a message with the barista and headed back home.

Seeing the computer on the counter reminded him to send the documents to Trip. He sat and punched the power button on the laptop. It didn't make the familiar whirring sound and the screen stayed dark. Nothing. *Odd,* he thought. He banged on the keys, and pressed the power button again. Still, nothing. Maybe the battery had died, he thought. He plugged in the power cord lying on the bar, but got the same result.

His phone buzzed. It was Sam.

"Where were you?" Warren said, answering the call.

"What do you mean?" Sam said. "I just saw where you'd called, and was calling you back."

"I went to Café Nation at 9:30, and you didn't show."

"Who said anything about Café Nation at 9:30?"

Warren was confused. "I got a text from you, telling me to meet you there then."

Sam laughed. "You sure it was from me? I didn't send you a text."

He took the phone away from his ear and looked at the message. It was at 9:12 and from *S Abrams*. He put the phone back up to his ear and relayed the information to Sam.

He opened the folder next to the computer. It was empty. The documents Sam had left with him were no longer there.

"You still there?" Sam asked.

"Hold on a sec." Warren looked around the house. Nothing was amiss. He checked the front door. Locked. Back door leading out to the deck. It too, was locked. Yet, the documents were missing and his computer was dead. Someone had been there.

"Somebody took the documents you left me."

"Are you sure?"

He thought about the boat near his dock when he got home. "Someone's been in my house."

"Maybe you left them somewhere—"

"I'm telling you, someone's been here." He told Sam about the computer and hearing a powerboat next to his dock.

"Did you get a chance to make a copy?" Sam asked.

Warren explained that he'd scanned the documents into his now worthless computer and that he'd not had a chance to send them to Carter. "Do you have a copy?"

"Some of it. And we probably shouldn't be discussing this over the phone. Why don't you meet me at Café Nation? For real, this time. If someone's watching your house, we probably shouldn't meet there."

Warren called Tabby and told him what had happened. Like Sam, Tabby questioned him about possibly misplacing the documents.

"No, I did not misplace them. And, how do you explain my computer conveniently dying?"

Tabby told him he'd come over and take a look around. Warren told him he was going to meet someone at Café Nation and he'd be home in an hour.

When he got to the coffee house, he found Sam sitting outside, a worried look on his face.

"You look upset?" Warren asked, as he sat.

"I am. I'm concerned about the source of the information. He may be in danger."

"Why? There was no doctor's name or patient-specific information on the list you gave me."

Sam shook his head. "I know, but there may be enough there that someone could work backward and trace it back."

"It's Benefactor, isn't it?" he asked, watching the doctor's face. "Is he—or she—in danger?

Sam looked around, then nodded. "Possibly. I don't know, but I'm concerned."

"Did you call and warn him?"

"I don't have any way to call him."

He shook his head. "How the hell do you contact him, then?"

"It's complicated. I leave a message at a pre-arranged location, and pick up messages at the same place."

"This sounds like spy stuff."

"You don't understand. These people are pros. The person who broke into your house wasn't some hack off the street. He spoofed my cell phone—which means he's been monitoring my calls, circumvented your alarm system, and wiped out your computer. All in less than an hour."

Warren considered what Sam had told him. Someone like this wouldn't come cheap.

"They're after Benefactor—not you or me. They want to stop this from coming out."

"What about Micah?" Warren asked.

Sam cocked his head. "I don't think she's in any danger. If so, they would've dealt with her some time ago."

He told Sam that Tabby was coming over to the house as soon as he got back.

Sam laughed. "And what exactly do you think the police are going to be able to do? These people don't leave a trail, Warren. And the locals are no match."

When he got back to the house, Tabby's unmarked car was parked in his drive. The big man emerged from around the side of the house as Warren parked his car in the garage.

"Find anything?" Warren asked.

Tabby shook his head. "Just got here. The grass was flattened underneath the telephone company box on the side of the house."

They walked into the house and Tabby looked around, starting with the alarm keypad. A few minutes later, he walked over to the refrigerator and took out a soda. Popping the top, he took a long drink, then looked at Warren seated at the counter.

"Nothing else missing or disturbed, right?" Tabby asked.

"No."

Tabby scanned the room, took another drink, and nodded.

"I'm wondering. Why would somebody go to this much trouble? What did they take?"

Earlier, Warren hadn't told Tabby exactly what was missing or where it came from.

"How much time have you got?"

"Depends on whether you've got anything to eat here."

Warren nodded and walked over to the refrigerator.

As he fixed a couple of sandwiches, he told Tabby about what he and Sam were doing. He told his friend about everything, including the trip to New York. He ended with the text message he'd received tonight. Tabby hadn't said a word the entire time. Listening, he ate his sandwich and chips, occasionally nodding.

"You think this is related?" Warren asked.

"I could get the crime scene techs out here, but doubt it would do any good. This was a pro. Came by water, probably watched you from a boat. Sent you a spoofed text message, then saw you leave. Disabled the phone system to prevent the alarm from dialing out, picked the lock, and jacked the alarm code."

Shaking his head, Warren said, "The alarm system has cell backup to keep someone from doing that."

Tabby chuckled. "Worthless. Easy enough to jam the cell signal. He came in, trashed your hard drive, took the papers, and left."

Warren slumped in his seat. "So much for my expensive alarm system and monitoring."

"Happens all the time. Keeps the amateurs out. Nothing's going to keep out someone like this. Somebody wanted this information. Bad."

"Should I be worried?"

Tabby shrugged. "Depends."

"On what?"

"What they're really after."

Chapter 31

Blaine sat at his desk, looking at the documents Mark had sent him. Patient information, highlighting the difference in care provided and correlated with the insurance level. So this is what Thompson was doing. He'd put the reporter on it and hooked him up with Samuel Abrams.

Clever, he had to admit. Thompson had the ten million and since he was out of the loop, he technically wasn't violating the terms of the gag order that was part of the settlement. But if an article on this appeared on the front page of the *New York Times*, it would still be disastrous for Forte.

He pulled his other cell phone out of his pocket and called Mark.

"I want Benefactor stopped. Cold. Whatever has to be done. Now."

When Warren told Trip what had happened, the reporter suggested they send whatever information they had via FedEx. He also suggested using a FedEx box in a very public location with lots of people around.

It was Friday before Sam was able to get more information from Benefactor. Sam remembered there was a FedEx drop box across the busy street that Café Nation fronted, and suggested they meet at the coffee shop.

They sat down outside, and when another man sat at the table next to them, they moved to the opposite corner.

"Sorry," Warren said. "I thought that guy was watching us."

Sam nodded. "I know. I'm seeing someone in every shadow, too. I freaked out this morning in Publix when I saw the same woman on two different aisles. I was about to accost her, when her boyfriend or husband walked up."

Warren took the papers and scanned through them. It was the kind of information Trip had asked for, though not as complete as the material that was stolen.

"It'll have to do. It's all we have," Warren said, returning the documents to Sam.

Sam pulled out a FedEx envelope, put the papers inside, and sealed it. "I'll drop this off at the box across the street when we leave."

"Is Benefactor going to be okay?"

"I think so. I told him about somebody stealing the papers from your kitchen."

"Tell him to be careful," Warren said. "Speaking of being careful, I think I figured out a way to use our phones securely."

He showed Sam the app on his phone that Lawrence Dalton had insisted on using. Sam downloaded and installed it while they were sitting there, and Warren showed him how it worked.

"Just make sure the Secure icon is lit."

Warren's phone rang. It was Trip.

"The draft of the first story is on my editor's desk. I suggested making it two articles and she agreed. This one is mostly background and the results of my research. It's up to her, but she told me it's running Sunday."

"Good," Warren said. He told Trip they were just sending the additional information that should arrive Monday.

"When I get your info, we'll follow it up the next Sunday with the second article."

Sunday morning, Warren walked out and retrieved the *Times* from his driveway. He waited to unwrap it until he got another cup of coffee and walked out to the table on the lanai.

Much to his surprise, the lead story was about the coal industry. Puzzled, he scanned the rest of the first section and the Financial section. Nothing by Trip Carter.

He picked up his phone to call his friend and find out what happened.

The call went straight to voice mail, and he left a message.

Later that morning, Warren's phone buzzed. It was Trip.

"What happened?" Warren asked as soon as he answered the call.

"I don't know. Last I heard it was running."

"Somebody got to her, didn't they?" He walked out on the deck, glancing around his backyard and searching the river for any boats near his dock. Nothing, but he was still uneasy.

Trip laughed. "If the *Times* killed every story based on a well-placed phone call, there wouldn't be a newspaper.

Some of the faux news outlets may work like that, but the *Times* is old school. In the eight years I've been here, I've not seen a single story killed that way. There's another explanation, but right now I don't know what it is."

Warren ended the call and slammed the phone down on the counter. Trip may have believed there was another reason, but Warren knew the truth. Forte had gotten to someone at the *Times* and managed to kill the story somehow.

Late that afternoon, Sam and Micah were over at Warren's house, out on the lanai. Gabe was over at a friend's, so Warren had suggested they come over to his place.

Dusk was settling in, and the boat traffic on the Caloosahatchee had thinned out. Carmela had prepared dinner for them: plantains, yellowtail snapper and asparagus. Dinner was delicious, but the mood was somber. They talked as they ate, Warren filling them in on his heated conversations with Trip Carter.

The reporter had called him earlier this afternoon and told him that his editor felt they needed more information.

"That's such bullshit," Sam said. "Why did we even bother sending another package?"

Micah looked at Warren. "They're winning, aren't they?"

"Maybe what we sent will be enough to convince Trip's editor." He said the words, but in his heart, he didn't believe them. Micah was right—Forte was winning.

"We can't give up. That's what they want. We've got to keep punching." He turned to Sam. "Can we get more detailed information, something that would 'wow' her?"

Sam shrugged. "I don't know. I'll give it some thought."

Mark sat in the rental boat, anchored fifty yards or so from the end of Warren Thompson's dock. After the close call last Saturday night, he was careful to keep more distance so as not to attract attention. A fishing rod hung over the side of the boat, connected to a bobbing cork in the water. If anyone looked, it was just another fisherman out on the river.

He had a clear line of sight to Thompson's lanai, which he'd learned was his favorite place to sit. From time to time, he looked through the binoculars at Thompson's house, although he was more cautious now since the break-in.

He recognized the doctor, but was surprised to see a woman. Taking out his digital camera with telephoto lens, he snapped a couple of photos. When he got back to his room, he'd figure out who she was.

Friday afternoon, he'd seen Abrams drop a FedEx envelope in the box across from Café Nation. After Abrams left the coffee shop, he walked over to check the next pickup time.

In disguise, he'd taken a chance and approached the FedEx employee picking up packages at the box. Dressed in a tie and slacks, he wanted to appear legitimate to the FedEx person.

As the uniformed employee was emptying the contents of the drop box, Mark walked up and introduced himself as a low-level employee of Dr. Abrams, asking if she could please just verify that she had an envelope going to a Trip Carter at the *New York Times*. He sheepishly said that Dr.

Abrams had told him he thought he'd dropped it off, and he just wanted to confirm it, since it was very important.

At first, the FedEx woman was skeptical. When Mark explained that all he wanted was to make sure that she had the package, she looked down at the contents of her pickup box. There were not a lot of packages, and since Mark knew where it was going and who sent it, she figured it wouldn't hurt. She pawed through the envelopes, and holding up one, she nodded and told him that yes, she had a package going to a Trip Carter.

It was marked Standard Overnight. He memorized the internal mail address on the envelope and thanked her profusely. He ambled down the sidewalk, waiting for the FedEx truck to leave. As soon as she drove off, he went back to his vehicle and called his contact in New York with the package information.

His associate at the *Times* would be able to intercept the envelope, but this was not a permanent solution.

Turning his attention back to Thompson's house, Mark figured that Thompson and Abrams were now using an encryption app on their phone. He could still intercept the signal, but could only pick up gibberish. This made things a little tougher, but he still had the tracking device on Abrams's Honda.

He had twenty-four, maybe forty-eight hours before they realized the package was missing. Harris had been explicit: *Stop Benefactor.* Since Mark had yet to identify Benefactor, he was going to have to move quickly.

Chapter 32

Samuel Abrams could hear the sounds of frogs and other creatures of the night. In the distance, he could hear an occasional vehicle, as if traveling on a highway. He was seated on a makeshift bench of some sort, his knees on the damp dirt. His legs were folded back underneath his butt, and his hands were tied to his ankles. Down the center of his back, he could feel a rough wood post that seemed to be securely anchored in the ground beneath his knees.

Someone removed the black hood that had been placed over his head. He blinked in the dim light. A lantern hung a few feet away, putting out a faint bluish-white light. Two men were standing in the shadows. In front of him was a well-built white male with a military-style haircut. His face was uncovered. *Not a good sign,* Sam thought.

Even in the weak light, the man's eyes were hard. His neck, if you could call it that, seemed to be no more than a solid foundation on broad shoulders on which his thick head rested. Sam felt a mosquito feeding on his cheek, and tried to scrunch his head down to his shoulder to dislodge it.

He sniffed, and wrinkled his nose. The smell was what he could only describe as primeval. He could see stars above, and the faint outline of bushes and small trees. There was a glow in the distant horizon. A splash off to one side startled him, but the man didn't flinch.

"I need information. You tell me what I need, we turn you loose, and you have a chance. You don't . . . well, let's just say things are going to get very uncomfortable for you."

"Who are you?" Sam asked.

The man shook his massive head once each direction. "I ask the questions here, doctor. If you need a name, you can call me 'Mark.'"

Another bad sign, thought Sam. They were not going to let him go.

"Who is Benefactor?" Mark asked.

Sam bit his lower lip. "I don't—"

The blow came out of nowhere, slamming against his left jaw, dislocating or breaking something. His head rolled back to center. What hit him felt too hard to be flesh, but he wasn't sure. His eyes watered, and he tasted blood in his mouth.

"We don't have time to play games, Doctor Abrams. I need to know everything you know about Benefactor. The sooner you tell me, the less pain you'll feel. And believe me when I say you *will* tell me."

"I don't know who you're talking about," Sam said, wincing and waiting for the next blow. It didn't come. He opened his eyes, and the man called Mark was staring at him.

"What did you take over to Warren Thompson's house?"

Sam was still dazed from the blow, and it took him a minute to adjust to the change in questioning. Mark was doing this deliberately to try and trip him up.

He tried to think about how this person could know that he took something over to Warren's house.

"What are you—"

He doubled over in pain. This time the blow was to the gut, and left him gasping for breath.

"I know you went over there, and I know you took him something. Again, I don't have time to play games. What was it?"

Sam's mind raced to try and figure out some way to buy time. *Why was Mark in such a hurry?* He got the impression that Mark knew more than he was saying. *What did he know?*

"It was a list of patients—patients who had similar diagnoses."

"Why would you be taking a list of patients to Thompson?"

"To show that the treatments aren't consistent." He decided to give him parts of the truth. He couldn't help but wince as he awaited the next blow. It didn't come.

"Where did you get the information?"

Now he was getting to the heart of the questioning. The man standing in front of him was the one who stole the list from Warren's house, but he didn't know the source. Sam knew he couldn't resist long, that he would eventually give him the name.

"Someone left it for me at the hospital. I don't know—"

His head snapped back. He saw stars and his head throbbed. Another blow to the face. Something felt loose in his jaw when he tried to open his mouth. Mark was deliberately placing the shots in different places to further confuse him.

"Who?"

After several more powerful blows, Sam was close to blacking out. It would have been a blessing.

"Benefactor," he mumbled.

Mark studied him for a moment, then a thin smile crossed his face.

"I know that much. *Who* is Benefactor?"

Sam tried to shake his head, but it felt more like it was lolling from side to side.

"There is no one by that name."

Mark took a cup of water, handed to him by someone in the shadows. He threw it in Abrams's face.

"Who is Benefactor?"

Close to losing consciousness, he gave Mark a crooked smile. "There is no such person."

After more denials followed by blows—the numbers he couldn't recall—he watched Mark out of his one barely open eye.

"One last time—who gave you the information?"

Sam spit blood and what he thought was another tooth out. His jaw ached, and it was work to form the words. "I told you. It was setup as a blind drop. I don't know who left it."

Mark looked over to the shadows, nodded, then turned his attention back to Abrams.

"You remember your old classmate, doctor? Remember Cam?"

Sam thought for a moment. Cam. Cam, his old roommate in medical school? Boston? That was years ago. What did Cam have to do with this?

"I caught up with him, doctor. Had a nice little chat with him. He's still in Boston, you know?"

Mark was grinning now, but it was a twisted grin, almost a sneer. Sam still couldn't figure out what Cam had to do with all this. He hadn't spoken to Cam in ages.

"Remember the pet he brought home with him? Cam said you weren't too happy."

Mark motioned to the shadows, and four muscular men emerged in the dim light, pulling what looked to be a cage on wheels. It appeared to be ten or twelve feet long and half that height.

Sam thought he saw movement. Something inside was alive. He was puzzled, then his eyes got wide with fear as realized what was in the enclosure. He whimpered and strained against his bindings, feeling a trickle of warm urine running down his leg.

Mark's white teeth gleamed in the faint light. "Looks a lot like Cam's pet, doesn't he? Just bigger. They do well down here."

It was a Burmese Python. The same kind of snake that his roommate had, though this one was larger. Much larger.

He knew that the snakes were thriving in the rich environment of the Everglades. Only a few months ago, the park service had captured one that was over twenty feet long and weighed over three hundred pounds.

"This one hasn't eaten in a while. Now, you've got one last chance to tell me who's giving you the patient information."

Chapter 33

Wednesday morning, on his way to the office, Warren received a text from Trip.

Didn't get FedEx pkg??

He was puzzled. The package should've gotten there Monday. He remembered Sam saying that it was for next day delivery.

He called Trip, and the reporter answered on the first ring.

"Hey, I didn't get a FedEx package. I thought you were sending me something."

"Sam did. I watched him put it in the FedEx box. Are you sure it's not in the mailroom? Maybe it was delivered to the wrong office?"

"I checked. It's a big place, but we're pretty good about not misplacing shit. I even got the clerk to check the receiving log. It was never checked in. Do you have a tracking number or anything?"

Warren didn't answer right away. He was trying to figure out how someone could steal a package from FedEx.

After hanging up with Trip, he called Becky and asked her to check with FedEx. When he got to the office, she started shaking her head as he walked in.

"FedEx sent the package to the *Times*. As you can imagine, they've got a pretty sophisticated tracking system." She looked down at a piece of paper she was holding. "It was picked up from the box Friday at 5:17 p.m. and left Fort Myers at 9:41 p.m. It was signed for in New York 11:22 a.m. Monday at the *Times* office. They sent me a fax with the log and the name of the person who signed for it."

She handed him the fax she was referencing. It was a copy of a manual log, and the signature was illegible. He glanced at it and handed it back. "Send this to Trip. ASAP."

Obviously, someone gave Trip erroneous information. He got to his desk and sat, perplexed. The package had to be somewhere in the building.

Four hours later, Trip called. Apparently, a temp signed for the package at the *Times*. It was entered on a manual log, but never entered into their computerized receiving system. The temp didn't show up for work today, and they hadn't been able to locate him.

Damn, Warren thought. That was everything they had. And no one had a copy, except maybe the person who gathered it for Sam.

He tried to call Sam, but no answer. Thinking he was in a meeting, he sent him a text, and asked him to call ASAP.

By the end of the day, Sam still had not returned his call or text, which was unusual. The doctor was always quick to respond.

He called Micah and asked her if she knew where Sam might be.

"No, funny you ask. I tried to call him earlier today and still haven't heard back from him."

"He didn't go out of town or something, did he?"

"Not that I know of. Why?"

He explained that he'd been trying to get in touch with Sam as well. As soon as he hung up, he called Tabby.

Something was wrong.

Around noon Thursday, Warren looked up from his desk to see Tabby walking in, unannounced. He shut the door behind him and said, "We found Abrams."

"That's great," Warren said, starting to rise. He stopped midway out of his chair. Tabby's trademark grin was pointed the wrong direction, and he was shaking his head. Warren eased back into his chair, waiting for Tabby to deliver the bad news.

"What was left of him. We had to identify him through dental records. Someone went to great lengths to inflict a lot of pain."

Warren dropped his head, his heart lodged in his throat. He looked up at the lieutenant. "Where?"

"A fisherman found him off the Alley yesterday. It took a while to identify him."

He was referring to the desolate section of I-75 that runs through the Everglades and connects Naples to Fort Lauderdale, known as Alligator Alley.

"What happened?"

"Trust me. You don't want to know the details."

"What did they do to him, Tabby?"

The big man exhaled, and seemed to deflate in front of him. "It'll probably come out in the news at some point. The Everglades is a scary place, even scarier with some of the animals that people have dumped there."

He waited for Tabby to continue.

"You know how a python kills its prey?"

Warren gasped. "A python? In the Everglades?"

Tabby nodded. "This one was over twenty foot long. And, according to the wildlife guys, it hadn't eaten in a while. Abrams was partially digested."

"My God."

The image was frightening. He tried to imagine how the man had suffered. He hoped it had been quick.

As if reading his mind, Tabby shook his head and continued. "They prefer to eat live prey."

He felt ill and felt the color drain from his face. He looked at his friend and wondered how anyone could be normal after seeing the things he'd seen. Warren thought he was going to be sick. The image his mind had constructed would haunt him forever.

"Who did it?"

"Don't know, wasn't much to go on." He rubbed his chin with his paw of a hand.

"Why?"

"That's what I wanted to ask you."

His mind was reeling, grasping at the implications. "You don't think it had anything to do with the break-in at my house, do you?"

Tabby shrugged. "I don't believe in coincidences."

"Are you suggesting that the same people behind breaking into my house had Sam Abrams killed?"

"I don't know. But if Abrams was getting patient information, that's a likely scenario. If I was trying to find out where the information was coming from, that's where I'd go. Somebody tortured him for a reason." His phone buzzed. He looked at it, then stuck it back in his pocket.

"I've got to go. I'm sorry, Warren. I wanted to tell you in person. We've kept it from the media, but that won't hold for long."

"I've got to let Micah know."

Tabby nodded. "Better do it soon." He turned to let himself out, then hesitated, turning back to Warren. "Be careful," he said, before walking out.

Warren sat there, stunned. First Dalton, now Abrams. The toll was climbing.

He sat there for a few minutes gathering his thoughts before he called Micah.

"Hey, Micah. Just checking to see if you're working."

"Until three o'clock. Why?"

He looked at his watch. It was only one in the afternoon.

"I've got to run over to the hospital for something. Can you grab a cup of coffee in a few minutes?"

"Probably."

Before she could ask anything else, he said, "Meet you downstairs in fifteen minutes. Gotta run—I've got another call I need to take." He hung up and took a deep breath.

When he got to the hospital, she was downstairs at the coffee shop. Ciel wasn't working, so he just got his coffee and walked over to Micah.

"Can we go outside?" he said.

She gave him a puzzled look. "What's wrong?"

"Let's go outside."

They walked out to the little garden area outside of the cafeteria. It was hot and humid. Since they'd eliminated smoking anywhere on the hospital campus, no one else was out there this time of day.

When they got to a table under an umbrella, providing some relief from the direct sunlight, he asked her to sit down.

He watched her with a heavy heart. She sat as if in slow motion, knowing he had something bad to tell her.

"Sam's gone," he said.

She sucked in a gulp of air, then shook her head, saying, "No. No, please don't tell me that. Please don't."

She reached out and grabbed his arm, squeezing it as if to verify this was indeed real. Her eyes searched his, waiting for the punch line, waiting for him to tell her that he was just out of town.

"I'm sorry. Tabby came by a few minutes ago and told me. They found his body off of Alligator Alley. I wanted to tell you before you heard."

She sniffled, and a tear rolled down her cheek. He sat next to her and she buried her face in his shoulder, the sobs racking her body. He held her, knowing there was nothing he could say to ease the pain.

He handed her a napkin from the table, and they stayed that way for a long time. At last, she looked at him, her blue eyes bloodshot and swollen.

"What happened?"

He thought about what to say to her. How do you answer a question like that? Especially knowing what he did.

"He was murdered. They don't know who, or why."

She started sobbing again. After she calmed down, he walked back upstairs with her. He waited while she told the charge nurse on her unit what had happened. She gathered her things and walked with him down to the employee parking lot.

He took her to her car. He asked if she wanted him to come home with her. When she hesitated, he told her he'd follow her home. She didn't protest.

When they got to her condo, he told her to sit out on the lanai and he'd fix them something to drink. Unfamiliar with where anything was located, he rummaged around until he found a bottle of white wine in the refrigerator. Opening cabinets until he found wine glasses, and drawers until he found the corkscrew, he uncorked the wine and poured them each a glass. He walked out on the lanai, handing her one.

"I don't understand. Why would anyone kill Sam? He was such a gentle man," she said, her cheeks wet with tears.

"I don't know, Micah. I wish I could tell you something, but I just don't know." He shuddered when he thought about what Tabby had told him about the snake. He hadn't mentioned that to her, and didn't plan to do so.

They sat there for several hours, saying little and watching the boats plough up and down the river. Gabe was going home from school with a friend, so he wouldn't be home until eight or so.

Around six, Warren ordered some takeout from the Greek restaurant nearby and had it delivered. Micah hadn't wanted anything, but he insisted on at least getting her a Greek salad, pita chips, and hummus.

"What do I tell Gabe? He loved Sam, too."

Warren shook his head. Gabe was mature for his age, but still this was going to be hard to accept.

Not waiting for Warren to answer, she continued. "I guess I'll tell him that he was killed by some bad people and he's in heaven. That's all I know to tell him."

"I think that's enough. We really don't know too much more, anyway."

"Thanks for coming to tell me. And for coming over here and staying with me. Will you stay till Gabe goes to bed?"

"Sure." He wished he could do something, anything to help ease her pain.

The food on her plate was untouched. She took a sip of wine and gazed out toward the river, a faraway look on her face.

"They killed Sam because he was providing information," she said.

He couldn't tell if she meant it as a statement or a question. He'd not told her about the rest of his conversation with Tabby, waiting for the right time.

"Sam died for nothing," she said. "There is no 'Benefactor.' Benefactor was an underground network started by a doctor here who had terminal cancer. After USCare was enacted, he made it his life's goal for the short time he had left."

"But Sam—"

"Sam perpetuated the myth that Benefactor was this single mysterious person. It served as a deception. It was a red herring."

"But someone was giving Sam information. I saw it. It couldn't have been Sam's patients—he didn't have that many."

She shook her head. "Sam didn't know who was providing him the information."

He was puzzled. Her explanation didn't make sense. She studied him a moment before speaking.

"You still don't get it, do you? *I* set up the initial contact, but it was blind. Sam asked me to recruit a physician on staff at Rivers to help the network. I set up a blind drop, and gave the person instructions on how to set up a new one. I told him to leave information on how to contact him. Sam picked it up, and from that point on, I had no idea on how they communicated. And neither of the two people knew who the other was."

Warren shook his head, the seriousness rolling in like fog, the realization hitting him like a punch from a heavyweight boxer.

"Who—"

"Robert Michaels."

"Robert Michaels? The cardiologist?" For a moment, Warren was confused. What did Michaels have to do— suddenly the pieces fell into place. Now he understood why Lawrence Dalton had asked him about Michaels.

"Michaels was the one getting information for Sam. And you were the only one who knew who the two people were? You were the common connection."

She nodded, tears rolling down her cheek.

"But, since you weren't involved, no one would think to question you?"

She kept nodding, the tears turning into more than a trickle. "That was Sam's intention. He couldn't tell anyone because he didn't know."

The tears were flowing again, and she had this tortured look on her face. He could see where she was going.

"Micah, don't—"

"I'm the reason he's dead."

The sobs broke free. He took her in his arms, and felt her whole body heaving as she cried. "That's not true, Micah," he whispered in her ear. "Sam knew the risk, and he made the choice."

Once she'd calmed down, he called Tabby's cell phone.

When Tabby answered, Warren said, "You've got to find Dr. Robert Michaels. His life may be in danger."

Chapter 34

The next morning at the office, Warren was yawning. Gabe had gotten home a little after seven, and Micah had told him that Sam was dead.

He had the usual ten-year-old kinds of questions, and they patiently talked to him, trying to give him answers to questions that they couldn't answer. Around ten, he fell asleep, and Warren carried him into his bedroom.

Micah had asked him to stay for a nightcap, and he'd obliged. She wanted reassurance that she'd handled things well with Gabe, and he assured her that she had. By the time he'd gotten home and in bed, it was almost midnight.

Tabby had reached Michaels, and gotten officers assigned to watch him and Micah.

"Where are you?" Warren asked Trip the next morning on the phone.

"Atlanta. Why?"

"How long are you going to be there?"

"Until tomorrow."

"Good. Let's have lunch today. I'll call you back." He hung up the phone and called Micah.

"Where are you?" he asked, for the second time in five minutes.

"Home. Why?"

"Where's Gabe?"

"He's down the hall at a friend's. Why are you asking me this? Is everything okay?" Panic was creeping into her voice.

"Just checking. The officer there?"

"Outside my door. He's taking Gabe to school."

"Good. I've got to go to Atlanta. I'll be back late this evening. I'll call on my way back. Don't go anywhere without that cop with you."

Before lunch, Warren took the Lear to DeKalb Peachtree Airport in northeast Atlanta and took a taxi downtown. When he told the driver his destination, the cabbie just laughed. The taxi dropped him off on North Avenue in front of the Varsity, the world's largest drive-in.

It occupies more than two acres of some of the most valuable real estate in Atlanta, the block on North Avenue between I-75/85 and Spring Street. The "hot dog stand," across the expressway from the campus of Georgia Tech, was started in 1928 by a Georgia Tech dropout named Frank Gordy.

Inside, the place was jammed with the normal lunch traffic. "What'll you have, what'll you have" echoed in the crowded room, the usual cry of the workers behind the counter, rushing to take orders.

He looked around, trying to figure out how he was going to find Trip in the shoulder-to-shoulder throng. He heard a familiar voice behind him.

"Don't turn around. Get your lunch and meet me in the CNN room." The rooms were designated by the channel of the large screen televisions on the wall.

He kept his stare focused on the menu board, as if he were trying to figure what he wanted. It was unnecessary, since he already knew.

"What'll you have, what'll you have?" said the woman behind the counter, as she placed a red plastic tray on the stainless steel counter in front of him.

"Two chili dogs, fries, and a Frosted Orange."

In less than a minute, the items were on the tray. He paid, and took the tray toward the room he remembered as the CNN room. The talking heads were chatting on the screen as he entered.

The room was filled with desk seats, similar to a classroom. Most of them were occupied. He saw Trip sitting on the other side, a vacant seat next to him. He made his way over to his friend and sat down. He didn't say anything, waiting for Trip to speak first.

"Thanks for coming, bro. Good to see you."

"You, too. Okay to turn toward you, or not?"

"Better if you don't. I don't think anyone was following you or me, but best not to take a chance. So, what happened to Sam?"

"Someone tortured him to get the identity of Benefactor."

He explained the setup to Trip and how it worked, but didn't supply any names. He was also more than a little vague about the existence of Benefactor.

"Sam tell you all of this?"

Warren nodded, not meeting his friend's stare.

Trip shook his head. "If Sam didn't know who Benefactor was, then how could they get a name from him?"

"Exactly. No one could torture him into giving up Benefactor's identity. They never asked the right questions. Best case is that they only asked him who Benefactor was, and he told them he didn't know, which was the absolute truth. Worst case, they were smarter, and asked for any names, anyone who would lead to Benefactor. Based on what my friend with LCSO told me they did to him, he would have given them his mother's name. Any of us would have."

"What names would he have given them?"

"I told you—names that would lead to Benefactor."

"Which would be . . ."

He pondered on how to answer Trip. Micah had been freaked out, and he knew there was no way she'd ever forgive him if he gave her name or Michaels's name to a reporter.

"I told you, Sam didn't know who Benefactor was."

Trip stuffed a French fry in his mouth and pondered Warren's response, staring at him.

"Yes, you did. But someone introduced him to Benefactor." He let the statement hang in the air as a question.

Warren shifted in his chair.

"What happened to the story? Why did your editor kill it? Someone got to her, didn't they?"

"What she told me is that I needed more proof—which I was supposed to be getting from you and Sam. She decided to make it one blockbuster story instead of two articles."

"Look. The package was stolen from your building. Sam was murdered. You're an investigative reporter. What else do you need?"

He noticed a man sitting two seats away from Trip who seemed to be taking an interest in the conversation. The reporter noticed it as well. Trip turned toward Warren and spoke in a lowered voice.

"Keep your voice down. I need facts. Proof. Right now, all I've got is notes from my conversations with you and Sam. Plus, a little background information I've gathered. Not exactly the kind of stuff that warrants headlines, especially to do a hatchet job on the biggest health insurance company around."

Warren finished his hotdog, and took a sip of his Frosted Orange, a frozen Dreamsicle flavored concoction that he'd not seen anywhere else. The eavesdropper had finished his meal, and was rising to leave.

"I'll do what I can," Warren said. "How do I get it to you?"

"You ever hear of Dropbox?"

"The term or something else?"

"Website. We use it all the time at the paper. It's a secure way to stash electronic info. The government has probably hacked into it, but as long as the stuff isn't related to them, it's relatively safe. I've put everything I've got there. Put anything you get in my box. Don't text me or leave voice messages. The ID is 'tecarter48.' It'll require a password to get to it. Remember that bar in the Village?"

Warren smiled. As many evenings as he and Trip spent in Greenwich Village, he couldn't forget. "I remember the bar well, but I'm not sure I remember too much about what happened there." The bar was O'Keeffe's.

Trip laughed. "I hear you. Anyway, the password is the name of the bar—spelled exactly like they did—plus my birthday. Remember that?"

Again, Warren smiled. Trip was born the same year as him. On February 29.

"I need something to work with. Watch your back, my friend. These people don't play." With that, Trip rose, taking his tray, and emptying the trash. He disappeared through the door.

Warren looked around. Now he felt like everyone in the crowded restaurant was watching him. He walked out and hailed a taxi on Spring Street, telling the driver to take him back to Atlantic Aviation at DeKalb Peachtree Airport.

Mark dialed Micah Rollins's cell phone number. He was spoofing Canterbury School's number, so he knew she'd answer, even though she was at work. As usual, he was on a throwaway phone.

"This is Micah Rollins."

She had a pleasant voice, but there was a question mark after her greeting. Good.

"Ms. Rollins. This is Stephen Hardwick with Canterbury School. Do you have a few minutes?"

"Certainly, Mr. Hardwick. Is anything wrong?"

He smiled. He could hear the worry and concern creeping into her voice.

"Not yet."

He paused to let that sink in before continuing. "Your son, Gabe, is a nice looking boy. I especially like that blue and white shirt he's wearing today at school. Looks better than the usual uniform."

There was a hesitation on the other end, then the voice of an angry, protective mother. "Who is this? Who are you?"

He grinned. Mothers were easy. Now there was a touch of panic in her voice, although she was trying to keep it under control. Perfect.

"Listen carefully. I don't have time to repeat this. Let's just say I'm an acquaintance of the late Dr. Samuel Abrams. I know everything about you and your son. Where you live, what you drive. I even know about the top drawer of your nightstand where you keep your vibrator." He heard her gasp.

"If I wanted to hurt you or Gabe, I could've already done so. What I want is real simple. Keep your mouth shut. Not a word to anyone about this call or about Benefactor or anything involving him. You say a word, and Gabe will pay for it. Understand?"

He heard her trying to catch her breath.

"Answer me, bitch!"

"Yes," she answered, in a meek voice just louder than a whisper.

He ended the call, and called Dr. Robert Michaels.

He'd crafted a similar personalized threat for the doctor he thought was Benefactor. After he delivered it, he wiped the phone clean and pitched it in a trash can on the street corner of downtown Fort Myers.

Later that evening, when Warren saw Micah, she was as white as a sheet, and her hands were shaking.

"What's the matter?"

She looked at him, and there was absolute terror in her eyes. She didn't answer and just shook her head.

He grabbed her shoulders. "What is it? Gabe okay?"

At the mention of her son, she burst into tears, sobbing. He pulled her close, and he could feel her body shaking against him as she wept. Stroking her head, he whispered, "What's the matter, Micah? Please tell me."

She pulled back and looked at him with red eyes. "I can't. He said—he knew—he said . . ." She started crying again, her eyes fearful of something monstrous out there.

"He who?"

"A man called." In between tears, she told him about the phone call she'd received from someone purporting to be from Gabe's school.

He pulled his phone out. "I'm calling Tabby."

Micah snatched the phone out of his hand. "No. You can't."

"Micah, we have—"

Her eyes pleading, she said, "I can't."

She told him what the caller had said, even including that he'd described personal items in her nightstand.

"He's been here in my condo, don't you understand?"

They argued for an hour, with Warren finally agreeing not to say anything. It was against his better judgment, but he wasn't going to risk alienating Micah. He'd have to find another way.

Chapter 35

The co-pilot, standing in the aisle, leaned over and touched Warren's shoulder. "Twenty minutes till touchdown in Salt Lake."

Warren had dozed off on the flight, wondering what he was going to say when he got there. For once, he was walking into a meeting with a major client and he didn't have a clue what he was going to say. He was flying to Utah to meet Clay Fortson at his house in Deer Valley to seek his help.

The story in the *Times* had been his last hope. With the threats Micah had received, he knew she couldn't be involved. She wouldn't even let him tell Tabby what had happened, although he was going to talk to her about doing so when he got back from Utah.

Everywhere he turned, he was thwarted, and had no more options. Clay was his last hope, and Warren hoped the hastily constructed plan he'd devised would meet with the billionaire's approval.

Looking out the window, he could see the Wasatch Mountains as they approached Salt Lake International. They flew just north of the city and when they turned to make their final approach, he could see the Great Salt Lake below.

They touched down, braked, and taxied to the TAC Air general aviation terminal on the east side of the airport. The limo was waiting. After deplaning, Warren handed his overnight bag to the driver and climbed into the car. Soon, they were headed toward the city on the forty-five minute drive to Deer Valley.

On the way, he called Micah. He'd told her he was flying out to Utah to meet with a client, but had left it at that.

"You okay?" he asked when she answered.

"Better, thanks. No more calls. Maybe I can sleep tonight."

"Tabby's guy still—"

"He's here."

"Good. I should be back tomorrow. Get some rest."

"Thanks."

He disconnected the call and realized they were already on the east side of Salt Lake City. He'd been to Clay's house on one other occasion several years ago. It was a massive home, over 15,000 square feet, with seven bedrooms and twice as many bathrooms. It set on top of Bald Eagle Mountain and had a commanding view of the area.

Arriving at the house, the limo was greeted by a valet who opened Warren's door. The limo driver removed the small suitcase from the trunk and handed it to the valet. The valet showed him to his room, and stated that Clay had asked Warren to join him in the library in thirty minutes.

Warren hung up his clothes, changed out of his travel duds and took a quick shower, more to wake him up than anything. He put on pair of chinos, a dress shirt, and a sweater. Checking himself in the mirror before he went downstairs, he adjusted his sweater and slipped on his loafers.

The valet had given him directions to the library, but he still got lost. He ran into the valet, and the young man escorted him to the appointed location. He opened the double doors and escorted Warren inside. The room was magnificent, with a breathtaking view. As he gazed around, it reminded him of the library in the Biltmore House in Asheville.

Clay's library was three stories tall, with glass from floor to ceiling on one entire wall. It overlooked Park City in the fading light. A fireplace occupied one corner, with a small table and two leather chairs. A fire burned there and beckoned. The other three walls were lined with bookshelves, all filled with books.

His gaze came to rest on the wet bar, tucked into a corner of the room opposite the fireplace. The bartender, spotting Warren, made his way over to him.

"May I offer you something?" he asked, in a quiet voice with an accent that Warren placed in South America. "A Macallan, perhaps? Mr. Fortson should be down in a few minutes."

"Yes, that would be nice." The bartender turned and headed back toward the bar, not bothering to ask Warren how he liked it. Warren figured he already knew, since he suggested it. In a few minutes, he returned with the Scotch—neat, and in a Glencairn whiskey glass.

Warren stood at the window, looking out and admiring the view. The Scotch was wonderful. He took a small sip and judged it to be a Macallan 25. He heard the door open behind him and turned to see Clay Fortson coming toward him.

"Warren. Good to see you. How was your trip?" the older man asked, as he greeted him with a firm handshake.

"Just admiring this view. I still think this is my favorite room in the house."

Clay chuckled. "I agree." The bartender appeared with a glass of bourbon on the tray and offered it to his boss. "Thank you, Don," Clay said, taking it from the tray. Warren noticed that Clay's drink was in a plain tumbler.

He saw Warren looking at it and said, "I have the fancy glasses for company. A plain one is good enough for me." He touched his glass to Warren's, and they both took a healthy sip.

"I decided to have dinner in tonight, if that's okay. We're the only ones here, and it'll be quieter."

"Perfect. I'd prefer that."

They stood by the window for a few minutes, chatting about current events. After they finished the first drink, Clay suggested they have one more before dinner, and sit in front of the fire.

As they made themselves comfortable, Don appeared with freshly filled glasses. Warren could feel the warmth of the fire, emanating from the hearth and warming him from the outside while the Macallan did its work from within.

Ever the gentleman, Clay continued the small talk, not wanting to rush things, waiting for Warren to bring up the reason for his visit. A creature of a different era, Warren could restrain himself no longer and started to say something about the purpose of his trip.

Clay held up his hand. "We've got all evening, Warren. I just want to catch up with an old friend, first. I enjoy your company, and I've been here alone for the last couple of days. No hurry to get into things on my account."

Warren smiled, and tried to relax, not wanting to appear rude.

The conversation changed course, and wound its way from one topic to another, in the comfortable way that only old friends can do.

Warren lost track of the time, and was surprised when Don came over and stated that dinner would be ready shortly, if they were ready.

Clay looked at Warren, then back at Don. "Don, why don't you set up a table in here? Seems kinda silly to sit in that big dining room, just the two of us. That okay, Warren?"

Warren nodded, and Don walked away. In a few minutes, two other men came in and set up a small table behind them with two place settings.

They moved, and Don had the two chairs and table they'd occupied shifted so that the view of the fireplace was unobstructed. For dinner, which consisted of potato-cased wild King salmon and asparagus, Don opened a bottle of 1998 Leroy Corton-Renardes Grand Cru, which Warren recognized as a French Burgundy.

Dinner was exceptional, and Warren found himself relaxing and enjoying not only the meal, but Clay's company. He was a remarkable man, and had accumulated an amazing repertoire of stories to regale his friends.

After dinner, they went back to the leather chairs where Don brought them each a snifter of port.

"I need some help, Clay," Warren said, taking a sip of the vintage port and seizing the opportunity.

The old man nodded, not saying a word.

Starting with the accident, Warren told him about Alex and what he'd learned about the health insurance system.

"I started out wanting to know what happened to her. I tried suing Forte, and they squashed that. I wouldn't have won anyway, but, I found out why she didn't get the treatment she needed. Now, I want to keep other people from getting screwed, people who don't know any better."

He told Clay the story about Ciel and her daughter, and also about Micah and Gabe. When Warren finished talking about Lawrence Dalton and Benefactor, he shook his head.

"I tried taking it to the media, but I underestimated Forte's reach. It dawned on me that I need to get them to play my game, and my game is hedge funds." He paused for a moment, then continued. "I want to go after Forte."

Clay nodded. "Why do you need me? You've got, what, twenty billion under management? Why don't you make a play?"

"It's not that liquid, Clay. You know that. Some of my investments are in real estate, and others are committed. I've got probably ten percent I could get my hands on immediately.

"Forte has seven hundred fifty million shares outstanding. Yesterday's close was $60 a share, which gives them a total market cap of somewhere around forty-five billion dollars. Their largest shareholder is Conrad Fischer, who owns thirty-five million shares."

"Interesting. I would've thought their market cap was higher than that."

"That's my point—I think they're vulnerable."

He pulled a sheet of paper out of his pocket that contained a handwritten column of numbers that illustrated his point.

"Everglades can acquire five percent—maybe a little more—at a market premium of between five and ten percent. I know—I've already checked."

Clay studied the sheet. "So you want me to buy ten percent? That still only gets you to fifteen."

Warren nodded and took another sip of port. "I'm hoping you can talk Fischer into voting with us, which gives us twenty percent control. Some of the other institutional investors will go with us. That's enough to swing the board our way."

"You're wanting to make a play for the largest health insurance company in the world?"

"That's right."

The drink, on top of travel and a good meal, was catching up with him, and he felt sleepy. Clay must have noticed, and set his glass down.

"Time for this old man to turn in. You're welcome to stay up if you'd like. Don's here as long as you need him." Clay stood, a little unsteady. "Let me sleep on this, Warren."

Warren finished his port and stood. "I'm beat, and turning in as well. Thanks for listening, Clay."

The old man nodded and tottered out of the room. Warren walked over to the window and stared out. He was drained and exhausted. He felt better, but didn't know if that was a result of the wine or talking to Clay. The lights of Park City twinkled in the near distance.

Nothing he could do now. Tomorrow would tell if he had convinced Clay to help him acquire Forte.

Chapter 36

The sunlight was streaming through his window when Warren awoke the next morning. He had slept soundly. He looked over at the digital clock on the nightstand. 7:14. He didn't feel bad until he realized that was after nine Eastern Standard Time.

After a shower, he made his way to the bar in the massive kitchen, hoping to find coffee. Following his nose, he wasn't disappointed. The sleek, modern Ratio coffee maker sat on the bar, its glass carafe full. Mugs sat on a warming tray next to it.

He poured a cup, and sat on a stool, looking out the massive picture window that framed a cobalt blue sky atop the mountains. Alex would've liked this.

He gritted his teeth, wishing he would stop doing that. He'd planned on asking her to come out for a week this winter to ski. Clay had been after him to use the place, since he rarely came out during the winter. Warren was angry that'd he'd lost her.

His thoughts were interrupted when Don asked him if he needed anything. He hadn't heard the man enter the room.

"No, thanks. Just coffee right now."

"Mr. Fortson is usually in here around seven thirty. We'll be having breakfast then, unless you'd like something before."

"That sounds good, Don. Thank you."

The man left as silently as he arrived. Warren wondered when he slept. He looked just as fresh this morning as he did last night.

"Good morning, Warren. Sleep well?" Clay Fortson asked, as he joined Warren at the counter and poured a cup of coffee.

"Yes, I did, thank you."

Clay took a sip of his coffee. "I know you said you were going back to Florida today, but do you think you could stay out here with me for another day?"

Warren hesitated. He was anxious for Clay's answer and he really wanted to go home today. Although Micah sounded calmer last night, he knew that was just from exhaustion.

Clay continued, "I've been up since five—when you get to be old, it's hard to sleep in. Got a few ideas on your situation, but I need a little more time."

Warren racked his brain, trying to think of an excuse that wouldn't come across as impatient or rude. Coming up empty, he nodded and said, "That'd be nice, Clay. I appreciate your hospitality."

The old man chuckled. "Hell, I get lonely in this place. Glad to have the company. Why don't we have some breakfast, then I've got some work to do. There's another little office downstairs you can use. Got computers and faxes and printers and all that shit you might need. If it's not in there, just let Don know, and he'll get it for you."

After breakfast, Clay excused himself, and Don showed him the office. The room was bigger than Warren's office back in Fort Myers, and had a spectacular view of the Deer Valley ski slopes and Park City. It contained everything he needed and then some.

He called Tabby, but got his voice mail. Warren left a message and called Micah.

"You on your way back?" she asked.

"Clay wants me to stay over one more day."

There was a pause, then, "Oh, okay."

He could hear the disappointment in her voice. "I'll be back tomorrow, for sure. It's just taking longer than I anticipated."

"I understand. I've got to go. Let me know when you are on your way home."

"I will."

He pressed End and sat there, staring out the window. One more thing he had no control over—the list was getting longer—but hopefully it'd be worth it.

He worked all morning, and around noon, Don came in and asked what he wanted for lunch. Clay was busy and unable to join him, but dinner was set for seven this evening in the library.

"You know," Warren said, "I'd really like a hamburger—and some fries."

"Certainly. We've got some nice, grass-fed bison. How would you like it prepared?"

Warren thought a minute. "Medium-rare, with blue cheese, lettuce, tomato, and Dijon mustard."

"It will be ready in thirty minutes. Would you like to eat here, or—"

"Could I have it in the kitchen? At the counter? I like that room. It's cozy."

Don smiled. "Certainly. That happens to be Mr. Fortson's favorite spot for lunch as well."

A half hour later, Warren found his way back to the kitchen and sat at the counter. Don, wearing an apron, had just plated the fries and set the plate in front of him. The burger was cooked perfectly, and the fries were obviously hand-cut.

"You're a man of many talents, Don."

"Thank you. I've worked for Mr. Fortson for fourteen years."

Warren raised his eyebrows and nodded. He took a bite of his burger. It was delicious. Several bites later, he complimented Don. "I honestly think this is the best burger I've ever had."

"Thank you. The bison comes from a ranch here in the valley."

Warren finished, eating every morsel of the scrumptious meal. He asked Don if it would be possible to take a walk to stretch his legs a bit.

Don left to fetch a map with instructions, and returned with a highlighted document showing a one mile, two mile, and five mile trail within Deer Valley.

The mountain air was brisk and clear. Although Warren was in good shape, the eight thousand foot altitude made breathing difficult for someone accustomed to sea level. He completed the two mile loop, and arrived back at the house an hour later.

That evening at dinner, Clay said, "I gave your proposition a lot of thought. Spent some time today going through the numbers."

Warren stopped chewing and held his breath.

"I appreciate your predicament, but . . . ." He paused and took a long sip from his wine glass. "I'm having a hard time justifying it from a business perspective."

Warren was devastated. He thought sure Clay would be willing to help.

"But, Clay. The stock is trading at sixty, which is a little low based on their earnings. It should be around seventy. You've got to admit, that's a pretty tidy profit."

"It's a sixty dollar stock, based on their current model. You gut that model, and it's maybe a forty dollar stock, not a sixty dollar stock anymore."

Warren closed his eyes and shook his head.

"At thirty, I'd buy a trainload of it. Not at sixty," Clay said. "I'm sorry."

Without Clay's investment, there was no way he could pull it off. And, he hated to admit, Clay was right. If Forte's model changed, it probably wouldn't be worth anywhere near sixty dollars a share.

"I may have another option," Clay said. "Your Micah— how well do you know her?"

Warren considered the question, and answered, "Pretty well. Why?"

"You know who her father was, don't you?"

He nodded. "She told me the story of their relationship."

Clay arched his eyebrows, waiting for him to continue.

He told him what Micah had shared with him.

"Did she mention anything about a trust?"

Warren squinted, and shook his head.

Clay proceeded to tell him that a blind trust had been set up for the grandson. Just before he died, Micah's father had established a blind trust with an attorney in New York as the trustee.

"Gabe has a trust?" Micah had never mentioned this to him. He wondered why not.

"My sources tell me that his mother probably doesn't even know about it. Old man Rollins wanted it that way. He didn't want people fawning over him just for the money."

He didn't understand, and Clay sensed his confusion.

"You're a wealthy man, Warren. But when you end up with as much money as I have, it can also be a burden. You learn not to trust anyone, especially family. They're the worst. You should go to a probate hearing sometime for a rich man. Damndest drama you'll ever see. Everyone jockeying for a piece of the pie. Beats the hell out of one of those reality shows.

"I don't know his reasons, but I can understand why he'd do it. I've done the same thing, though Jeb doesn't know it."

"What does Gabe's trust have to do with my problem?"

Clay grinned. "More than you might think. It contains a sizeable chunk of Forte stock."

The next day, flying back to Fort Myers, Warren called Micah, asking her to come over to his house that evening after he returned.

Shortly after he arrived, Micah drove up.

"Where's Gabe," he asked when he opened the door. He'd told her to bring Gabe along.

"A neighbor down the hall is babysitting. He hadn't finished his homework, and I didn't want to bring him out."

He was disappointed. He led her out to the lanai, asking if she wanted anything to drink. "I've ordered takeout from Greek Islands."

She asked for a glass of wine. He opened a bottle of Sancerre and poured two glasses.

"How was your trip?" she asked.

"Okay," he said, taking a sip of wine. "Learned a lot."

"Like what?" Micah asked.

"Like your father left Gabe a trust fund." Micah's shocked look told him she didn't know about it, and he was relieved to know that she hadn't been keeping secrets from him.

"Are you sure? I've never heard—"

"It was a blind trust, and he never intended for you or Gabe to know about it until he reaches eighteen. Apparently, that's not unusual for the ultra-wealthy."

"What does it mean?" Micah asked.

"For starters, you and Gabe are set—financially."

She pondered that and nodded. "That's good. What else?"

"The trust includes a substantial amount of Class A shares of Forte stock."

He went on to explain about classes of stock, and how the Class A shares of Forte stock had the real power—votes. The shares traded publicly were the Class B shares—widely traded, but no votes.

"In essence, Gabe will end up with a controlling share of Forte stock."

She looked at him, excitement in her eyes. "That's awesome. So does that mean we can control—"

He held up his hand. "Gabe's ten years old. Eighteen is a long way off." Her grin turned into a frown.

"I've asked my friend Tim, an attorney who specializes in estate planning, to review the trust document and see if there's any provision for accelerating the timetable."

"What if there's no way to do that?" Micah asked.

Warren shook his head. "I don't know." He didn't tell her that Clay Fortson had refused to invest in Forte stock. Right now, all of their hopes were riding with a ten-year-old boy who was at the babysitter's doing his homework.

Tim called the following afternoon. "Can you come over to my office?"

"Sure." Tim hardly ever requested a meeting at his office. Most of their business had been conducted at Barney's or on a boat. "Four okay?"

"See you then."

Tim's office was only a few blocks away, so Warren walked. He got off the elevator on the sixth floor, and walked in. The receptionist, an attractive young girl with long blonde hair, asked him to have a seat while she called Mr. McLaughlin. Before he could find a seat, Tim walked out.

"Hi, Warren. Come on back."

He followed his friend back to his office. Although a partner, Tim had a rather modest office, overlooking the river and downtown Fort Myers. Tim shut the door behind them, and walked over to the conference table and sat.

"It's either real good, or real bad," Warren said, as he pulled out a chair and sat.

Tim smiled, but it was forced. "Not good, I'm afraid." He opened the folder in front of him, and pulled out a page of handwritten notes.

Warren's heart sank.

Tim looked at the paper, but Warren knew his friend well enough to know that he didn't need to do so. It was the classic *breaking the bad news* scene.

Tim cleared his throat and spoke. "Gabriel Rollins didn't leave much wiggle room—in fact, none. And— unfortunately for us—he had a damn good attorney draw up the trust." He set the paper back on top of the folder.

"I'm sorry, Warren. This trust is bulletproof. You could challenge it, but in my opinion, you'd be wasting your time and money."

He looked out the window. A sailboat, sails furled, was motoring down the river, headed for the Gulf and parts unknown. Warren wished he was on board. God, he hated to lose. Especially to the likes of Blaine Harris and Pete Manning.

But this was worse. This wasn't about him losing. It was about Alex losing. And Ciel. And Micah. An exceptional attorney lost his life. And a brilliant physician. All of it sucked. And he was powerless to stop it.

He was out of cards. Game over.

"Did you hear me?" Tim was saying.

Warren shook his head. "Sorry. What?"

"I asked if you wanted to go down to Barney's and get a beer? My treat."

He got up to leave, and shook his head once. "No, thanks. Some other time. Thanks for trying, Tim. I appreciate it." He turned and walked out of the office.

Instead of walking back to his office, he walked down to Harborside Park and sat on a bench. It was in the shade of a group of palm trees and faced the river. Boats of all shapes and sizes plied the waterway in front of him. For once, his brain was in full neutral. He wasn't thinking about next steps, or analyzing what had happened. It was as blank as the cloudless blue sky above.

He didn't hear the person coming up behind him. He felt a hand on his shoulder. Surprised, he turned.

"Mind if I join you," Micah said. She didn't wait for his response. She came around and sat on the bench next to him.

"I tried to call," she said.

"I turned my phone off."

"That bad, huh? Becky said you might be here. She said you come here sometimes to think."

He couldn't think of anything else to say.

"So tell me. What's the bad news?"

He looked back out to the river. "The trust is ironclad."

"I'm not surprised. My father wouldn't have been that sloppy. Not when it came to money."

They sat there for a few minutes in silence, watching the boats on the water.

She broke the ice. "Clay wouldn't invest in Forte, would he?"

He shook his head, unable to look her in the face. "I'm sorry, Micah."

She touched his chin with her hand, turning his face toward hers. Her brow was wrinkled and she looked displeased. "Sorry? What are you sorry for? Giving it your best effort? Busting your hump to help me, Gabe, and the others?"

She moved her hand to his arm and shook her head. "I can't accept that, and I won't let you do that to yourself. You're a good person, Warren. You tried to do the right thing."

He looked in her eyes, and all he could see was good. She wasn't just saying the words, she believed them.

At that moment, he realized the important thing was she believed in him. And he couldn't let her down.

Chapter 37

Warren knew it was a long shot, but he and Micah had stayed up past midnight, working out the details. Convincing her had not been easy. It was the only thing left he knew to try, and he wasn't going down without swinging.

Clay's comment about buying a trainload of Forte stock if it was at thirty had given him an idea. Maybe there was a way after all.

He picked up the phone and called Trip.

"What's shaking in Florida, my friend?"

"I have a proposition for you."

There was a slight hesitation on the other end.

"Talk to me."

"I want you to go to your editor and ask if she'll reconsider running the insurance story."

"Tell me why—"

"I can give you access to Benefactor."

He'd talked with Micah, and she'd agreed to his plan, if and only if the *Times* was willing to run the story.

"You've got my attention."

"Exclusive access—direct access." He was careful not to give away too much. He wanted Trip to take the hook.

"You've piqued my curiosity. But how do I know it's the real thing? Before, you didn't know who this mysterious 'Benefactor' was and now you can give me exclusive access? Sorry, my friend, but it smells a little off."

He decided to take another tack. "Look, what do you have to lose? All I want you to do is ask. If she agrees, you get access and you decide if it's the real thing. No harm, no foul, right?"

There was hesitation on the other end. Trip was thinking it through, nibbling on the bait.

"No promises on our end, right?"

Warren smiled. Now was the time to play his hole card.

"Your call. Just act in good faith. But, you heard it here first—this is a Pulitzer-caliber story. If you turn it down, I'm taking it to the *Washington Post*."

He hung up the phone and breathed a sigh of relief. Trip had taken the bait. Now, he had to wait and see if Trip could sell it to his editor. He was counting on his friend to succeed. The whole plan depended on it.

That evening, his cell phone buzzed. It was Trip.

"What's up, New York?" Warren said, trying to be casual.

"How soon can I see Benefactor?"

The next morning, Becky met Warren at his house, and they drove to Micah's condo. Micah and Gabe were packed and ready when they arrived. Micah was nervous about going forward, but Warren had assured them they'd be fine.

They drove out to Base Operations at Page Field, where Warren kept his jet. The general aviation airport, formerly the main airport in Fort Myers, was convenient to downtown and only a few minutes away from Micah's condo.

Gabe was excited. His mom had told him that they were flying to New York City on a private jet, and he had hardly slept last night.

They parked and went in to the terminal, where the co-pilot was waiting for them. The Lear was parked out on the ramp next to the building, the pilot standing in the door.

They walked outside and up the steps into the sleek jet. Gabe was asking one question after another. He was fascinated at the beverage center in the galley, the first thing he spotted walking into the cabin. Chip, the pilot, was laughing at the child's enthusiasm, and offered to give him and his mom a quick tour while the co-pilot finished the pre-flight checklist.

"Thanks for coming along, Becky," Warren said, as they settled into their seats. Becky sat in the seat across the aisle from Warren, leaving the seats facing them vacant. With only two seats abreast, everyone had a window.

She gave him an incredulous look. "You're kidding, right? A trip to New York, on a private jet, with nothing to do but show a ten-year old the sights? Throw me into that briar patch anytime," she said, laughing.

Becky had lived in Manhattan, so she was familiar with the city. She was also good with kids, and made a good tour guide for Gabe.

Micah and Gabe came back from their tour. Becky patted the seat opposite her, asking Gabe to sit there so she could get to know him on the way up. Holding a Coke he'd conned out of Chip, he jumped in the seat, and she helped him fasten his seat belt as he looked out the window.

Micah sat down across from Warren.

"Thank you for doing this," he said.

"We're doing it for Sam—and all the others." Her eyes welled up when she said his name. She looked at Gabe, who was talking and pointing out the window, already fast friends with Becky. "It's worth it for him."

Two hours later, they landed in Teterboro. A car was waiting to take them into the city, where the driver dropped Warren and Micah off in front of the *New York Times* building on Broadway.

At the reception area, they waited for Trip, who came down to meet them.

He could tell Trip was surprised, but he said nothing in the lobby as Warren introduced him to Micah. They made their way upstairs to a small conference room that Trip had reserved for them.

They settled in and after everyone had their coffee, Trip could no longer resist.

"You're Benefactor?" he said.

Micah smiled and looked at Warren before looking back at Trip. "Not expecting a woman?" she replied, without answering his question.

Trip stumbled over his faux pas and tried to make amends while Micah let him suffer for a few minutes. Warren was enjoying the show, and couldn't help but laugh at his friend.

At last, she shook her head. "There is no Benefactor."

Trip smiled, then realized she was serious. His smile turned into a serious frown and he looked at Warren. "What do you mean, there's no 'Benefactor?' You told me—"

"I told you, and I quote, 'I'd give you access to Benefactor.' Those were my exact words."

"But, you let me—"

Warren held his hand up. "Don't panic. I'm giving you what I said. Listen to what she has to say. As you are wont to remind me, 'you're a reporter.'"

They spent the rest of the day leading Trip through the 'Benefactor' persona, with Micah sharing copies of documents that she and Sam had accumulated. Trip was so impressed, he took them upstairs to meet his executive editor.

While Micah had excused herself, Trip whispered to Warren, "Nice looking lady. Sharp, too. Very impressive."

"I told you she was the real deal," he said, oblivious to Trip's intimation. "Is your editor going to run it?"

Trip laughed. "I neglected to tell you. She was going to run it anyway. She only pulled it because 60 Minutes was doing a piece on the coal industry that weekend, and she didn't want our story to compete with theirs."

Warren stared at his friend. "You son of a—"

Trip held up his hands. "Hey, you only asked me to ask her, right?"

He thought about it. "So, nobody got her to kill the story?"

"Nope. She said she'd gotten pressure, but it didn't influence her decision. I believe her. She's a tough cookie, and like I told you, big names have tried before to intimidate her."

The conference room door opened, and Micah walked back in.

"How much longer?" she asked.

Trip looked up at the clock on the wall. "Maybe another hour. That should do it for today. I may have some more questions when I do the draft. Khaleesi wants to run it next Sunday," he said, comparing his executive editor to the Mother of Dragons in *Game of Thrones*.

"That soon?" Warren said.

Trip shrugged. "I had most of it done. Just a matter of updating it based on my interview with 'Benefactor' today."

Warren looked at Micah and smiled. *Time to implement phase two,* he thought.

Becky and Gabe showed up around five, and Trip had an intern give them all a tour of the *Times* while he went to work on the article.

When they got ready to leave, Warren found Trip at his computer, papers scattered all over the desk. It looked like a tornado had touched down.

"You going to be able to join us for dinner?" Warren asked.

Trip looked at his clock. "Maybe a quick bite. Where are you going?"

"Dina's?"

He nodded. "What time? I'll just meet you there, so I can come back and work on this."

"Six? It'll have to be quick, because we've got an eight o'clock curtain."

"Works for me." Trip turned back to his computer screen. "See you later."

Warren had booked three rooms at the Intercontinental. They went over and checked in, then strolled over to Times Square as dusk was falling.

Gabe had not stopped talking the entire time. Becky had taken him to the Empire State Building, Central Park, Rockefeller Center, and of course, Times Square.

Trip had arranged second row seats for *The Lion King* that evening. They had a quick bite at Dina's, then walked over to the Minskoff Theatre on West 45th. Gabe had insisted on sitting between his mother and Becky, his new best friend. Warren let everyone go in first when they got to their seats, so he ended up sitting next to Micah.

Gabe was mesmerized by the production. Warren hadn't seen it, but had to admit, it was enchanting. Micah was happy, and poked Warren a couple of times during the show to look at Gabe, sitting on the edge of his seat, eyes wide open, and mouth matching.

On the way back to the hotel, Gabe was yawning.

"I think he's finally tired," Micah whispered to Warren.

They were all on the same floor. Micah and Gabe had one room, Becky was next door to them, and Warren was across the hall. Gabe yawned, tugging on his mother's hand. After agreeing to meet for breakfast in the morning, everyone said goodnight, and retired to their rooms.

Once inside, Warren switched on the television, then shed his clothes. He hung his slacks and draped his shirt over the back of one of the chairs, then went to the bathroom to get ready for bed. After finishing his nightly routine, he climbed into bed, stacking the pillows behind his back. He picked up the remote and started surfing through the channels, spending a couple of minutes each on the few that he found interesting.

Settling on what appeared to be a documentary of sorts, he eased under the covers and turned the nightstand light down to its lowest level. He'd just settled in when he heard a knock at the door. *Probably room service,* he thought, *at the wrong room.* He slipped on a pair of boxers and went to the door.

When he opened it, he was surprised to see Micah standing there, holding a bottle of port and two wineglasses. She was barefoot and wearing scrubs.

Holding up the bottle of wine, she said, "Thought you might be interested in a nightcap. Not a stellar vintage, but this was the best I could do at this hour."

"Uh, sure. Come in," he mumbled. He was conscious that he was wearing nothing but boxers, but she didn't seem to notice.

She stepped inside and he closed the door behind her. He got a faint whiff of perfume as she passed, a scent he recognized from earlier in the evening.

"What are you watching?" she asked, looking at the television.

He shifted his gaze from her to the television, trying to recall what was on.

"Nothing," he said. "Nothing really. I just turned it on for background noise."

She nodded, then walked over and set the wine and glasses on the small table by the window. Turning to his bed, she picked up the remote and switched the television off. After placing the remote on the nightstand, she removed the cork from the wine and poured a few fingers of port into each of the glasses. With only the dim light from his nightstand on, he could swear she wasn't wearing anything under her scrubs.

She turned around holding the partially filled glasses and saw him still standing by the door.

"I don't bite. I promise," she said, laughing, and holding up a glass for him.

He shook his head and walked over, taking the glass from her.

As she touched her glass to his, she said, "To a wonderful evening with a delightful host in my favorite city."

He took a bigger swallow than normal, trying to settle his nerves. She sat in one of the chairs at the table, and patted her hand on the tabletop, indicating for him to sit and join her.

Seeming to read his mind, she said, "Mine and Becky's rooms are adjoining. Gabe is sound asleep. I opened the door between and asked Becky if she would mind keeping an ear out for him while I came over."

He blushed as he thought of what was running through Becky's mind. And his.

Micah smiled. "She said it was fine, that it would do you good." Micah took a sip of her wine and looked out the window. "What a beautiful view."

Looking back at him, she said, "Thank you for a very nice evening." She wrinkled her face as she studied him. "Are you okay? You haven't said a word since I came in. Would you rather I leave?"

"No," he answered, a little too quickly.

She smiled, not missing his prompt response.

"I'm just . . ." He shook his head.

"Yes?"

"I'm glad you're here."

She laughed, but this time it was a gentle laugh. "Good. I was beginning to wonder."

Now it was his turn to chuckle. "I'm just feeling a little self-conscious, sitting here in nothing but . . ." He glanced down at his lap.

She shrugged. "I'm a nurse—I don't pay any attention to that. Anyway, I've seen you in your swim trunks, remember?"

He could feel the warmth of the port, and his nervousness was beginning to dissipate. He shrugged. "It's just not fair. I mean, I've seen you in a bikini, but you're wearing way more than that now."

She smiled, but it was a devilish grin. "Did you like what you saw?"

His mouth was getting dry and he swallowed, hard. "Very much."

She finished her wine, licked her lips, and said, "So, what are you going to do about it?"

He awoke the next morning with daylight streaming through the window. He inhaled the hazy fragrance of another person. Micah. He shifted and realized she was lying in his arms. The rumpled sheet was over them, the only thing covering their bodies. Memories of the evening flooded over him, and he couldn't help but grin.

She opened her eyes, blinked, and looked at him.

"Good morning," she said, a smile appearing.

"Yes, it is," he answered.

Chapter 38

Warren slowed the boat as he approached. The boat he was looking for was anchored behind Sanibel in Tarpon Bay. He glanced around, and no other boats were nearby.

He'd not told Micah about this part of the plan, knowing she wouldn't have approved. She'd agreed to talk to Trip, believing in the sole power of a front page article in *The New York Times*. Warren wasn't that trusting.

He pulled alongside the other boat, port side to port side, so they were pointed in opposite directions. As expected, there was only one person in the other boat, watching him as he eased closer. The man was shirtless, wearing a ragged Winchester cap and holding a faded blue foam can cooler that Warren knew contained a cold beer. A cigarette dangled from his mouth.

He set his beer on the helm, then held his hand out toward Warren. Warren tossed him a line and he secured it so the boats were lashed together.

"Can I offer you a beer?"

"No thanks. I'm good."

Garrett Thomas picked up his beer and took a drink while eyeing him. "Long time since we've been fishing. This used to be our favorite spot."

"Yeah, we caught a lot of fish here. And drank our share of beer, too. I miss those days," Warren said. "I appreciate you coming." He hesitated before continuing. "I'll get to the point. I'm going to tell you how you can make some serious money. Fast."

"Always interested in serious money. Especially when it's quick."

"Short as much Forte Insurance as you can, as quickly as you can. It's selling for sixty. It's going to half that. You'll know when to pull the trigger."

Garrett finished off his beer, slid the empty out of the cooler, crushed the can, and threw it in the ice chest by his feet. He reached down, brought another out, and popped the top, replacing the foam insulation around it.

"You sound sure. Easy to sound confident with someone else's money."

Shorting was a risky investment strategy, not for the faint of heart. A million shares at sixty dollars a share would cost $60,000,000. Going short meant that the investor was in effect borrowing stock he didn't own and promising to cough up the shares later. If the price fell, the investor could replace it with cheaper stock, pocketing the difference. The risk was that if the stock rose, the investor would have to replace it with more expensive shares.

In this case, if Warren's predication came true, Garrett Thomas stood to make nearly $30,000,000, a fifty-percent return in a matter of weeks. If he was wrong, the penalty was severe. A ten-dollar-a-share increase would cost $10,000,000.

Warren handed him a Ziploc bag. Garrett held it up to apprise the contents, then looked at him. He didn't even open the bag.

"Looks like Eurodollar bonds."

Eurodollar bonds were one of the few bearer bonds left. Unregistered, they were payable to whoever happened to possess them.

Warren nodded. "Ten million dollars' worth, to be exact. You hold them. If what I tell you doesn't come true, they're yours. Otherwise, I expect to get them back."

Garrett chuckled. "Damn, if you don't have big, brass ones. Always did. What do you want out of this?"

"After you cover the short, I want you to buy enough stock in Forte to get you at least one seat at the table. And go long—it'll pay off—you'll see. You'll have to move quickly. Once you cover, you'll have maybe a week before the price goes up. If you're not convinced, then hang on to those bonds."

Garrett wrinkled his face, took off his cap and rubbed his head. "Why the hell would you want a seat on the board of Forte?"

"I don't. I want you to make sure that the person I name gets it. That's all."

"All this and the only thing you want out of it is a board seat for someone else? That's a lot of work and a big risk for that. Don't suppose it'd do me any good to ask how you know all this?"

He smiled and shook his head. "The less you know the better."

Garrett studied him for a few seconds, then tossed the Ziploc back over to him.

"I don't need this. I've pissed away more than that in my life. My call, my money. I know you. If you're willing to put it up for no gain for yourself, that's all I need to know. Who's the person?"

"Robert Michaels. Doctor Robert Michaels. He's local. A good man, and he won't embarrass you."

Garrett nodded.

"You know I'm going to catch a lot of flak?"

Warren nodded. "That's why we had to meet like this. I don't care what kind of story you make up—that's up to you. Say it was a hunch or whatever. Much as I enjoy your company, we can't have any contact for a while. Not until everything settles. And I can never handle your money again."

Garrett studied him for a minute while he polished off another beer. "I figured something was up when you had Paco deliver the message about meeting out here. Didn't figure you for this, though. You've always been a straight arrow. Not like me."

The words cut more than the man realized. Warren swallowed hard. "Not the way I wanted this to play out. Sometimes a man's got no choice."

"A man always has a choice. Sometimes there's just not a good one." Garrett untied the line and tossed it to him.

Pete Manning and Blaine Harris were seated in the forward seats of the Gulfstream passenger cabin, on their way to New York for a last minute meeting with the debenture issuer. The back of the plane was full of suits, going through reams of paper, crossing T's and dotting I's.

Pete stared out the window. He looked calm, Blaine thought. His boss turned to him, and said, "You did a good job containing that mess in Florida, Blaine. I'm not sure how you do it, but you always come through in the clutch. I don't know what I'd do without you."

Blaine smiled, accepting the accolades. That one had been a bitch. One of the toughest he'd had to deal with since working at Forte. Killing the story at the *Times* was the coup de grace. He didn't think he was going to pull that off, but thanks to a couple of compromising photographs that Mark had managed to acquire, it became a reality. It was a one-time play, but that was all he needed.

"Excuse me." A tall, gray-haired man stood in the aisle next to them. It was Tony Grayson, the CFO of Forte.

"Have a seat, Tony," Pete said, nodding toward the vacant seat opposite him. "You look like you have the weight of the world on you? Your dog die?"

Tony shook his head. "Bad news. There's a lot of unusual activity in our stock this morning."

Blaine's ears pricked up.

Tony continued. "Somebody's shorting big blocks of our stock."

Pete frowned, his good mood evaporating. "Why?"

"Not sure. Could just be a hedge fund manager gambling the bond issue is not going to sell. Or a classic case of 'short and distort.'"

Now, Pete's look turned into one of apprehension, as if watching a car about to go off of a cliff. "That's absurd. Anything on the wire?"

"Not yet," Tony answered.

Blaine had a sick feeling in the pit of his stomach. Hedge fund managers were notorious for shorting stocks, then releasing negative news about the company, hoping the stock price would drop. The strategy was called short and distort. They would also short stock if they knew of any pending bad news. Pete was asking if any negative news had appeared on the news wire. Tony didn't make mistakes like this.

"Who?" Blaine asked Tony.

Tony shrugged. "We've got our people trying to find out. Most of the shares are being bought in street name, so it's difficult to see who's behind it."

A young lady tapped Tony on the shoulder, handed him a sheet of paper, and left. He read it and looked at Pete. "Garrett Thomas."

"Garrett Thomas? Who the hell is that?" Pete asked.

Blaine squeezed his cheeks with his hand. Not many people on this plane knew who Garrett Thomas was. While not quite in the same club as Warren Buffett and Bill Gates, he was still in the one percent of the one percent. Real fuck-you money.

Garrett Thomas had been one of Warren Thompson's biggest clients. Blaine had gotten Mark to call Thomas, posing as a reporter, knowing that the call would prompt the reclusive billionaire to close his account with Everglades. Less than a week later, Thomas had done exactly that.

This was too much of a coincidence. It had Thompson's handwriting all over it. Now he knew who was really behind it.

"He's a billionaire who lives in Fort Myers. Owns a lot of land in southwest Florida. Big developer," Tony said.

Pete looked puzzled. "So, he's not a hedge fund manager?"

Tony shook his head.

"Do we have anyone who knows this guy?" He looked at Blaine, who shook his head.

Pete picked up the phone and dialed his assistant's number. "Get me a number for Garrett Thomas." He hung up and turned his attention back to Blaine and Tony.

"I'll get this straightened out. There's got to be an explanation for this."

Blaine took a deep breath. There was an explanation alright, but not one Pete wanted to hear. He figured he'd keep his mouth shut for the moment. Maybe it was something else. He hoped he was wrong.

A few minutes later, Pete's phone rang. "Yes?" he said, when he snatched up the phone. His face turned angry and red. "What do you mean, he doesn't have a number?" Pete's voice went up an octave. "Everybody has a fucking number. I pay you to get me information, so get it. Find a way to get in touch with the man." He slammed the phone down, venom in his eyes.

He slammed his fist against the side of the plane, causing everyone to jump. "Son of a bitch, who does he think he is? Tony, what can we do to block this?"

Tony adjusted his tie, uncomfortable to be the one under the gun. "He's doing this on the open market. Nothing's required if someone buys stock that way."

"Well, dammit, figure something out. Don't just stand there."

"Yes, sir," Tony said, walking away, glad to be out from under the glare of the spotlight for a moment.

Blaine steeled himself, knowing he was next.

"Blaine, what the hell is going on? I thought you had this under control?"

He started to say, *I don't have any control over someone who's one of the wealthiest persons in the world, and neither do you,* but he thought the wiser of it. "I'm as surprised as you. I'll get on the phone and see what I can find out."

Pete smirked. "That'd be nice. Why don't you do that?"

Blaine got up to retreat to the back of the plane to make a few calls. He sat next to Tony.

The CFO looked suicidal. "Hell, Blaine, there's nothing we can do. If a rich son of a bitch wants to short Forte stock on the open market, there's not a damn thing we can do about it. I know that's not what Pete wants to hear, but—"

"I know that. But, you better come up with a better story than that. You know how he is."

"What's going on with Forte's stock?"

Warren had expected the call from Trip. "Don't know. I haven't been paying attention."

"Garrett Thomas—one of your former clients, I'm told—is shorting Forte. To the tune of millions of dollars' worth."

"Really?" There was a silence on the line, as Trip waited for him to say something else. When he didn't, Trip plowed ahead.

"What's going on?"

"Look, Trip. Garrett Thomas closed his account with me months ago." He clicked on the keyboard as if he were looking it up, although he didn't need to do so. "Back in June, to be precise. His entire account. I haven't talked to him since, and I have no idea what he's up to. Frankly, I don't care."

"Has the exchange contacted you, yet?" Trip was referring to the investigative arm of the New York Stock Exchange, where Forte's stock was listed.

"No, and if they do, I'll tell them the same thing I just told you. I have nothing to hide."

"I hope so. For your sake. By the way, I talked to Khaleesi this morning. The article's coming out Sunday."

"Great. Can't wait to read it."

Chapter 39

Blaine watched as Tammy opened the door and bent over to pick up the Sunday *Times*. The sheer, green babydoll left little to the imagination, especially since she wasn't wearing panties. He'd just shaved her earlier, so she had no cover at all. *Nice,* he thought.

She was his newest fling, an intern from Alabama. She wasn't the sharpest knife in the drawer, but she was model-gorgeous with an incredible body, and insatiable in bed. With those qualities, he was willing to overlook the fact that she was not exactly a Rhodes Scholar candidate.

She shut the door and walked back over to him, holding the paper in front of her generous chest to tease him. As she slowly lowered the newspaper to the table, he could see her nipples, highly visible through the wispy material. *Thank God for Viagra*, he thought.

She sashayed over to the coffee pot and refilled his mug, sitting across from him and picking up her *People* magazine she'd been reading when he asked her to get the paper. She may not have excelled in college, but she knew her assets and how to work them to her advantage. Tammy was destined for big things in life.

He forced his eyes down to the paper, and unfolded it, first sneaking another peek at the blonde goddess across from him. The headline was like a bucket of ice-cold water dumped over his head. He blinked twice to make sure he wasn't seeing things.

Health Insurance-Not What You Think

Front page, above the fold, Sunday's paper. The article was attributed to Trip Carter.

"What the fuck?" He unfolded the paper and started reading.

When his phone rang, he wasn't surprised. When he didn't answer, Tammy looked up from her magazine and said, "You want me to get that, baby?"

He shook his head.

Sensing something was amiss, she put her magazine down and walked over behind him, putting her arms around his neck. Her long, blonde hair tickled his face. Whispering in his ear, she said, "What's wrong, baby? Maybe I can make it better." One of her hands started down his chest, and he could feel her pressing her breasts against his shoulders.

He brushed her aside, and he rose from his seat. All desire for an encore had evaporated. "Time for you to go. I've got work to do today."

"I can come back later," she said, not willing to throw in the towel yet.

"We'll see." He turned and brushed by her, walking over to the window of his penthouse apartment.

She pouted, but could tell he wasn't in the mood to play. She walked out and went into the bedroom to get dressed.

He closed his eyes and massaged his forehead with his hand, trying to stop the headache that was creeping in. Successful for the moment, he looked out the window. The city was just beginning to wake. It was cloudy, and a layer of smog hung over the area. It was going to be a long day.

He poured himself a tumbler of vodka and choked down three Advil.

The fourth time his phone rang after Tammy left, Blaine answered.

"Where the hell have you been? I've been trying to reach you."

The screaming voice of Pete Manning grated on his ears like fingernails on a chalkboard, despite the Advil and glass of vodka. He held the phone at a distance as Pete continued his tirade.

"You told me you'd taken care of everything. What are you doing about this? I need answers, Blaine. *Now*."

"I'm on it, Pete. I don't—"

"I want you at my house in an hour."

You've got to be fucking kidding me, Blaine thought. Pete had a place in the city, but his house was out in Sagaponack, three hours by car.

"Pete, it's three hours—"

"I don't give a damn if you have to steal a helicopter. You be here in an hour."

The next thing Blaine heard was a click, indicating that Pete had disconnected the call.

He poured himself another vodka tonic—minus the tonic—as he called the car service to arrange for transportation.

"You see the paper?" Trip said.

Holding his cell phone, Warren grinned from ear to ear and looked over at Micah. Gabe was down on the dock, fishing. They had just finished breakfast, and Warren had read the article twice, savoring it before giving it to Micah to read.

"Every word. Twice. You did a good job on it. This should send the rats scurrying."

Trip chuckled. "My phone's been ringing off the hook. Thank Micah for me, will you?"

"Will do. She's reading it now. Later."

He hung up and watched Micah's facial expressions as she read. Once she frowned, but mostly, she grinned. When she was done, she looked up at him.

"Nicely done. Sam would be pleased."

The article, while mentioning Warren by name, did not mention Micah's name. It did refer to a loosely-knit group of health care professionals working collectively under the banner of Benefactor.

Warren nodded. "Now let's hope the dominoes keep falling."

The next morning at work, Warren was itching for the markets to open.

As soon as they did, he watched Forte's stock start drifting downward. By noon, it had dropped ten points. When the markets finally closed at four, it was down another two points, to finish the day almost twenty percent lower than it opened.

While that was good, he hoped it was just the beginning. He wanted the story to get legs and go viral. The stock had a ways to go before Garrett would be able to cover his shorts.

Waiting until after the close, Forte released a response to the article, hoping to ride the evening news cycle.

Warren read their response with amusement. Without mentioning names, Pete Manning accused unnamed forces of trying to sabotage the successful program that had brought affordable health insurance to tens of millions of previously uninsured people. He expressed confidence that this was just another hatchet job by the liberal-biased media and had no basis in fact.

The next morning, Forte's stock inched upward as a few buyers waded in. He wasn't too concerned with daily variances, but he'd hoped that the downward momentum would have continued a bit longer. He prayed there wouldn't be another major news event for the next few days.

It didn't take the talking heads long to latch on to the *Times* article. By the end of the week, every major news outlet was running stories on it.

Warren was receiving dozens of calls from people wanting interviews. He'd instructed Becky to refer everyone to Jim Woodward.

He'd decided to let the young attorney run point. Although young, he was bright, photogenic, and would benefit from the exposure. It was his way of paying Woodward back for Forte underestimating him and letting Woodward get revenge on Forte for killing Dalton.

By Friday, Forte's stock was still hovering around the high forties. Warren spent the weekend wondering if the last shoe was going to drop.

On Tuesday of the following week, Senator Collin Frederick, the senior statesman from Illinois, held a press conference that was carried by all of the major news outlets. He announced that Congress was opening an investigation into health insurance industry practices.

Epilogue

Warren walked into Barney's. The only person there other than Barney was Paco, sitting at the bar in his usual spot. Warren pulled out the stool next to him and sat.

"Sup?" he asked the biker.

"Not much."

He noticed a copy of the *Wall Street Journal* on the bar in front of Paco.

"You reading the *Journal* these days?"

"Hey, I'm treasurer. Gotta keep up."

Barney brought a Newcastle over, nodded, and set it in front of him. He turned and walked back over to the other end of the bar and resumed watching the baseball game on the small television screen.

Paco slid the paper over in front of Warren. "Good article on page four. You should read it when you get home."

Warren took a deep drink from the frosty mug.

"I've got a copy at the office."

Paco tapped the copy in front of Warren. "Take this one. I'm done with it."

He gave Paco a puzzled look, then shrugged. "Sure." He slid the paper over to the side. "I appreciate your help." Another drink and another pause. "How's he doing?"

"Good. He took a lot of heat, but he's a tough old bird." Paco laughed, followed by a nicotine-laced cough. "A reporter stuck a mic in his face and he told them to fuck-off."

Warren laughed. That was Garrett.

The price of Forte stock never made it to thirty. But, it did drop to almost thirty-two. Garrett Thomas pocketed somewhere around $25 million in less than a month. When the price hit thirty-two, Clay Fortson jumped in, just as Warren had predicted. The stock climbed back up to around forty-five where it settled.

With their combined block of Forte stock, Garrett and Clay had persuaded Conrad Fischer to join forces and they fired Pete Manning. Manning's pit bull, Blaine Harris, was also gone. As promised, Garrett had Doctor Robert Michaels appointed to the board.

"Saw you on the news. How was Washington?" Paco asked.

Warren had testified at the congressional hearing on health insurance, his first time. Jim Woodward had worked in the office of a Florida senator where he'd participated in several hearings. He knew the routine, and what to expect.

The young attorney had done a good job of prepping him for the event. Warren felt like he'd done a credible job and hadn't committed any major faux pas.

The biggest surprise had come a few weeks later. Apparently, Clay Fortson had accumulated enough Forte stock to get him a seat on the board. The billionaire and his wife were still planning on traveling and didn't want to be burdened with business obligations. He called Warren and asked if he'd be interested. Warren Thompson was now the newest Forte board member, compliments of Clay Fortson.

Warren heard footsteps behind him and turned.

Tabby walked up. "Interrupting anything?"

Paco shook his head. "Just jawing. How's it hanging?"

"Not bad. Ready to go for a ride. How's this weekend look?"

"I ride every day. You wannabes are another story."

Paco couldn't resist gigging them every chance he got.

Warren shook his head. "Sorry, guys. I'm out. I promised a cute nurse and her son that I'd take them fishing." He finished his beer and looked at his watch. "I should be running."

He stood and reached for his wallet.

"I've got it," said Paco, as Tabby eased onto the stool next to him.

"Thanks. See you later," Warren said. He turned to walk out and Paco slapped his arm with the *Journal.*

"Don't forget your paper."

He took the paper and walked outside, squinting in the bright light until he could get his sunglasses on. The paper folded under his arm, he walked to his car—a new red Corvette.

He'd sold the BMW and decided to go American. Throwing the paper in the passenger seat, he started the car and waited for the air conditioning to start cooling down.

He glanced over at the *Journal* in the seat next to him and wondered what the hell Paco was talking about. Picking up the newspaper, he unfolded it and flipped over to page four. A piece of paper dropped out in his lap.

He picked it up and turned it over. It was a Eurodollar bond for a million dollars. Laughing out loud, he shook his head. He set it down and put the car in gear, heading home.

Acknowledgments

Many thanks to the following people for taking time to read my manuscript and offer much-needed feedback and support: Mary Jo Burkhalter Persons, Otis Scarbary, Cindy Deane, Shirley Scarbary, Clara Blanquet, Fred Blanquet, Barry McIntosh, and Jay Holmes. You guys are the best.

Also, continued thanks to Lt. Karl Steele for putting up with my questions on police procedures. My son, Ben Bollinger, is a professional firefighter and gave me valuable information on first responders. I appreciate the jobs you do and your service to us all.

Thanks to my friend Tim McLaughlin for the use of his name. I hope he enjoyed his new incarnation as an attorney.

Carl Graves, a brilliant cover artist, once again delivered a stunning cover. Thanks to Anitra Mayhann Photography for the new picture on the back as well as many that appear on my website.

A special thanks to my editor, Heather Whitaker. She pushes me to make my writing better, and I appreciate her advice and counsel. As always, any mistakes that remain are mine.

I'm still buying books for my granddaughter, Breanna. I can't wait until she graduates from college and starts buying me books.

Thanks to my wife, June, for supporting me and having faith in my writing. I couldn't do it without you.